A RESCUE FOR A QUEEN

The eleventh enthralling adventure to feature Ursula Blanchard, reluctant spy in the service of Queen Elizabeth I.

February, 1571. Ursula is once more plunged into affairs of the state when she escorts her foster daughter Margaret to the Netherlands to meet her suitor. The queen's spymaster, Sir William Cecil, learns that the wealthy Italian banker Roberto Ridolfi will be hosting their forthcoming wedding – a man who he fears may once again be plotting to put Mary Queen of Scots on the English throne. But Ursula is also about to come face-to-face with her greatest enemy – and the exiled Countess of Northumberland is not the only figure from Ursula's past to put in a surprising appearance.

A RESCUE FOR A QUEEN

Fiona Buckley

Severn House Large Print
London & New York

This first large print edition published 2014
in Great Britain and the USA by
SEVERN HOUSE PUBLISHERS LTD of
19 Cedar Road, Sutton, Surrey, England, SM2 5DA.
First world regular print edition published 2013 by
Severn House Publishers Ltd., London and New York.

British Library Cataloguing in Publication Data

Buckley, Fiona author.
  A rescue for a queen.
  1. Blanchard, Ursula (Fictitious character)--Fiction.
  2. Great Britain--History--Elizabeth, 1558-1603--
  Fiction. 3. Detective and mystery stories. 4. Large type
  books.
  I. Title
  823.9'14-dc23

  ISBN-13: 9780727897053

Severn House Publishers support the Forest Stewardship Council™
[FSC™], the leading international forest certification organisation. All
our titles that are printed on FSC certified paper carry the FSC logo.

Printed and bound in Great Britain by
T J International, Padstow, Cornwall.

Dedicated to the memory of Hope Muntz
And Kate Morton
To both of whom I owe so much

ONE

The Straight and Empty Road

The funeral was over. Hugh Stannard, my dear husband, to whom I had been married for six of the happiest years of my life, had been buried in the graveyard of Hawkswood parish church. It was early in February, 1571, and the day was as raw as February usually is. Mercifully it wasn't raining, but it had rained for several days beforehand, and the grave was a muddy wound in the grass of the churchyard. To see Hugh's coffin lowered into that had been a horror to me.

I wanted to cry out loud but I didn't because I shouldn't, really, have been there. It isn't customary for bereaved spouses to attend the burials of their husbands or wives, because they might become hysterical and mar the solemn dignity that such occasions should have. I broke with custom because I wanted to be with Hugh until the very end. I had watched beside him as he died in our bedchamber at Hawkswood House; I was determined to go with him on his final journey, to stay until the moment when he was laid in his grave. But I would have to behave, so

I did.

By evening, it was all done with. Food and drink had been served in our great hall, which was one of the features of Hawkswood House and now, most of the guests had gone. The hall looked forlorn. The white damask tablecloth was littered with crumbs, empty wine glasses and used platters; the rushes underfoot were scuffed and trampled. Chairs and benches had been pushed carelessly about. I thought of Hugh's belongings, his clothes and his chess set and his gardening tools. He had loved his rose garden and often tended it himself. When he was alive, those things had had meaning, been part of him. Now, like the scattered objects in the hall, they were unconnected bits and pieces, mere debris, their meaning lost.

I was not, of course, all alone in the hall. I was standing near the hearth with my gentlewoman Sybil Jester and Margaret Emory, who was more or less my ward. That is, she had taken refuge with me some months before, when her father Paul Emory rejected her because she would not marry the man he and his wife Cathy had chosen for her. Since then, they had left her entirely to me.

In addition to our little group, Gladys Morgan, the elderly – and frankly unprepossessing – Welshwoman who had long ago attached herself to me and did small jobs about the house, was crouched close by, engaged in mending the fire, while my manservant Roger Brockley and his wife, my tirewoman Fran (out

8

of habit, I still called her by her former name of Dale) were busy lighting extra candles now that the daylight was fading.

My married daughter Meg, the child of my first husband, Gerald Blanchard, and her husband George Hillman were still with us, too. They had a long journey to their home in Buckinghamshire and as they had used a coach, they wouldn't travel fast. Meg was expecting their first child, and riding was unwise for her. She and George would not start for home until the morrow and for the moment were at the far end of the hall with the steward, Adam Wilder, talking to the most illustrious guest of the many who had come to say farewell to Hugh: Sir William Cecil, Secretary of State, and shortly to be raised to the baronage.

It had been kind of him to attend the funeral, though I had been hard put to it to accommodate his entourage as well. They too were present, talking among themselves: a physician, a clerk, several liveried retainers, two grooms and a coachman. I had been a little disconcerted too, during the graveside ceremony, during which Cecil stood opposite to me, to notice that he was watching me in a curiously intent way. He knew me too well to fear a hysterical scene. I suspected something else.

He was here, I knew, to represent Queen Elizabeth as well as himself. No one talked of it much, but Elizabeth was my half-sister. Her father King Henry had had a roving eye. Also, I had in the past undertaken certain missions on behalf of the queen, and it was Cecil who had given me my instructions. That intent gaze worried me, for I was determined that my last mission should really be my last, for ever. It had nearly killed me and Brockley and actually had killed one of our companions.

I had only let myself be drawn into it to help Hugh out of a financial crisis and later I and also my dear Sybil nearly became the victims of a revenge plot spawned by an angry woman whose treasonous scheme I had thwarted. No, I would not dip my toe into the waters of intrigue again. I would *not*.

I knew nothing, then, of a tragedy which had occurred two months previously, before Christmas, when, on a still grey December morning, Captain Benjamin Danby, skipper of the *Trusty,* a coastal trading ship then sailing up the Thames, leant over the rail to swear at the steersman of a barge that had swung too close while overtaking the *Trusty*, and received a nasty surprise.

Danby's annoyance was justified. The *Trusty* was bringing sea coal from Newcastle in the north-east of England, and she was heavy laden. She was slow and anything but manoeuvrable. The barge, under sail, had come dangerously near, throwing up a wash that splashed the *Trusty*'s deck. Danby's curses were loud and imaginative, but they suddenly stopped short, for the wash had not only thrown a wave against the *Trusty*. It had also flung a horrid, pale thing with a human face and human hands that for a moment had brushed the deck rail as if seeking a hold.

'Christ almighty, there's a bloody corpse trying to get aboard!' bawled Captain Danby.

Within moments, the quarrel was forgotten. Bargemen peered over the side of their vessel and began to shout and point, as shocked by the corpse as Danby. The barge was past by now, but it changed course towards a mooring on the north bank, and a dinghy was lowered. Two bargemen rowed quickly back towards the *Trusty*, where the sails were coming down and crewmen with grappling gear were leaning over the side, reaching for the poor thing in the water.

A crowd, summoned by the mysterious forces that draw people to the scene of a disaster, was already gathering on the bank. Somehow, the body was caught and raised aboard the *Trusty*. It was the corpse of a man, perhaps in his thirties. He lay on the deck, streaming. He still had some clothing, a torn shirt and hose but his boots had gone. His feet were bare, white and oddly pathetic. And round his right ankle, there was a red, rasped line.

Danby, staring down at him, pointed at it and said: 'He's had a rope round that.'

'Poor sod,' someone else said. No one spoke the word *murder* but everyone was thinking it.

The body was transferred into the dinghy, and Danby went with it. By the time it reached the bank, someone in the crowd had found a make-

11

shift bier in the form of a disused door found propped against the wall in a nearby watchman's hut, and someone else had summoned a constable, who had taken charge. The body was borne ashore and set down on its wooden bed. The constable looked round at the throng, most of whom were watermen of one kind or another, and asked if anyone knew him.

One man stepped forward. 'Reckon I do! Leastways, he looks like a man that came over from Antwerp on my ship the *Saint Catherine*. Same big nose, anyway, and those ears – they're a bit pointed. Put him ashore when we docked upstream, just beyond London Bridge. Ebb tide carried him down, maybe.'

'His name!' said the constable irritably. 'If he was your passenger, you surely know that!'

'He wasn't a passenger. I don't carry no passengers, just cargo. Silk cloth, tapestries, spices, German wine – they're what my owner deals in. This fellow signed on as a deckhand. Said he wanted to get home quickly – family matters, he said. He was English and I needed an extra hand, so I took him. He was good, a proper seaman. No complaints about him. His name was Jacky Wickes.'

'You must be very tired,' Sybil said to me. 'You have borne up so well but it must have been exhausting, presenting such a calm face to all those people.'

'Hugh had so many friends,' I said. 'I was touched to see such a crowd.'

12

'You could have done without Jane Cobbold,' Sybil said.

I sighed. 'That's true enough.'

Anthony Cobbold and his wife Jane were old friends of Hugh's, and had known him long before I did. With Anthony Cobbold I got on well, but Jane did not like me. For one thing, she knew a good deal about my past adventures, and disapproved of them. She considered me unwomanly and she didn't hide her opinion. Just as the Cobbolds were about to leave, Jane had managed to annoy me considerably.

She had been standing with us at the fireside while Anthony Cobbold went to see if their horses were ready. We were exchanging small talk; about the weather as it happened, which ought to have been harmless enough, but...

'At least today was dry,' Jane said. 'Funerals are always worse when it's raining. Muddy graves are so depressing, I always think.'

'Yes,' I said, thinking that I had never met anyone more tactless than Mistress Cobbold. Due to the recent rain, poor Hugh's grave had been quite muddy enough. I did not want to be reminded of that wound in the grass.

Jane didn't notice my tone. 'How do you intend to pass the days now?' she enquired. 'Will you keep the rose garden up? I expect Hugh would have liked you to do that.'

'Yes. I shall look after the roses,' I said. 'I expect I shall do some of the pruning myself, as Hugh used to do.'

'And we'll practise music and study Latin and

13

Greek,' said Margaret. 'I began both languages as a child and Mistress Stannard has studied them too and is instructing me. We are reading Homer, and Virgil's Aeneid.'

Margaret was small, freckled and sandy-haired, and her best claim to good looks lay in her big grey-green eyes. But she was intelligent and enjoyed studies. Her eyes sparkled now, thinking about them. Jane's carefully plucked eyebrows rose. She took trouble with her hair and eyebrows even though she was not at all an elegant woman, being large, with a soft, fleshy face and big blue eyes which were too earnest for beauty.

'Do you feel that such things are truly suitable for ladies?' she said. 'We never encouraged our daughters to study Latin and Greek. Music, yes, but not too much book learning. Needlework and household management are what I consider important for girls.'

'The queen takes pleasure in the study of languages, including classical tongues,' said Sybil mildly.

'Ah. The queen. Well, her position is different from that of most women. Though even so,' said Jane, 'many feel that she might have done better to concentrate less on ancient tongues and more on finding a husband and providing the realm with a prince to follow her. Even a baby princess would be better than no heir at all.'

I longed for Hugh to help me deal with this tricky conversation. To discuss daughters with

14

Jane was perilous, since the younger Cobbold girl had married a man her father Anthony did not like, though he had allowed the match. I was relieved when Anthony reappeared at that moment, to announce that the horses were standing at the door.

'I don't suppose,' I said now, 'that I shall see much of the Cobbolds in the future.' I turned as Meg came over to me. She looked at me with concern and then, like Sybil, told me I looked tired.

'I am,' I said. 'I think I'll go to bed. You and Margaret and Sybil can do whatever entertaining is still to be done. Look after Sir William. I just want ... to retire. Tell Dale I won't need her tonight.'

Yes, I would retire. To the big bed where Hugh and I had made love, where he had died, where I must now sleep alone. I wanted to be alone. In private, behind the closed curtains of that bed, with no one to see or hear, I would be free to cry.

Before I lay down, I looked at myself in the silver mirror which was part of the bedroom furniture, a costly item that Hugh's father had bought in the previous century. It gave flattering reflections but I still looked terrible, older by far than my thirty-six years. My hair, dark like Meg's, had no gloss and my eyes, which were actually hazel, looked dark as well, with weariness. My black mourning gown turned my complexion sallow.

Not that it mattered. How I looked would

never matter again.

I went to bed. And lay awake, wondering about the future. It seemed like a road, stretching across an empty plain and vanishing over the horizon into the unknown. A straight and empty road, leading nowhere.

In the morning I still felt weary and jaded and I was not pleased to learn that Cecil had woken with an attack of gout and couldn't leave that day, after all. He and his companions would have to be looked after. Another worry, I thought unhappily.

I said farewell to Meg and George, promising to be with them in August when the child was due, and begging Meg to take care of herself. Meg would be sixteen by the time the child was born and she was sturdily built, taking after her father in that respect, but I had always had trouble with childbirth. I had conceived three times, but Meg was the only child I had brought living into the world and I had had a dangerous time even with her. *Oh, please God, don't let anything happen to Meg! I couldn't bear it; not after losing Hugh. Let her come through safely and give me a healthy grandchild, to lead my thoughts to the future, so that the past won't hurt so much.*

But I must not say any of this. Meg and George were laughing at me and Meg told me that she was feeling very well.

'Travel safely,' I said, and stayed in the court-yard to watch the coach disappear through the

16

arch of the gatehouse before I went back indoors. My next task was to enquire after Sir William Cecil. That was how my days were going to be, I supposed: a series of tasks, duties to be done, from now until my own life ended.

Cecil's attack was sharp. His physician gave me details of the diet that his employer should follow, which meant no red meat and no wine or even ale but well water and fresh milk to drink, chicken, rabbit and also fish if obtainable. I visited him in his room and he said that if Gladys knew of any good potions that might relieve his discomfort, he'd willingly take them.

'But for the love of heaven, don't tell my physician,' he added dryly.

In the past Gladys had annoyed local physicians by concocting remedies – some of which were better than theirs – for anyone who asked her and she had outraged more than one vicar with her unfortunate habit of cursing people who annoyed her. It had brought her within inches of being hanged for witchcraft.

'I expect she can make a painkiller for you,' I said, 'and I'll smuggle it to you when your doctor is otherwise occupied.'

'My thanks,' said Cecil, and smiled.

He was a serious man, who worked long, hard hours in the service of Elizabeth, and she was no easy taskmistress. He had a permanent line of worry between his brows. Elizabeth needed a good deal of protecting because she was a constant target for conspiracy. Her cousin, Mary Stuart of Scotland, was in England, halfway between guest and prisoner, having been driven out of Scotland because of the suspicion that she had been a party to the murder of her husband, Henry Darnley. Darnley had been dissolute and treasonous but there were other ways of dealing with him besides murder.

Whether Mary had known of the plot or not, she had married the chief suspect and then the Scots would have no more of her. She was constantly manoeuvring to get herself reinstated on the Scottish throne or, alternatively, on Elizabeth's. She was a Catholic and in Catholic eyes, Elizabeth was a usurper whose mother had not been legally married to her father. While Mary lived, there would be plots, which Cecil must constantly defeat. It was no wonder that he looked anxious and – as I knew in my more honest moments – no wonder either that he was sometimes ruthless in pursuing his duties. He had in the past shown ruthlessness towards me. I had never quite forgiven him and yet I understood him.

'I know I can trust you to look after me, Ursula,' he said. 'Probably better than I have looked after you, at times.'

'That may well be,' I said and again, uneasily, I recalled that considering gaze he had directed at me from the far side of Hugh's grave.

Three days later, he was so much better that he joined the rest of us at the breakfast table and said he would leave for London the following

18

morning.

'If I am to become a baron, I had better not be late for the ceremony,' he said. He glanced towards a window that gave on to the courtyard. 'I hope my coach horses have been kept exercised; I don't want to be jolted about by an excitable team on my way to London. I can hear hooves out there now. Are my horses being taken out at this moment?'

Margaret, who had been seated beside me, rose and went to the window. 'No. It's visitors. A man and a woman have just ridden in ... Mistress Stannard!'

'What is it, Margaret?'

'It's my parents!' said Margaret.

TWO

The First Bend in the Road

I hadn't set eyes on either Paul or Cathy Emory
since the day, some months ago, when Margaret, in highly dramatic circumstances, had
declined their choice of husband and her father
immediately cast her off. Previous to that, I had
known them only slightly. They were virtual
strangers to me.

I had been glad enough to take Margaret in,
for I was missing Meg. Fond though I was of
Dale and Sybil, they were not young as Margaret was. Her youthfulness brought a gaiety
into the house, and a sense of a future to be. She
had been good for me during the bitter days of
Hugh's last illness.

I joined her by the window, to watch as the
Emorys dismounted and our grooms took their
horses. I found myself stiffening. If they had
changed their minds and come to take Margaret
home, they would be within their rights but I
would be sorry and Margaret, who was no
doubt wondering the same thing, looked positively alarmed.

But the courtesies must be observed. Adam

Wilder, who had evidently seen them arrive, had stepped out to greet them, a tall and dignified figure no matter how much the wind ruffled his grey hair. He was bringing them indoors. I drew Margaret away from the window.

'They may only have come to assure themselves that you're well,' I said to her. 'They may be worried about your religious life.'

This was quite possible, as the Emorys were Catholics. Margaret was supposed to be a Catholic too, but at Hawkswood, she had come to the village church with me and seemed perfectly content with Dr Fletcher's Anglican form of worship. Her parents certainly wouldn't approve of that.

Margaret said nothing. 'We'll go to the large parlour, everyone,' I said. 'No need to welcome guests amid a litter of the breakfast things. Sybil and Dale, come too, and Sir William, would you join us as well?'

'For moral support?' said Cecil dryly. 'Certainly. Lead the way.'

In the parlour we settled ourselves in formal – or perhaps I should say defensive – fashion, skirts arranged neatly and hands folded. The only discordant note was the Secretary of State. Sir William Cecil took a window seat and put his gouty leg up on it.

'This is a pleasant surprise,' I said with a smile, when Wilder brought our visitors in, followed by Brockley with a wine flask and glasses on a tray. Margaret rose to make her curtsy and Brockley set the tray down on a

21

small table and unstoppered the flask. My heart sank as I saw that these welcoming gestures hadn't induced the Emorys to smile back. 'Will you be seated?' I asked them, gesturing towards a comfortably cushioned settle near the hearth where, as always in winter, there was a fire.

Brockley filled the glasses while I introduced my companions. The Emorys did look impressed when I told them who the man with the bandaged leg was and the conversation began in a polite and conventional fashion.

'We were sorry to hear of your loss,' Paul Emory told me as he accepted his glass of wine. 'We couldn't get to Master Stannard's funeral because our river flooded and we had much ado to keep the water out of the farmhouse. But Master Stannard was much respected in this district. We're here to offer our condolences, even if they're late.'

'And, of course, to see our daughter,' said Cathy.

'I try to take care of her,' I said, offering them another smile.

They still didn't respond in kind. Not that they were much given to that anyway, I reminded myself. Paul Emory was a weather-beaten man whose bleak blue eyes had no laughter lines at their corners. He was plainly dressed in brown fustian, with no ruff, just a white linen collar open at the neck, and his powerful hands were calloused with farm work. His wife bore similar signs of a hard-working life, since her white collar and cap were not perfectly clean. Their farm, Greenlease, was prosperous; in fact, the Emorys were quite well off. But you couldn't guess that from the way they dressed.

Margaret's interest in languages had come about because they had had ambitions for her, and as a girl, had let her share the tutor who instructed a neighbour's son. They had been good parents in many ways and they had meant well when they planned Margaret's marriage. She had had reasons for her defiance but those reasons were not her parents' fault.

Brockley handed me my wine and I sipped it, which heartened me, and began to talk about the studies Margaret and I were engaged on. But then Paul Emory, after drinking half his glass, suddenly set it down on the flat wooden arm of the settle, and cut across me.

'Let's not waste time. We are here for a very special purpose. We are grateful to you, Mistress Stannard, for taking our daughter in. I was angry enough last year to say I didn't want her back, but neither of us really wished her to be turned out into the world all alone. However, as you know, ours is a Catholic household and yours is not, which means that Margaret cannot follow her own religion while she is with you. Also, it is time that she was married – if we can find a man she won't reject!'

He gave Margaret a sharp look, and she stared at the floor.

'But we think we may have done,' said Cathy, more gently. 'It's someone you've met, Mar-

23

garet. You seemed to like him and he is most suitable.'

Margaret looked up. 'Who ... who is he?"

'You maybe remember,' said her father, 'that though I myself don't go in for travelling, I buy and sell stock from other parts of England or even abroad in France and the Netherlands, hiring agents to make the journeys, and sometimes the people I do business with come and stay at Greenlease. Do you recall a young cattle farmer called Antonio van Weede, from the Netherlands? Half Italian and half Flemish, but he spoke good English, and has a farm just north of the city of Brussels.'

'Yes, Father. I remember him,' Margaret said doubtfully.

'He remembers you very well indeed,' said Paul. 'In a letter that I wrote to him just after you came here, I told him of your broken betrothal. It was just a matter of mentioning family news; I meant nothing by it. But a week ago, a letter arrived from him in which he offered himself as your husband. He's not yet thirty years old and good-looking, if you recall. He is quite wealthy, too. It would be the kind of life you're used to, but better. His letter says that you won't have to work, either in the house or outside, unless you wish. And, of course, he's Catholic. Margaret, your mother and I urge you to agree to this marriage. It is a good match; we do still want the best for you, no matter how intransigent you may have been in the past.'

'You won't have to look after a mother-in-law,' Cathy added. 'Master van Weede's mother died when he was still a lad. He is an only son, who inherited his farm intact when his father also died three years ago.'

'Does this farm have a name?' Cecil asked.

'It's simply called van Weede's, I think,' Paul Emory said. 'It's been in the same family for generations.'

I said: 'Will the gentleman come to England to collect his bride?'

'There's a difficulty there,' Paul Emory admitted. He picked up his wine glass and swirled the remaining contents round, peering into them as if for inspiration. 'He doesn't wish to leave the farm just now. He's negotiating to buy some adjoining land and it's taking time. If he came to England, he can't tell how long it would take. Ships can't cross the Channel at will at this time of year. On the other hand, he'd like to get the matter settled. He suggests that we should bring Margaret to him ourselves, so that we can see with our own eyes what he has to offer her. Only...'

'We've never travelled abroad, or even as far as London, in our lives,' said Cathy. 'We'd hardly know how to go about it. Can you advise us, Mistress Stannard – or suggest someone who could go in our stead?'

Smoothly, Cecil cut in once more. 'Mistress Stannard is used to travelling,' he said. 'And just now she is, more or less, Margaret's guardian. Are you not, Ursula? You could escort her

– if Margaret is agreeable to the match, of course. If so, Margaret, you will feel quite at ease, travelling with Mistress Stannard.'

'That 'ud be a good idea. I've not much spare time to go on journeys, anyhow, with the farm to look after,' Emory said.

I almost gasped aloud. Brockley had not left the room but was standing aside, quietly listening. His eyes met mine and he had no need to say what he was thinking. *Brussels! But that's in the same country as…*

His wiry hair, more grey now than brown, had begun to recede, so that his high, gold-freckled forehead seemed higher than ever. Just now, his eyebrows, like mountaineers on a cliff, seemed to be trying to climb it.

I steadied myself and said: 'First things first. Margaret? What do you think of this proposal?'

Paul Emory, tiresomely, began to bluster that it was Margaret's business not to think but – this time, please God – to do as her parents told her. I let him finish and then looked at Margaret.

She had been considering. 'You have been very kind to me, Mistress Stannard,' she said. 'But I must marry someone sooner or later, and I remember Master van Weede quite well. He seemed a pleasant gentleman.' She turned to her parents. 'I think I should accept him, as you suggest.'

The Emorys, who had I think been braced for objections, looked almost startled but then, at last, they smiled. With happy exclamations,

26

they embraced their daughter, forgiving her past disobedience and promising her a trousseau of charming new dresses. I turned quickly to Cecil.

'Brussels is in the Netherlands,' I said. 'And Anne Percy, the exiled Countess of Northumberland, is in the Netherlands, in Bruges. She hates me. Well, she has her reasons. But you know what she tried to do to me last year! She managed to attack me even from the other side of the Channel. If I go with Margaret, I'll be putting myself within arm's reach of her.'

Brockley had moved to stand beside me. 'Mistress Stannard is right. Master Cecil, you know what happened last autumn. You know that this journey wouldn't be safe for her.'

Cecil said calmly: 'I doubt if there's much to fear from the lady now. I get reports from the Netherlands, you know. These days, Anne Percy lives a most pious and secluded life with her infant daughter and she is in Bruges, not Brussels. They're a good seventy miles apart as the crow flies. Why should she ever learn of the marriage of a cattle farmer, even a prosperous one, who lives so far from her, or care who accompanies the bride from her home?'

'It's not just Anne Percy. There's a branch of the Inquisition in the Netherlands,' I said.

'You and the Brockleys here – I suppose they'll go with you – can quite well pretend to be Catholics. You could travel under your former name of Mistress Blanchard, too, to hide your real identity.'

27

Before I could stop myself, I said: 'Not Madame de la Roche?'

Cecil didn't blench. Still with perfect calm, he said: 'That might not be a good idea. But I think it *would* be a good idea for you to take Margaret to her new home. It will give your thoughts a new direction. You are grieving, which is natural, but this would help you through. I'm sure of it. Seize the opportunity, Ursula!'

'I wish you would, Mistress Stannard. *Please!'* said Margaret.

Her parents joined in. It emerged that neither of them had ever been further from home than Guildford in their lives. It seemed impossible to refuse and in any case, grief had sapped my energy for arguing. I did try, for a while, but the Emorys' anxious appeals and Margaret's pleading eyes were hard to resist and Cecil's calm persistence had something inexorable about it. It overcame my protests just as an iron roller crushes worm casts. I began by being determined not to say yes, and ten minutes later, I had done so.

Margaret, though somewhat reluctantly, agreed to go home with her parents for the time being, though she would return to me a few days before we set out. 'After all, we may not see her for years once she's married,' said her mother.

I was to organize the travel arrangements and help to prepare her trousseau although Paul Emory would pay the bills. In the Netherlands I would use the name of Blanchard, as Cecil sug-

28

gested. We would start as soon as possible, and hope that winter weather wouldn't delay us too much.

When the Emorys had gone, I went to the rose garden that Hugh had loved so much, wanting to walk by myself and think. But Cecil came to find me there, falling in beside me. He was limping and using a stick but we walked slowly on together, while he said what he had come to say.

'There are things we should clear up,' he told me, without preamble. 'I know you are still bitter, towards me and towards your sister the queen, because we deceived you over Matthew de la Roche but you yourself know that you could never have been happy with him for long.'

I was silent, because it was true. Matthew de la Roche was the man I had married when I had got over the loss of my first husband, Gerald Blanchard. I had lived with Matthew for a while in France. But Matthew was a passionate Catholic and a supporter of Mary Stuart, and was continually up to his eyebrows in plots to put Mary on Elizabeth's throne and drag England back to what he called the true faith. I didn't agree with him, and that is a mild way to put it.

'You left your daughter with foster parents in England, because you didn't want her to grow up in his house,' Cecil reminded me.

'And you used her to draw me back to England, and then kept me here by telling me that Matthew had died of plague,' I said. 'And

29

you and the queen told him the same tale about me!'

'And you married Hugh Stannard and were so content with him that even when you learned that Matthew was still alive, you didn't go to him.'

'The queen had annulled our marriage.'

'And would that have stopped you, if you had really wanted to go?'

Again, I was silent.

'At that time,' said Cecil, 'only I and the queen knew that you were her sister, but these things have a way of getting out. If that had become known to Mary Stuart's supporters in France, then...'

'I know. I could have become a hostage.' I said it sourly, but I knew that it was true.

'You are better as you are,' Cecil said. 'And I think you know it. That you stayed with Hugh is proof enough. Now, let us deal with the present day. I do indeed think taking your young friend Margaret on this journey will benefit you in this difficult time. Don't worry about Anne Percy. The queen and I do try to assure your safety, you know, even if you aren't always aware of it. Do you remember the Ridolfi business?'

'Of course I do! It was only two years ago!'

Roberto Ridolfi had been – well, still was – a Florentine banker who had been in London at the time and been involved in another of the plots that so bedevilled Cecil's life. He had conspired with the Spanish ambassador and others, including the Duke of Norfolk, to get Mary Stuart reinstated on the Scottish throne, after which, they hoped to snatch Elizabeth's throne for her as well. I had helped to uncover the conspiracy. It wasn't the kind of thing anyone was likely to forget.

'And do you recall me telling you,' said Cecil, 'that I had taken steps to see that Ridolfi never learned of your part in his downfall?'

'Yes. Did you succeed?' I asked.

'I trust so. He spent six weeks in the custody of my protégé, Francis Walsingham, so that Walsingham could question him and lay traps for him, though we never got anything out of him beyond the fact that he wanted to see Mary Stuart back in Scotland as its queen. He admitted that. He never admitted anything else, and the queen didn't want to press too heavily on a wealthy international banker. Bankers are useful people,' observed Sir William. 'On Walsingham's recommendation, we let him go – Walsingham said he hoped that Ridolfi would get up to further mischief and then we could have him in the Tower with the queen's goodwill. The queen was very distressed by the whole affair, especially Norfolk's part in it. He is one of the principal men of the realm and not just that – he's related to her. His father was her great uncle. He confessed everything to her, you know, and knelt at her feet, in tears. She forgave him. It would break her heart if he ever failed her again. She has said as much to me. But that's by the way. The point is, that I

31

ordered Walsingham to be very very careful what was said in Ridolfi's hearing. To him, you are almost certainly still just the Englishwoman who acted as companion to his wife for a time.'

'To have Anne Percy wanting revenge on me is bad enough,' I said. 'I would rather not have Signor Ridolfi as well. I must thank you for taking care of that.'

'Well,' Cecil said. 'That's all. I wish you well, Ursula, always that, and both I and your sister have valued the help you have given us. I must prepare to leave for London tomorrow. My thanks for your hospitality, and for Gladys Morgan's potions! I was very careful not to let my physician know about them.'

I let him make me laugh. But my feeling of unease persisted. I was afraid of this journey to the Netherlands. I also kept on asking myself why Cecil seemed so determined that I should go.

Later that day, while Cecil was upstairs, resting his gouty leg before tomorrow's coach journey, I settled myself and Sybil in the large parlour to discuss the items of Margaret's trousseau we had promised to make for her. We were interrupted, however, by the arrival of Brockley, Dale and Gladys. They were unmistakably a deputation and I knew at once what that meant.

'Very well,' I said. 'Sit down, all of you, and tell me the worst. Is it about the Netherlands?'

'Madam,' said Brockley, 'it's most unwise for you to undertake this. Mistress Jester and Fran and I will escort Margaret to Brussels. Margaret knows us. You would come, would you not, Mistress Jester?'

Sybil nodded. Dale said candidly: 'I can't abide travel, but I'll do it for that nice lass Margaret, and to help you, ma'am. But will you really want us all to pretend to be Catholics? I don't know as I can do that.'

'If you visit the Netherlands, you must,' I said. 'It's no good looking mutinous. It's necessary for your own protection. Otherwise, I shall have to leave you here, and I'm sure you'd rather come with Roger. I'd want him with me anyway. Yes, Brockley, I am going to make the journey. I must. I have given my word.' I added bravely: 'I'm sure Cecil's right. Who is going to tell Anne Percy in Bruges about a private wedding party bringing a girl from England to marry a farmer seventy miles away?'

'It's Sir William Cecil I'm worrying about,' said Brockley. 'He was watching you at the funeral, madam. I saw him. Didn't you? He pounced on this chance to pack you off to Brussels, as quick as a cat when a fledgling falls out of a nest. He's up to something,' said Brockley ominously.

Gladys had seated herself beside the fire. 'If that's so,' she remarked, 'it'll show itself afore long, I dare say. Be quite like old times!'

She emitted the dreadful cackle which had probably done as much as her curses and her potions to get her accused of witchcraft. That and the knowing look in her dark Welsh eyes,

33

and the brown fangs which did duty as her teeth. 'We've had some lively times, look you, and maybe there's more ahead. Remember Signor Ridolfi and that shocking topiary garden of his.' She dissolved once more into eldritch mirth.

'Stop that cackling!' I said. Brockley was trying not to grin, but Gladys had just stirred up memories which had their comic side. When Cecil arranged for me to enter Roberto Ridolfi's London household to help Ridolfi's wife Donna find her feet in a strange country, the Brockleys had been with me and so had Gladys, who – to our amazement – had then been pursued by an elderly and lustful gardener with a most impure imagination. He had clipped the topiary into thoroughly suggestive shapes. Brockley declared he was scandalized and discouraged Dale from going there but judging by the grin he was now trying to suppress, he hadn't been as shocked as he claimed.

I had liked Donna. She was a sweet young woman and I was glad for her sake that Elizabeth had decided that it was improvident to throw wealthy foreign nationals into dungeons or to chop their heads off.

'I hope,' I said repressively, 'that my journey to the Netherlands will *not* be like old times! Please don't create bogies, Brockley. I intend to escort Margaret to her new home, see her married and settled, and then come back to Hawkswood. I can't see how that can be connected with plots or affairs of state.' I said it very firmly, so as to convince myself.

The long empty road to the horizon seemed to have a bend in it after all. I could only hope that what lay beyond would be interesting and cheerful and that nothing dangerous lurked there in ambush.

THREE

Just a Simple Farmer

We set out in March. The journey was planned without much difficulty because there was a foreman at Greenlease who had been to van Weede's farm once before. He was dispatched in haste with a letter accepting Master van Weede's proposal and was lucky with the weather. He got back a week before we left, bringing a delighted reply to the Emorys, a most affectionate letter for Margaret herself and the news that the land he had hoped to buy was now his and he regarded it as a gift for his bride. He also included some useful information about the route to take once we reached the Netherlands, information that was supplemented by the foreman.

Margaret came back to me two days before our departure. I realized then that she was nervous. She showed me the wedding gown that a Guildford dressmaker had made for her, but stood doubtfully fingering the deep cream brocade overgown and the blue silk kirtle with its silver embroidery, and then whispered to me: 'I hope I shall like him. I didn't take much

36

notice of him when he visited us. What will I do if when we get there I suddenly find I *don't* like him? My parents will never let me come back to Hawkswood. They'd keep me at home – as a sort of prisoner.'

'If the man is quite impossible, I'll do my best for you. But I'm sure he won't be,' I said calmly. 'Don't panic before there's need!'

'I'll be glad you're there, though I know you don't really want to make the journey,' Margaret said.

'I've promised your parents,' I said. 'Now, do remember that since the Netherlands are under Catholic rule, I shall be representing myself and my companions as Catholics. Also, as Sir William Cecil recommended, I shall call myself Blanchard instead of Stannard, as a protection against Anne Percy of Northumberland who now lives in the Netherlands. You know how she tried to injure me last year. You must remember to address me as Mistress Blanchard. I am trusting your discretion.'

'Yes, of course!' Margaret said.

'Thank you,' I said, and then took the opportunity of mentioning something else that had been on my mind. 'Margaret, I take it that your mother has told you everything you should know about marriage. Is there anything you want to ask?'

'Mistress Stannard, I grew up on a farm. I am a little nervous, but I expect I'll live, just as every married woman does.'

I hoped to heaven that the unknown van

37

Weede would be gentle and affectionate and would be able to coax this restrained enthusiasm into something warmer. Still, it was better than ignorance, or fear.

On the morning of departure, Margaret's parents came to Hawkswood to say goodbye. Those who were to go were Margaret, myself, Brockley and Dale. Dale never liked to be separated from him and was in any case to attend on me. Sybil was to remain behind and look after Hawkswood and there was of course no question of taking Gladys with us.

Margaret had no maid and said she didn't need one; she had never had one at Greenlease. However, I told Dale to help her when necessary. Some of her new gowns were difficult to put on without assistance, and I hoped that Master van Weede would provide his bride with a tirewoman. He had said that she wouldn't have to work unless she chose, which sounded as though his household was well served.

Our belongings and Margaret's comprehensive trousseau, which included linen and some silver plate as well as clothes, occupied a big pile of hampers but Margaret and Dale (who was thankful not to be on a horse) were to travel to London in the coach that Hugh had once used and the coach could carry the luggage as well. Arthur Watts, our head groom, drove it. Brockley and I rode. Once in London, we embarked on a ship called *The Lucky Chance*, and set sail down the Thames.

Margaret loved it all. She was thrilled by

38

London and its crowds, even inhaling the town air with joy, though, as ever, it smelt of a mixture of horse droppings, human ordure, coal fire smoke and rotting leftovers on kitchen middens. The ship too was a whole new world to her and she explored it with the curiosity and venturesomeness of a female Christopher Columbus, bemusing the sailors by asking questions.

The hostelry we found in Ostend was another new experience for her. We spent a night there, and in the morning, we set about hiring transport for the rest of the way. Our coach, of course, had been left in England and Arthur Watts would by now have driven it home to Hawkswood, with the horses Brockley and I had ridden, tied behind. We now had to arrange a wagon and driver for Margaret, Dale and the luggage, and saddle horses for Brockley and myself.

It took the best part of four days to reach our destination. The weather stayed dry, though there was continual wind, blowing unhindered across country markedly flatter than the rolling landscape of Surrey. We saw many fields in which crops were sprouting, and Margaret was particularly intrigued by some tall wooden structures with great sails on top, arranged like the spokes of a wheel, that spun in the wind. She leant over the side of the wagon to ask me what they were.

I didn't know, but Brockley did. 'I've heard of them though I've never seen them before,' he said. 'They're windmills. They use the power of the wind to move grindstones, just as we use strongly flowing rivers and streams in our watermills.'

Our driver, Pieter, who talked to us in French, remarked: 'Plenty of wind here,' and Dale, who knew enough French to understand him, muttered: 'That's true enough,' and drew her cloak more tightly round her.

The Emory foreman had described the approach to van Weede's. 'There's an avenue of trees, quite long, with fields to either side, leading to the house. There's no gatehouse or courtyard in front – just a flat space and then a tall wooden house with a tiled roof. The farm buildings are behind it and so are the farmyard and the fowl pen. You'll know it when you see it.'

We did, for it was an accurate description. The trees of the long avenue were tall and straight, with quivering, silver-tinged leaves and Margaret wondered at them, having never seen such trees before. 'They're poplars,' I told her.

The house was in sight by now. It had overhanging eaves, and as we drew near, I saw that the walls were made of dark, narrow horizontal planks, overlapping downwards. Presumably the design was meant to drain rainwater off easily. The windmills we had seen were much the same. No other buildings were visible from the front. I thought the place looked stark and lonely and was just wondering whether it had struck Margaret in the same way, and what I should say to encourage her, when the main door opened, and a man came out and walked to meet us.

As we drew nearer, I saw that he was not tall, no more than five feet five inches. He held himself well, however. When we were close enough, he swept his cap off in greeting, and I saw that he had brown eyes and a brown beard, and hair to match, a rich, warm colour. He was smiling broadly.

'I am Antonio van Weede,' he said, in excellent English. 'I was looking from a window and I saw you arriving. And this is Margaret!'

He had identified her at once, and held out his hands to assist her out of the wagon. 'You are welcome,' he said as her feet touched the ground. 'Very, very welcome.'

'I am happy to be here,' said Margaret. She made him a curtsy, but he drew her up for a kiss of greeting and then they smiled at each other and with relief, I saw that liking had already sparked between them. Margaret, I hoped, would bask in his kindly greeting and not notice the starkness of his house. Probably, in time, she would introduce improvements.

'I would like to present Master Roger and Mistress Frances Brockley,' I said. 'They are in my service, but they are also my friends and travelling companions. And this is Pieter, our driver, who will take the wagon and horses back to Ostend.'

'You are all welcome! Ah, here are my

41

grooms.'

Two men, dressed in breeches and leather waistcoats over their shirts, had appeared round the side of the building. 'They will help Pieter to see to your horses,' van Weede said. 'You may safely leave your animals in their care.'

Brockley, who had dismounted and was helping Dale out of the wagon, grunted uneasily. Brockley never trusted anyone to look after our horses properly without his supervision. I caught his eye and he subsided. In this not entirely friendly land, I preferred to give my servants status enough to keep them near me.

'Come indoors,' said van Weede.

The moment we were inside, the air of starkness disappeared. There was warmth here, and a human population. As we stepped on to the slate floor of the entrance vestibule, we were surrounded by van Weede's servants. There were three women, all middle-aged, with clean white headdresses and aprons; a man who looked like a valet, and a cook with a white cap on his head and a rolling pin in his hand, as though it were a badge of office. Everyone looked pleased to see us. We were led into a snug parlour, warmed by a wood fire and with deep red woollen curtains to shut out darkness and the draughts from doors and windows. The plastered walls were painted a pleasant cream and there were settles with cushions, a lute lying on a table, and a shelf holding books, a chess set, a backgammon set and a statuette of

42

the Virgin and Child.

We took off our cloaks and the maids whisked them away. Van Weede waved us all to seats and one of the maids reappeared almost at once with a tray of wine, ale, and some delicacies that were new to all of us, little confections of pastry and toasted bread, variously topped with nuts in cream, a kind of smooth brown cheese, bits of fried bacon and what seemed to be spoonfuls of a savoury beaten egg concoction. It was all very tasty. Van Weede, having made sure that everyone had something to eat and drink, came to sit beside me.

'You are Mistress Blanchard?' he said quietly. 'Margaret has stayed in your household, I think, according to the letter I had from her parents.'

The Emorys, who were well aware of Anne Percy's machinations the previous year, had willingly agreed to refer to me as Blanchard when they wrote to van Weede about Margaret's acceptance, and her travel arrangements.

'I agreed to bring her because I have travelled a little and her parents have not,' I explained.

'So they said. I hope Margaret will be happy here. Most people here speak French and I understand that she has the language.'

'Yes, she speaks it very well,' I said, in that tongue.

'That will make it easier for her to settle down,' said van Weede, also switching to French, with an air of relief. 'It isn't long since I last saw her, but I didn't then pay her much heed. I understood that she was spoken for and

43

in any case, I was too busy talking cattle with her father. Now I see that her appearance is pleasing. She has lovely eyes. Mistress Blanchard, have I your permission to talk to her aside? I think we should get to know each other somewhat before the final decision is made. I don't expect a bride to be handed to me on a plate like a trussed chicken, with no say in the matter. From the letter they sent me, I think her parents think all is settled, but though I am just a simple farmer, I have more delicacy than that.'

'Of course.' Margaret had sat down beside Dale, opposite to us. 'Dale!' I called. 'Change places with Master van Weede and let him exchange a few words with Margaret!'

For the next half hour, Dale, Brockley and I sat together, nibbling the refreshments, talking in low voices and pretending to ignore the couple on the other side of the room though I, of course, was trying to catch something of their conversation, which was in French.

'...you grow crops as well as rearing cattle, do you not? I saw fields with crops growing in them. What are they? Wheat and barley?'

'Wheat and oats. I have chickens and geese too, and a vegetable garden. Eggs, capons, vegetables can bring in useful extra income...'

Dale's voice, admiring the red curtains, briefly drowned Antonio's and when Margaret's voice reached me next, she was asking whether Antonio used oxen or horses for the ploughing.

'My father employed oxen,' he told her, 'but I

44

have horses, Percherons.

'Percherons?'

Brockley was always interested in anything to do with horses. He pricked up his ears and signalled to Dale not to speak.

'Ah. You would not know,' van Weede was saying. 'Back in the days of knights in heavy plate armour, huge, strong horses were bred to carry the weight. Guns have made such massive armour useless and the enormous horses weren't needed as chargers any more. But farms can use them, and also, when crossed with lighter breeds, you get a sturdy animal, not so huge and cheaper to feed but still powerful enough for most farm work. A Frenchman in Perche has created a whole new breed that way and it's called the Percheron. I have two. They're dapple grey – most of the breed are. They're mild tempered, as well. Would you like to see them?'

'I would like to see everything; the house, the farm, everything!' Margaret's exclamation sounded eager.

'Indeed you shall.' Van Weede rose and came over to us. 'Mistress Blanchard, I would like to show you and your companions round my property, house and farm alike. Margaret is clearly interested, and knowledgeable, too.'

'Well, she is a farmer's daughter,' I said.

Master van Weede grinned. 'One of the reasons, Mistress Blanchard, why I have stayed unmarried so long, is because here, there is a modern fashion for keeping girls, even farmers' daughters, what their parents call innocent. It's the Lutheran influence, I think. It seems to infect the air and change the way people think even when they're not Lutheran at all. I have had hopeful mammas trying to tempt me into marrying their daughters, but I don't want a wife who won't discuss the realities of life, such as horse breeding. Farms are *full* of reality. Not that my life is quite without luxuries. This is a comfortable place, as you and Margaret will see. Shall we start our tour of the premises? We'll start in the kitchen. Any future lady of the house will want to inspect that.'

As we left the parlour, he and I were foremost, walking side by side. He had something more to say to me.

'One thing I can promise,' he said to me, 'is that Margaret, if she chooses to stay and marry me, will have a splendid wedding. It will be held in Brussels, in the church of St Michele and Gudule, a very fine church indeed. We shall stay with a kinsman of mine, by marriage. I am half Italian, as I think you probably know, and on that side, I am well connected. My Italian relatives mostly live in Florence, and a cousin of mine – a delightful girl called Donna – was in a position to make an excellent marriage. Her husband is wealthy and as it happens, they are due to arrive in Brussels from England, any day now. He travels a great deal – he's one of those men who seem to be forever in the saddle. I regularly correspond with him and Donna and he knows all about my impending nuptials. I wrote to them in England as soon as I heard that my offer to marry Margaret had been accepted. He wrote back saying that he would be over-joyed to provide the reception and arrange the ceremony at St Michele and Gudule. He expect-ed to be in Brussels in time. He's a Florentine banker with international contacts and friends in high places. There will be some notable guests at the wedding! His name is Roberto Ridolfi.'

FOUR

Committment

After that, van Weede walked with Margaret while I walked with the Brockleys and joined with them in making suitably admiring remarks about the big, well-appointed kitchen and the comfortably furnished dining room and bed-chambers. But below the surface, I was grimly thoughtful, and I wasn't thinking about Margaret.

A suspicion was churning in my mind. I tried to push it away but it fitted too well with the suspicions that Brockley had aroused before we set out. When we had finished with the house and were crossing the farmyard to look at the Percherons, van Weede once more appeared at my side and I seized my opportunity.

'Tell me,' I said, 'what really made you offer for Margaret's hand? Was it just because you thought she would be a good wife for a farmer? Or did her parents suggest it after her first betrothal fell through?'

'No, it wasn't their idea. It's odd how it happened.' He spoke easily, without any sign of guile. 'I was in England in the early autumn last year, to see Margaret's father. I saw Margaret then without really noticing her. After that, I came home by way of France – I wanted to see a breeder about a new bull I thought of buying. And who should be there at the same time, accompanying a friend who was on a similar errand, but a man whose name you'll probably know! He is at present the English ambassador to France. Francis Walsingham.'

'Indeed!' I had been vaguely aware that Walsingham had now been sent to take up an appointment in France, but had given it little thought.

'He made me nervous,' said van Weede with a chuckle. 'He was most courteous to me but there is something intimidating about him.'

'Yes,' I said. 'I know what you mean. I've met him.' Walsingham was ardently Protestant, a devoted servant of the queen and said to be an affectionate family man. He was also tall, lean, swarthy, usually dressed in black and his reputation in the world of politics and conspiracies was one of total ruthlessness. I could well believe that van Weede had found him alarming.

'We actually had quite a long conversation,' van Weede said, sounding awed. 'In the course of it, I spoke of the Emorys. I also mentioned that I was thinking of marriage and looking for a wife. And what do you think happened next?'

'I can't imagine,' I said.

'Just before Christmas,' said van Weede, 'much to my surprise, I received a letter from Walsingham, saying that he had mentioned the

Emorys in his correspondence with Sir William Cecil in England and that Cecil knew of the Emorys. And had heard that their daughter was no longer betrothed. Walsingham said that if I were indeed seeking a wife, it was Cecil's opinion that she might be suitable. Margaret's parents also mentioned the broken betrothal in a letter that I received a few days later. As I already knew Margaret was free, I had had a little time to think the matter over. What little I did remember of her seemed agreeable. And when two such important men had kindly troubled to concern themselves in my small affairs, well, it would have seemed rude to ignore them. So I wrote to her father.'

'I see!' I said.

Shortly after that, he detached himself from me to rejoin Margaret. I fell in once more beside Brockley and Dale and said quietly: 'Tonight, when we all retire, I have something important to say to you two.'

'What kind of thing, madam?' Brockley asked.

'Wait for tonight,' I said. 'It can't be discussed here and now.'

When I retired, I found my room was agreeably warm. A fire had been lit for me, with a well-filled wood basket beside it. The bed was curtained with heavy woollen hangings and made up with linen sheets, puffy pillows, a thick blanket and a fur coverlet. Definitely, I thought, this is a well-run house.

Dale, less impressed, helped me undress,

wrapped me in a stout dressing gown and put fur-lined slippers on my feet, remarking that the wind was fairly whistling over the fields and she couldn't abide to live here.

'*You* won't have to,' I pointed out. 'Now, fetch Brockley. It's time to talk.'

I settled the three of us on stools near the fire, to which Dale at once applied the poker. Brockley said: 'Madam?'

'I wish to state,' I said in formal tones, 'that if Sir William Cecil were to walk into this room at this moment, I would probably kill him.'

They stared at me and Dale nearly dropped the poker. 'I mean it,' I said, and recounted my conversation with van Weede in the farmyard.

'But...' Dale said.

Brockley said: 'I don't follow. Madam, are you saying that Francis Walsingham and Sir William Cecil between them, for some reason, suggested to van Weede that he should offer to marry Margaret? But why? And why does that make you angry with Cecil? I just don't see...?'

'Cecil knows all about the Emorys,' I said. 'He knows everything that happened last year and that, as a result of that, Margaret came to live with me at Hawkswood. Look, Brockley, you yourself said Cecil was up to something. I think he wanted me to come to the Netherlands. He saw a way of getting me here. He knew very well that I didn't want any more assignments, but this way I wouldn't realize it was an assignment until it was too late! His ploy might not have worked, but he probably decided it was

51

worth trying.'

Dale sat back and hung the poker on its stand. 'But, ma'am, it's all so roundabout and complicated!'

'Not really,' I said. 'All he had to do was tell Walsingham to dangle the idea of the marriage in front of van Weede – and let it be known that the idea was his originally and that he was recommending it. It's clear that Antonio was impressed by the interest they were taking in him – as he said himself, they're both important men. And well they knew it. That alone would probably encourage van Weede to take the bait, and if he did, and Margaret's parents were agreeable – and the marriage took place during Ridolfi's visit to Brussels, well and good...'

'Ridolfi?' said Dale and Brockley together.

'Yes. He's here, or will be at any moment.'

'What do you mean, madam? Ridolfi is here? Where?' Brockley actually looked round the bedchamber as though he half-expected Signor Ridolfi to emerge from a clothes press or creep out from under the bed. 'I thought the Ridolfis were still in England,' he said.

'They were, but at the moment they're on their way to Brussels, according to van Weede. Cecil presumably knew about their travel plans. He has his methods of keeping himself informed about people he keeps an eye on. Ridolfi's wife Donna,' I explained, 'is van Weede's cousin. They're going to attend the wedding. In fact, Ridolfi intends to host it. When Cecil heard that Walsingham had come

52

across a relative of Ridolfi's, living near Brussels and looking around for a wife, he must have thought heaven was fighting on his side. I wonder how long it took him to think of thrusting Margaret at him and me along with her? About five minutes, I should imagine.'

'But how would Cecil know that van Weede is related to Ridolfi?' Brockley asked, puzzled.

'I said, he keeps himself informed! Or maybe van Weede mentioned the connection to Walsingham, who passed it on to Cecil as an interesting snippet. Anyway, it seems that – assuming the marriage now goes ahead – Antonio and Margaret are to be married in Brussels, from wherever the Ridolfis are staying. It's my belief that Cecil has new suspicions about Ridolfi and wants to bring me into contact with him. After all, Ridolfi has conspired on behalf of Mary Stuart before.'

'But...' Brockley was frowning. 'Even if Cecil did secretly encourage this marriage, and did know that Signor Ridolfi meant to come to Brussels, he couldn't be sure that the two things would coincide!'

'No, but there was a good chance. Because of the relationship between van Weede and Ridolfi's wife. It would be natural to invite Ridolfi to the wedding and probably he would want to accept. If nothing came of it – well, the gamble had failed. But it looks like succeeding. If van Weede and Margaret marry, they'll do so from Ridolfi's very house.'

'Cecil,' said Brockley, 'seems to have had

providence on his side.'

'He has a gift for exploiting opportunities,' I said. 'Even if her bridegroom had come to England to collect her, I expect he would have found a way to pitchfork me into accompanying her here. It would be natural enough for her to have an English woman as a companion just at first, as she found her feet in a new country. I expect it seemed providential that because of his attack of gout, he was actually present when the Emorys came to Hawkswood with the proposal. But he would have managed somehow!'

'In other words,' said Brockley, 'Cecil made use of what was there.'

Between him and me there was a brief moment of intimate silence. *Use what's there* had been a favourite saying of the friend who had been killed on my last official mission. It was invaluable advice, which we had taken on one very dramatic occasion. Each of us knew that the other was remembering him. Then I saw Dale glancing from one of us to the other in a puzzled way and I said briskly: 'It isn't the first time I've known Cecil treat people like pawns on a chessboard – and Walsingham is as bad if not worse.'

'But won't this man Ridolfi know that you helped to stop him two years ago?' Dale was alarmed. 'He'll recognize you, even if you are calling yourself Mistress Blanchard.'

'Cecil says he doesn't know of the part I played two years ago,' I said. 'In that case, he'll

54

only recognize me as the lady who kept his wife company when they were in London. Well, there it is. I think Cecil has managed to manoeuvre me into Ridolfi's path. I've been nicely trapped.'

'Does Master van Weede know you've met Ridolfi before?' Brockley asked.

'Not yet, but I'll have to mention to him that we met the Signor briefly in London some time ago – there'll be no hiding that! I don't suppose,' I said bitterly, 'that Cecil foresaw that Ridolfi would want to host the wedding. Excellent luck for him; it will bring our little party closer to Ridolfi than ever and he knew,' I added with even more bitterness, 'that when our paths crossed, I would realize it was no accident, and I wouldn't be able just to walk away. I would guess at once that he suspected Ridolfi of something and I would feel I had to find out if he was right.'

'It's outrageous!' said Brockley. 'Margaret's been made use of as well as you, madam.'

'I feel,' I said, 'like a ferret being thrust into a rathole. Dear God! Cecil *reminded* me that Ridolfi knows nothing of what I did to uncover his plot when he was in London! He actually spoke of it, when I had a few words with him alone, in the garden at Hawkswood. He was preparing me! He said something about the Duke of Norfolk, too – said it would break the queen's heart if he betrayed her again, or words to that effect. I'm wondering if he's sent me to find out not only what Ridolfi is doing but if

Norfolk is involved in anything he shouldn't be. Believe me, I really would like to kill Cecil!'

'Can't we just not attend the wedding?' Dale asked. 'Ma'am, couldn't you invent some reason for going home at once?'

'No,' I said slowly. 'I think Margaret and Antonio will make a match of it and I don't want to upset that. I don't suppose,' I added, giving reluctant credit where credit was due, 'that either Cecil or Walsingham meant any harm to Margaret. I expect they felt they were furthering a worthwhile match for her and they could well be right. But I think I must stay until the ceremony is over and preferably a little longer. I don't want to leave her alone in a strange country with no one of her own to talk to or encourage her. Besides ... as I said...'

I had no need to repeat it. Willy-nilly, I had been pushed into the position of being on duty and my instinctive loyalty to Elizabeth had taken over. I could not now back out. I said: 'I wish Hugh were here.'

But Hugh was not there. Suddenly, the need for him, for his kindness and friendship, for the reassurance of his love, poured over me like a wave. I put my hands over my face. Brockley said worriedly: 'Madam? Are you well?' and Dale quietly pulled her stool closer so that she could put her arm round my shoulders.

Making a fierce effort, I conquered the fit of grief. I lowered my hands and Dale offered me a handkerchief. Taking it, I wiped my eyes.

'I'm sorry. I'm better now. Please forgive

me.'

'What is there to forgive?' Brockley said in a low voice. 'Master Stannard was a good man.'

'Yes. He was. And he isn't here so I must manage this business without him.' Somehow, I achieved firmness. '*If* he were here, he and I would act together as representatives of Margaret's parents. I expect Hugh would give the bride away. Since he is not, Brockley, I am going to suggest that you should undertake that duty.'

'Ridolfi may offer to do that.'

'You're more suitable. Margaret knows you and you are part of her escort from England. Brockley, Dale, I want to keep you both close to me, closer perhaps than servants normally are. This is one way to ensure that. As soon as matters are settled between Margaret and van Weede – as I think they will be – I'll speak to him about this. She'll surely prefer to be given away by someone she knows. Since he calls himself a simple farmer, it's quite in order that his bride should have a dignified manservant as her father's representative. Indeed, you've always been much more than just a manservant as far as I'm concerned, Brockley.'

I strongly held the opinion that our neighbour at home, Jane Cobbold, was a remarkably tactless woman. Now, only a split second after I had spoken, I saw Dale's face and knew that I had been supremely tactless myself. And it couldn't be retrieved. To try to do so would only make things worse.

I did try, though, carefully. 'You are both more to me than servants,' I said. 'You have been through danger with me, again and again.'

Dale said: 'Thank you, ma'am.' But I had hurt her. She knew very well that Brockley's part in my secret work, was greater and deeper than hers. She had sensed the intimacy of that silent moment when Brockley alluded to our one-time friend, and now I had tacitly admitted that intimacy.

I was so very sorry. Dale had always looked after me so well, and so kindly. I was still clutching her handkerchief.

FIVE

Luxury and Dread

I knew from experience that it was best, when I had committed myself to a given course of action – especially one that frightened me – to make the commitment complete. It was wiser not to keep looking over my shoulder.

I didn't wish Margaret to rescue me from Cecil's schemes by deciding against the marriage, since I thought it would be a good thing for her. Next day, I went with the couple to see the new fields that van Weede had purchased. He talked of enlarging his cattle herd and declared that if Margaret married him, the extra cattle would be regarded as hers. She looked happy and asked questions and I was not surprised when, at dusk, he called everyone in the house to the parlour and announced formally that they had agreed to be betrothed.

They wanted someone to join their hands, so I gave Brockley a push, and with great aplomb, he stepped forward and placed Margaret's left hand in van Weede's right, whereupon the servants all cheered, and trays of wine and delicious snacks appeared so fast that it was clear that in the kitchen, this outcome had been taken for granted and preparations made in advance.

Next day, early, van Weede mounted the sturdy roan gelding which was his personal mount and rode to Brussels. He was back after dark, smiling broadly.

'When cousin Ridolfi wrote to say he wanted to arrange the wedding, he told me where the house was that he was arranging to rent, but I did wonder if it would be easy to find. It couldn't have been simpler! They were just moving in when I got there, with the courtyard full of horses and a wagonload of goods blocking up the archway from the road! But they were glad to see me, and yes, arrangements will be made forthwith for my marriage to take place in the church of St Michele and Gudule in Brussels.' Meanwhile, he added, the wedding party was invited to go to Brussels at once to join the Ridolfis in their rented house.

'Signor Ridolfi has meetings arranged with various men concerned with the Spanish administration here in the Netherlands,' van Weede explained, evidently most impressed by the status of his cousin Donna's husband. 'Including the governor himself, the Duke of Alva! Signor Ridolfi says that the duke may actually attend the wedding reception for a while. It will be held in the Ridolfi house, which is large, and has a fine dining hall.'

'It's Lent,' I said. 'Is it usual here for marriages to be allowed during Lent? The feast will have to be rather austere, won't it?'

'Signor Ridolfi has obtained a dispensation.

He wrote to Rome for it the moment he received my letter telling him I was to be married. The feast won't be a fast,' said van Weede, beaming. 'For that one day, we shall be allowed all the meat we can eat. We can set off for Brussels tomorrow, if that is agreeable to everyone.'

'How exciting!' said Margaret.

'Indeed,' I echoed, and sent forth a silent prayer that Cecil really had made sure that Ridolfi knew nothing of my part in wrecking the schemes he had laid in England. In the folds of my skirt, I secretly crossed my fingers as well. A sadly pagan practice, no doubt, but in the circumstances, I preferred to placate as many powers as possible.

In the process of crossing my fingers, I felt the outlines of things that, as was my long-established custom, I carried in a pouch stitched inside the skirt of my black overdress. All my gowns were divided, to reveal elegant kirtles below, and I had stitched pouches inside the split skirts, to carry things that I might suddenly need. I would never have undertaken a journey to a place like the Netherlands, infested with such dangers as Anne Percy and a branch of the Inquisition, without those useful items to hand. They included a set of picklocks, a small but very sharp dagger in a leather sheath and some gold and silver coins in a little velvet drawstring bag.

And this time, in case of emergency, I had one more secret item about my person, not in the pouch, but in a sheath that I wore inside my clothes, on the left-hand side, under the edge of my buckram stomacher. It was a very small, very sharp knife. If unfriendly hands discovered my pouch and took away my dagger, the knife was small enough, perhaps, to escape notice long enough for me to use it. I had made sure, before we set out, that I knew exactly where my heart was, and could find it instantly. I had made sure that both of the Brockleys carried such knives, as well.

I hoped we would never need them but I was glad to have them there. I feared the inquisition more than I feared Anne Percy.

Pieter had departed, to take our wagon and horses back to their stables, but van Weede had wagons and horses of his own. Next day, Margaret, myself, the Brockleys, van Weede's valet and the luggage were all stowed into a stout four-horse vehicle with a weatherproof covering, and with van Weede riding alongside on his roan, we set off.

Ridolfi's rented house was in the Upper Town of Brussels, and was a tall, imposing place, with an arched gateway leading into a spacious courtyard. I learned later that it was one of several owned by the Duke of Alva who rented them out to visiting dignitaries, and no doubt made a useful extra income from them.

We drove straight into the courtyard and as I climbed down from the wagon, I saw two familiar figures at the top of the steps up to the front door of the house. Short, dark Roberto

Ridolfi, with his smooth olive-tinged skin and his pleasant smile, looked much as he had when I last saw him, except that he had put on a little weight and now had a decidedly plump midriff. Beside him, his young brown-haired wife Donna was as sweet of face and as elegantly dressed as I remembered. I would have known them anywhere.

Van Weede was already out of his saddle, handing his reins to a groom, and striding towards the steps. While Brockley and Dale and van Weede's valet coped with the luggage, I helped Margaret down. We followed Antonio up the steps and he at once plunged into introductions, in French.

'Cousin Roberto, Cousin Donna, meet my future bride, Mademoiselle Margaret Emory. And here to represent her mother, is Madame Ursula Blanchard.'

'They are very welcome,' said Ridolfi, also in French. Just as Donna, with a glad cry, leapt forward, seized me in her arms, and exclaimed: 'Ursula, dear Ursula! How wonderful to see you again! But why are you Madame Blanchard now? Surely you used to be called Stannard!'

'Dear Donna!' I said, hugging her back and not answering the question. There was no immediate need, anyway, since mild confusion had overtaken our arrival. Ridolfi was greeting Margaret with a kiss and simultaneously trying to steer us in through the door, just as a number of his servants were coming out of it to help with the luggage, and in the courtyard, a head

63

groom was shouting instructions to his minions about unhitching the wagon horses and putting the wagon away.

Somehow, on a tide of talk and laughter and orders and exclamations and people bumping into each other, we were swept inside. In the flagged entrance hall, where there was a life-size statue of Our Lady, a table with flowers on it and a growing stack of hampers as Ridolfi's servants brought the baggage in, Ridolfi presented his butler to us. He was not the same man that I had met in London, but a younger and leaner individual whose name, we were told, was Giorgio Bruno, and who was also, when required, Ridolfi's secretary.

Then, to my surprise, Ridolfi beckoned a young man out of the busy flock of attendants and said: 'This is Timothy Kingham, who assists Bruno in his work as a butler, though not as a secretary. His French and Italian are not of the necessary standard. But as he is English and can talk to you in your own language, I have told him to devote himself to my English guests and to serve you in any way that you need.'

'I shall be very happy to do all I can,' said Kingham, bowing graciously. He was a lanky fellow, long both in arms and legs, with bony wrists sticking out beyond his shirtsleeves, and a long chin to match, and mousy hair that to my mind was in need of trimming. But he had a smile that was in his light brown eyes as well as on his mouth. 'I'll begin by getting your belongings to your rooms,' he said. 'I will then

64

return to escort you to them. Will that suit?'

I said: 'Of course,' and smiled back at him. Ridolfi, meanwhile, was saying to van Weede: 'Antonio, you never told me that your guests were old acquaintances of mine.'

'I only found that out the other day, myself,' said van Weede. 'An odd coincidence.'

'A small world!' said Ridolfi. Timothy Kingham had rounded up some assistance and our bags and hampers were already disappearing up the stairs. Ridolfi observed this with approval and then turned a beaming face to me. I had never exactly disliked him, despite his conspiracies. If anyone had asked me to sum him up, I would have said he was devout but naive. And I certainly hadn't disliked Donna, who was lovable, if somewhat clinging and not unduly intelligent.

But here came the dangerous question, once again, this time from the Signor himself. 'But why *have* you changed your name? I heard Donna ask you but I don't think you replied. Have you been widowed and married again? But you are dressed in black?' It was a question rather than a statement.

I had shied away from answering Donna but I would have to answer now. I had anticipated the question, of course and invented what I hoped was a convincing explanation.

'It's a complicated tale,' I said. 'You may remember, Signor Ridolfi, that when I stayed in your house in London, I told you that I had been brought up in a Catholic household, but in adult

65

life, had chosen to attend Anglican services as law-abiding citizens were and are expected to do, and as my Anglican husband expected, too.'

'Yes, indeed. A cruel dilemma if at heart you wished to worship as a Catholic,' Ridolfi agreed.

'Quite. Well, recently, my dear husband Hugh did pass away and yes, I am in mourning. But I have found myself troubled at the thought of still using his name. You see, I was married to him by Anglican rites and I am not sure that the true Church would recognize them as valid. In that case, I was not truly entitled to use Hugh's name and now that he is gone – well, I have decided to revert to the name of my first husband, Gerald Blanchard, for I have no doubts about the validity of my marriage to him.'

My marriage to Gerald had been a runaway match, and the ceremony was conducted not only by an Anglican vicar, but also very secretively. It was far more dubious in Catholic eyes than my wedding to Hugh. But with a little luck, Ridolfi would never find that out.

He was smiling more broadly than ever. 'So you now regard yourself as a Catholic?'

'Yes, indeed. As is Margaret here, and, I am happy to say, as my two good servants, Roger and Frances Brockley. They have followed me into the fold.' Dale bit her lip. Dale loathed all things Catholic and for very good reasons. But she had agreed to the pretence and would not betray us. I would have to remind her to genuflect to that statue of Our Lady.

'This is the most delightful news,' Ridolfi exclaimed. 'We are all of one mind, happy brothers and sisters in the true body of Christ. I will have a Mass said in the chapel here tomorrow morning before we break our fast. Ah, here is Kingham. He will show you to your rooms and see that hot washing water and mulled wine are served to you. How I hate this cold grey weather. It makes me homesick for Florence, it does indeed.'

I was given a room to myself. Brockley and Dale had an adjoining one, which had probably been meant as a dressing room for whoever occupied mine, since it was much smaller, and there was a connecting door. Their room was also plain, while mine was elaborate, its walls panelled in glossy light-coloured wood, its ceiling beams carved with leaves and fruits. There were fur rugs and padded stools and a couple of small tables as well as a wide bed with a coverlet of bronze-coloured moleskins, and a washing stand topped with a slab of greenish marble. In one corner stood a prie-dieu of white marble with a gilded crucifix hanging above it and a softly padded kneeler to make praying comfortable. The casement looked out on a wintry garden, but crocuses were showing. Spring was not far away.

A fire was laid and a maidservant came to put a taper to it. Dale did some unpacking for me, poured the washing water and then helped me to change into a fresh gown as the one I had on was creased from travelling. When she was

67

done and I was alone, I set quietly about transferring my picklocks, dagger, money and knife to my new ensemble. Then, on impulse, I knelt down at the prie-dieu. I have never known whether I actually believe in God or not. I have seen little evidence of any deity's existence. But conformity offers safety and there were times when one longed to feel that somewhere, somehow, there was a power one could call on for help.

So I knelt there and prayed for protection and guidance and then I rose to my feet and stood looking round the beautiful room.

I had often known danger, but this time it seemed to be worse than ever before. I was in hostile territory, for here there were Inquisitors whose greatest joy in life was discovering and destroying heretics like me, and who would be doubly delighted to catch one masquerading as a Catholic. The Netherlands also contained an implacable personal enemy who would very much like to get her hands on me. And I seemed to be committed to a task about which I knew nothing. Cecil, I was sure, had steered me into contact with Roberto Ridolfi but for what purpose? If Ridolfi was plotting against England again, how was I supposed to find out? I needed help, if anyone ever did.

I also needed courage. In the past, I had been a prisoner, more than once, locked in a cellar or a cell, and very much afraid. Here, I was surrounded by luxury but I was as frightened now as I had ever been.

SIX

Other People's Conversations

When my daughter Meg was married the previous summer, it was a homely ceremony in the
Hawkswood parish church, a pretty enough
place but modest in size, with no gilding or
Popish statues.

The Brussels church where Margaret Emory
was married on that cold day at the end of
March was as lofty and spacious as a cathedral,
with golden images to proclaim that it was
dedicated to the Archangel St Michael, the
patron saint of Brussels, and to St Gudule, a
female saint who had lived in the seventh
century. An immense and very beautiful stained
glass window depicting the Last Judgement
threw a pattern of rich red and sky blue and
warm amber over the interior, imparting colour
to the pale stone of walls and pillars; even
gleaming on the cream silk of Margaret's gown.

Margaret was not plain but I would not,
hitherto, have called her beautiful. Her sandy
hair was fashionable, because Queen Elizabeth
had pale red hair as well, but Margaret's needed
a great deal of washing and brushing to make it

69

shine, and she was sadly freckled and had white eyelashes, though she had learned how to darken them. Only her big grey-green eyes were really striking. But today, glowing with pleasure at being the centre of so much good-hearted attention, and clad in a gown which suited her perfectly, she did have beauty. Van Weede evidently thought so; he kept on looking at her in a way that exuded admiration.

The church was nearly full, as Signor Ridolfi apparently had a wide acquaintance in the town and had invited everyone. Most of the gowns I had packed were of black wool, but knowing that if the marriage ceremony took place, I would replace Margaret's mother, I had a couple of better gowns as well, and was in lavender and silver brocade, with a lavender silk kirtle. I had a place at the front, while Dale, acting as a matron of honour and dressed in a pale blue that echoed but did not challenge the deeper blue of Margaret's kirtle, carried the bride's train. Brockley, suave in a suit of black velvet that I thought he must have bought just before we left home, had indeed been granted the duty of giving the bride away, and with a great air of ceremony, he once more laid Margaret's hand in that of van Weede.

The service began early but it was long and was followed by a Mass that seemed even longer, and though the day was bright, it was also cold. I was relieved to get back to the Ridolfi house for the reception. The great hall there was warmed by a good fire and a long table had been spread with white damask and laden with food and silverware. Polished dish-covers and the facets of a vast and elaborate silver salt reflected the ceiling paintings of cherubs and saints, and the dancing flames of the fire. Seats and small tables were scattered everywhere; this was to be a buffet meal that would let people move about and talk to whom they would.

The food was inviting. Signor Ridolfi had made good use of his dispensation, and there were beef and chicken dishes, though beaver meat was on the table, as well, no doubt for those who didn't wish to break the fast. Beaver, being a water-dweller, was often classified as fish and during the long weeks of Lent could provide a blessed escape from eels and cod. I could remember Aunt Tabitha and Uncle Herbert making use of it. Dale considered the spread with awe.

'The Ridolfis have only been here a few days. However did they arrange all this so quickly?'

'Brussels is a town full of merchants anxious to outdo each other,' I told her. 'At times, by holding feasts too big for their own cooks to manage. So they hire help from catering businesses. It's expensive, but a wealthy man like the Signor need only snap his fingers and it's done.'

The bridal pair had led the procession from the church and, together with Signor Ridolfi and Donna, were at the hall door to receive their guests. I and the Brockleys had been invited to join them but I had said graciously that four would be enough, and that we would rather subside into being ordinary guests. I wasn't eager to be too prominent.

Looking about me as the Brockleys and I made our way towards the table, I thought that this was without doubt a brilliant occasion. The guests were all beautifully dressed and the air was fragrant with perfume and appetizing food. The guests' jewellery, like the silverware, picked up points of light. Timothy Kingham, very elegant in blue velvet and a ruff edged with Spanish blackwork, was performing introductions and shepherding the guests towards the food and there was a happy hum of talk and laughter.

So why, I wondered, was Ridolfi casting so many anxious glances past the arriving guests as though searching for someone who wasn't there, and why did Donna keep on watching him with such a worried air?

Brockley had noticed, too. 'Who is it our host is expecting?' he said, as the three of us helped ourselves to glasses of white wine, and to warm white bread, hot game pie and cold gilded chicken quarters. 'Someone who wasn't in church? I thought most of Brussels was there!'

Dale cocked her head. 'I think someone important's arriving now. Listen.'

She was right. Outside in the street, hooves were clattering and orders were being barked; the typical sounds of a mounted escort being brought to a halt. Then the butler appeared in the hall doorway and pounded on the floor with his staff.

'His Excellency Duke Fernando Alvarez de Toledo, Governor of the Netherlands!'

Watching, we saw relief replace the anxiety on Ridolfi's face, while at his side, Donna smiled and looked shy. The Duke of Alva stepped past the butler and bowed to her and to Margaret. Because of the press of people, I couldn't see him clearly, and received an impression only of a tall man dressed in black. But I knew that he controlled the Netherlands on behalf of King Philip of Spain, wielding virtually royal power. I remembered suddenly that van Weede had said that the duke might call in at the reception and wondered why. After all, this wedding party was for a very ordinary couple. Probably, money lay at the bottom of it. Roberto Ridolfi was, after all, a banker and Spain was known to have financial problems.

But in that case, why should Ridolfi look worried until Alva appeared?

Across the room, Margaret caught my eye and made a beckoning signal. With slight reluctance, I set down my wine and my plate of food on the nearest small table and went to her.

'Ah, Mistress Blanchard!' Ridolfi beamed. 'My lord duke, may I present the lady who has accompanied the bride from her home, and taken the place of her mother on this happy day. It was her manservant who gave the bride away. Margaret's parents are not accustomed to foreign travel.'

73

He was using French and I replied in the same language. I could see Alva properly now. He was indeed very tall and also lean, with a long, olive-skinned face and although he was smiling amiably, his black outfit gave him an ominous air. It was relieved only by his white ruff and the flash of his jewels. His hair was jet black, his dark eyes hawklike. He reminded me of Francis Walsingham and had the same effect on me, which was to make me nervous.

However, he was here to be sociable, and he made conventional conversation like any other guest, asking how long I had been in the Netherlands and what the sea crossing had been like. When I sensed that the right moment had come, I excused myself and returned to my companions. All the guests were now in the hall and the receiving was over. The Brockleys had seated themselves at the table where I had abandoned my platter and wine, and I joined them. Dale, nibbling chicken, remarked: 'That man looks frightening. Is he really governor of this whole country?'

'He is,' I said. 'But I don't suppose we'll ever see him again, so there's no need to be afraid of him.' I turned slightly as I spoke, to see where the duke had got to now. He and Ridolfi had come over to the buffet table. The duke was holding a silver wine goblet but neither man was eating. Instead, Ridolfi seemed to be speaking to the duke in a curiously urgent way. It didn't look like small talk.

It didn't look anything at all like small talk! I

caught Brockley's eye and we both began to watch them, though as unobtrusively as possible. The duke shook his dark head vehemently and banged his goblet down on the buffet table, so hard that some of his wine slopped over, staining the damask cloth. Ridolfi made an appealing gesture with both hands. Then I noticed that someone else besides us seemed to be taking an interest.

Once more, I met Brockley's eyes. His steady blue-grey stare was comment and question all in one.

Our host and the duke are not discussing the weather. And we're not the only ones who know it. Timothy Kingham is hovering as near as he dares. Why? And what do we do?

'Brockley,' I said in a low voice, 'you and I are going to fetch some extra food, and move as close to Ridolfi and Alva as we can. They're near that splendid salt. We can stand and stare at it in riveted admiration.' Out of the corner of my eye, I saw Donna and Margaret making their way towards us. Conversation with them just now would be a hindrance. 'Stay here, Dale, and talk to Margaret and our hostess.'

As Brockley and I rose and made for the buffet table, I saw Dale's mouth droop, as it sometimes did when I was off with Brockley on some ploy or other. One of these days, I thought distractedly, I would have to seize the nettle. I would have to sit down with Dale and explain to her, once and for all, that there was nothing between Brockley and me but comradeship and

75

that it in no way threatened her bond with him as his wife.

It would be an awkward occasion, I thought and this wasn't the moment for it. Something was going on, between Ridolfi and the Duke of Alva, and as I was now fairly sure that I was here because Cecil believed Ridolfi was making mischief in some way, I must try to find out what. If possible, with more subtlety than Kingham, who in my opinion was being obvious.

I brought us up beside the salt. We both seized extra chicken patties to add to our platters and then stood still, our eyes fixed on the glittering silver thing, two impressed guests, concerned only with eating and admiring and not of course in the least interested in Ridolfi and Alva. They were only a few feet away but our backs were turned towards them.

With my spare hand, I pointed to the complex arabesques chased into the front of the salt. Brockley nodded and also pointed, pretending to draw my attention to some other feature. Behind us, the conversation between Ridolfi and Alva now had a decidedly irritable tone. We strained our ears.

Presently, we edged away, and sought a quiet corner. 'What did you make of that?' I asked him.

'It was in French and I didn't follow all of it,' Brockley said. 'Signor Ridolfi has an Italian accent and the duke has a Spanish one and my French couldn't quite cope. I *think* I heard the name of Mary spoken, and I believe the Signor

76

also mentioned the word Ross. He was grumbling. He said something about it being difficult to get to this wedding because he had to delay his journey from England in order to get a letter of introduction from Ross. An introduction to Alva, would that be? Doesn't Mary Stuart use that Scottish bishop who never seems to be in Scotland, John Leslie, Bishop of Ross, as an ambassador to Elizabeth's court? And I did hear the duke say, very indignantly, that he needed all his troops to keep the Netherlands in order. He was annoyed and he let his voice rise. He spoke of dangerous Lutheran influence ... only then, I think he moved, and I lost him.'

'I didn't,' I said. 'I heard what you did, and a little more. I was just a fraction nearer to him. He said he couldn't spare even one thousand men, let alone ten, and could do with more guns and ammunition himself, and as for money, Spain was in debt already.'

'And after that, Ridolfi did finally pick up something to eat and between his accent and the way he had his mouth full, I couldn't make out anything more,' said Brockley.

We stopped talking because Timothy Kingham was coming towards us, offering a big silver platter of delicacies. We hurriedly donned smiles and reached out to choose. I took what looked like a piece of salmon tart and then nearly dropped it, as he said quietly: 'I know who you are, Mistress Blanchard. I work for Cecil too. Are you here on his behalf? I think, just now, you were listening to a certain conversation.'

'I really don't know what you're talking about,' I said. 'I'm here in place of the bride's mother, nothing else. I think you have confused me with some other lady.'

Timothy merely smiled. 'You are very properly discreet. But I really do know who you are. I was listening to that conversation too. I have difficulty in communicating with Cecil just now and Cecil should know what we overheard. It will relieve his mind. I am one of Sir William's secretaries. I speak some French and Italian and Spanish – not too fluently but I understand them quite well. I was bidden to get into the Ridolfi household which I did last summer, while the Signor was still in England. He has only just come to Brussels. I was able to let Sir William know, months ago, that the Signor meant to come here this spring, and a contact was arranged here, who could get messages to England for me. However, he has disappeared and I haven't been able to send anything to Cecil since. If you have a way to contact him, I'd be glad to know of it'

So that was it. I was here to reinforce Timothy Kingham, and how cunningly Cecil had gone about it, making sure I didn't know I was being thrown into Ridolfi's path until I actually got there. I had read somewhere of people who believed in reincarnation. If their ideas were true, then in a previous existence, Cecil had probably had a sharp nose, a red-brown coat and a bushy brush of a tail and all the foxy cunning that went with them. But Timothy seemed to have no cunning at all.

'Please, Master Kingham,' I said. 'You shouldn't talk so freely, least of all with so many other people close by. Please go and offer your platter elsewhere.'

I had noticed that a number of people were moving towards us, into earshot, and Dale, who had all this time been talking to Donna and Margaret, was glancing towards us. Kingham walked obligingly away, peddling his platter as he went. I gave Dale a tiny shake of the head and moved myself and Brockley deeper into our corner. When I felt safe from other ears, I said: 'And what do you make of *that*?'

'He's English all right,' said Brockley. 'I fancy he really is genuine. But not experienced. The duke and the Signor were so engrossed with their talk that they didn't notice him listening but that was just good luck. And this certainly is the wrong time and place for him to approach you. '

'He saw us trying to eavesdrop,' I said. 'He seems to think that Cecil will be relieved by what he overheard, but that's naive. Ridolfi was trying to persuade Alva to provide men and arms for something. Alva's objecting but what if he changes his mind? It's a scheme against England. It has to be. The Signor's one of Mary Stuart's ardent supporters. I think – I thought it two years ago – that he sees himself as a knight errant, rescuing a queen in distress. And I'm sure the names Mary and Ross were both men-

79

tioned.'

We looked worriedly at each other. 'What if Ridolfi does talk Alva round?' I said. 'Or finds help somewhere else? I don't like this at all.'

SEVEN

Messengers

I wanted to go home.

There in the midst of the reception's hubbub, my brain humming with alarming ideas that should have driven everything else out of my head, I found myself yearning for Hawkswood. I wanted the comfort and companionship of my memories. I wanted to walk in the rose garden Hugh had loved so much. I wanted to sit by his grave in the Hawkswood churchyard and tell him how it fared. I was homesick as I had never been before in my entire life.

But here I was, at Margaret's wedding reception, representing Margaret's mother. I must stay in the hall, eat, drink, make conversation. I must join in the robust jokes when the couple were bedded. In the midst of luxury and celebration, I was as much a prisoner as if I were in a dungeon.

The reception dragged on. The Duke of Alva took what looked like a somewhat brusque leave of Ridolfi and departed. The buffet meal was finally cleared and then there was dancing, well into the evening, and then came the time

81

when bride and groom were stowed away in a bedchamber with cherubs painted on the ceiling, pomegranates (a traditional emblem of fertility) embroidered on the bed-hangings, a fire in the hearth, and a supper tray at the bedside. Some of the guests then left, and the rest of us partook of supper in the hall where a new set of dishes had appeared on the table.

Eventually, and it felt as though several years had elapsed since the morning, I was able to retire to my own bedchamber, taking both of the Brockleys with me. Brockley, by then, had had time to tell Dale what we had overheard, and who Timothy Kingham was. Dale was astounded.

'You mean that Master Kingham talked to you so openly ... how sure is he, really, that you're who he thinks you are? I think he might be dangerous to work with.'

That was Dale all over. She was not a highly intelligent woman but sometimes she produced surprising shafts of insight about people. She added: 'One thing's plain as the nose on my face. If Signor Ridolfi wants the Duke of Alva to lend him ten thousand men, then that means he's trying to raise an army. For what? I think he wants to lead an invasion.'

'Quite,' I said. 'And we think the Bishop of Ross was mentioned. He's Mary Stuart's ambassador to Elizabeth. Alva seems to be saying no to Ridolfi, but that could change. I think we should leave for England as soon as we possibly can.'

Just to think of it lightened my heart. I would report what I had learned to Cecil and then I would sink back into the peace of my own home and draw it round me like a protective cloak. I would sleep in the bed where Hugh and I had loved. I would get out his chess set and play a few games with Sybil, and tell myself that I could feel Hugh standing close by, shaking his head when I made mistakes.

'Time to say goodnight,' I said. 'Dale...?'

'Goodnight, madam,' Brockley said, and withdrew, leaving Dale to help me out of my lavender gown before bidding me goodnight in her turn and going to join him in the room next door.

That night, when I was alone, I cried for Hugh, but the thought of soon returning to Hawkswood was nevertheless a warmth and a comfort deep within me.

In the morning, I rose early, called Dale to help me once more into the lavender gown, and then we went down to breakfast, which was served round the big table in the hall. Brockley had already risen and gone out to the stables to make sure that the horses we had brought had been properly cared for. Brockley would always be a groom at heart.

The Ridolfis were at the table when Dale and I came in. We greeted each other in the usual fashion, everyone hoping the others had slept well, and remarking on the fact that it was another sunny day. Bruno came in with jugs of small ale, followed by Timothy Kingham with a covered dish that smelt of fried fish. I let my nose twitch and he smiled and said: 'Fresh trout, madam. I recommend it,' and I let him help me to some of it.

What no one was mentioning and everyone was wondering, of course, was how the newly-weds had fared last night. I had seen a tray being taken up, so evidently they were break-fasting in their room. I could not speak of plans for departure until I was sure that all was well with Margaret. I remembered the morning after my daughter's wedding and how ineffably smug she and George had looked when they came downstairs. I hoped that for Margaret and Antonio van Weede, it would be the same.

When breakfast ended, however, there was still no sign of them. I went out with Dale to walk about in the garden. When we returned, we caught sight of van Weede, cloaked, appar-ently going out of the front door on his own. I frowned, wondering where Margaret was.

'Dale,' I said, 'go upstairs and begin packing our hampers. I must find Margaret. I very much hope we'll soon be on our way home.'

'I'll be glad, I don't mind saying so,' Dale told me. 'I'm not easy in my mind here, pre-tending to worship in a way I don't like, and I didn't like that duke we saw yesterday. He looked frightening. So *Spanish*.'

'Not so loud,' I said. 'And next time you pass that statue in the vestibule, do remember to genuflect. You forgot when we came back from

84

the church yesterday. Go and pack.'

Dale muttered a somewhat sullen apology and hastened away. I found Margaret in a small parlour, doing embroidery in the company of Donna, who rose to her feet as I came in.

'Margaret has been wanting to see you, Madame Blanchard. Have you been out? I will leave you together.'

She gathered up her frame and workbox and left the room. I took her place and said: 'Well, Margaret. How quiet it seems today, after yesterday's excitement. You and Antonio – I suppose I can call him that – will be going back to the farm before long, I imagine.'

'Oh, Mistress Stannard!' said Margaret, forgetting that in the Netherlands I was Mistress Blanchard and reverting to my real name by mistake. 'I ... am so grateful to you for bringing me here and looking after me and ... and ... but...'

'Margaret!' I said. 'Margaret, my dear, what's the matter? Surely ... *Margaret!*'

For she had dropped her embroidery frame on the floor and thrown herself into my arms, and warm, wet tears were spilling on to my shoulder, soaking into the brocade of my gown.

'What is it? What's the matter?' I hugged her but then lifted her gently away from me so that I could see her face. 'My dear! Surely ... surely Antonio hasn't been unkind? I would never have expected...'

'No, no, it isn't that!' She drew back from me, found a handkerchief and wiped her eyes. 'No, he was kind, patient. Gentle. And worried. I was sorry. I wasn't being what I ought to be. He's gone out now. He said he wanted a walk, on his own. He looked so unhappy and it's my fault but I didn't know ... I never guessed ... it *hurt* so much!' said Margaret, and dissolved into tears once again.

Oh, dear God. In my head, I could see Hawkswood shrinking away into the distance, further and further out of reach. Perhaps Eve felt like this when she and Adam were thrust out of Eden. I put my arms round Margaret once again and held her until she was quiet.

'Now, listen,' I said. 'You were unlucky. For some girls, it can be like that, to start with.' It hadn't been like that for me and clearly not for my daughter Meg either and I hadn't anticipated that it would be so hard for Margaret, but at least I'd heard of the problem before. 'It doesn't stay like that,' I said. 'The next time, it will be quite different. Remember that it will be different and don't be frightened, because being frightened will make you tighten up and create the very thing you fear. You see...'

I spent the next hour giving Margaret advice, thankful for my own varied past, because in the course of it, I had learned much that could be helpful to her and to van Weede, too. Antonio might, gently, offer one or two suggestions. From what she said, he was concerned by her distress and would want to ease it.

Margaret was essentially a sensible girl. She listened to me with attention, and when I had finished, she said: 'I know that it isn't supposed to be the way it was last night, and I do understand that I'll get over it. But it was just such a shock, and ... well, that's not the only thing. I mean, not the only reason why I'm upset.'

Now what? I looked at her anxiously. 'What else is there? You must tell me everything that's worrying you. You can't be worried about the language – you can speak French with Antonio and you'll soon pick up Dutch. Everyone here seems to speak both. Are you worried about taking charge of a household? Because...'

'No, no. Or I wouldn't be if I were in England. But this is a strange country. I don't ... I don't know how things *work* here. I don't know the names for half the dishes we've eaten! Everything is so foreign. No one here is English except Master Kingham and he won't be there at the farm. Mistress St— Blanchard, you aren't going to go back to England at once, are you? You aren't going to leave me here alone until I'm used to the place and have begun to feel at home, are you? I need you to stay with me, just for a while. *Please* say you'll stay! We didn't talk of this before; I never thought about it; I didn't know how I'd feel. Please, please, say you won't go away yet. Antonio's still a stranger. I only met him first a few days ago. I'm not ready to be alone with him. Not yet!'

'You can unpack the hampers again,' I said to Dale.

To Margaret, I had made the only promise I

87

could possibly make, in humanity. I would return to the van Weede farm with her and stay there as a guest, until she felt sure of herself. The ache for Hawkswood was almost physical, a dragging in my stomach, but there was nothing to be done about it. And how on earth, now, was I to make that essential report to Cecil? What we had overheard should certainly be conveyed to him (though I would put in the possibility that Ridolfi might yet persuade Alva into cooperating with him). If Kingham had no means of contacting England, then I must see to it instead.

Dale, who was in the very act of buckling a strap round the last hamper, looked at me with so much astonishment that her expression was almost comical. 'We're not going home after all, ma'am?' she said blankly.

'Not yet.' I started unstrapping a second hamper. Briefly, I explained the difficulty. Understanding came into her eyes.

'Poor lass. I can imagine just how she feels.' Dale lifted out a pile of dresses and began putting them back in the press from which she had taken them only a short time ago. 'She'll get over minding his love-making, but being left here in a foreign land – that's different. I'd be terrified, myself. Her parents shouldn't have pushed her off as they did. I never thought it was right. Just wanting to be rid of her because she wasn't as biddable as they thought she ought to be. And wanting her to marry a Papist. It's a marvel they didn't send her to Spain and be done with it!'

'It's done now,' I said. 'And I have to see her through. Is that someone tapping on the door. Who's there?'

'Brockley, madam.'

I called him in and Dale at once began to regale him with the news that we weren't going home yet, on account of Mistress Margaret was upset over being left among strangers and had begged me to stay awhile longer. I helped to finish the unpacking and then said: 'We have things to talk over. I have done some thinking since yesterday. Sit down, both of you.'

They did as I asked. I said: 'We have to get word to England, to Cecil, about the conversation we overheard. I suspect that Roberto Ridolfi wants to assemble an army to invade on behalf of Mary Stuart, with the Bishop of Ross caught up in it somewhere.'

'I agree, madam,' Brockley said.

'Then it's likely that messages are going to and fro. Wouldn't Ridolfi – and any other conspirators – want Mary Stuart to know what is being planned on her behalf? Before we send word to Cecil, I'd like to find out who is carrying messages to England for Ridolfi. I fancy Cecil will want to get hold of him.'

'Master Kingham might know,' Brockley said. 'He's supposed to look after the English guests. Say you want him to escort you and Dale round the town. I shall go back to the stables and occupy myself there.'

* * *

It was a simple ploy, and it worked very well. Antonio van Weede was still out and in case Donna had any ideas of coming with us, I had a few words with Margaret. 'Tell her you want to make sure you're here when Antonio comes back, but say you don't want to be on your own.'

Margaret looked at me with widening eyes but asked no questions and did as I wished. In half an hour, Dale, Timothy and I were on our way, ostensibly to look at the market in the Lower Town. When we were a safe distance from the house, I said: 'Master Kingham, yesterday, you told us – Brockley and me – that you applied for a post in this household on the instructions of Sir William Cecil. Was that true?'

'Yes, Mistress Blanchard, indeed it was, last July, while Signor Ridolfi was in London.'

'And now Cecil has arranged for me to be in Brussels too,' I said. 'There are things I need to know. If I ask questions, will you answer them if you can?'

'Of course I will. I am relieved to see you. This is the first time I have had an assignment like this and it isn't at all easy.' He sounded despondent. 'I do have some knowledge of languages but not enough, and I can't decipher codes or pick locks. I have heard you can do both. I am sure the Signor uses codes sometimes. It has worried me.'

'I hope there'll be no need to crack ciphers or force locks,' I said. I added, with curiosity, 'I

90

take it that it was you who kept Cecil informed of the Signor's plans. Someone, I think, must have let him know when the Signor decided to come to Brussels.'

'Yes, it was just as you say. The Signor was planning it back in last September and I reported that immediately. I also told Cecil when the Signor offered to host the wedding. Master van Weede wrote to him the moment he heard his proposal was accepted and then the Signor made a great to do over sending word, at once, that he wanted the privilege of arranging the ceremony – he couldn't leave for Brussels at once, but he sent a messenger dashing off ahead of him, so as to get there before van Weede did any arranging on his own account.' Timothy's face became dejected again. 'I got a glimpse of the letter before he sealed it – I often tiptoed into his office to see what was on his desk. The letter wasn't in cipher, naturally, but it was all in Italian instead and I could only make out part of it. Still, I knew the gist, because the Signor talked about it so much. So I passed on the news. I passed on everything I learned, as a matter of course.'

In inveigling me to Brussels, I thought savagely, Cecil had had a great deal of luck. Walsingham's fortuitous encounter with van Weede, a relative of Ridolfi's, had been lucky. So was the fact that van Weede was so easily impressed by men of importance, and therefore so malleable. And when Cecil heard that Ridolfi was actually going to be in the forefront of the wedding arrangements, bringing me into close contact with him, he must *indeed* have felt that the cohorts of heaven were fighting beside him. Cecil was a practical man and hard-working. I had heard that midnight sometimes found him still at his desk. It wasn't likely that on hearing that final item, Cecil had forthwith repaired to his nearest church and spent the night on his knees before the altar, offering prayers of gratitude. But he ought to have done.

'Tell me,' I said, 'does the Signor now correspond with anyone in England? And if so, who carries his messages?'

'Messages!' Master Kingham groaned. 'Didn't I say yesterday that I haven't been able lately to get word to Cecil at all? I was told that when I reached Brussels, a contact would make himself known to me if I went to a certain tavern in the evenings. So I did and someone did make himself known to me, and said we'd meet there the next evening too. But on the next evening he didn't come, and then another man tapped my arm and said to me, very quietly, in French – my French is better than my Italian – that yesterday I'd been keeping dangerous company. The fellow I'd been talking to had been taken up by the Inquisition.'

'Dear God!' I said, horrified.

'So what do we do now?' Timothy was clearly frightened as well as dejected. 'I daren't write direct. Oh, I could address letters to a cousin of mine – my closest relative as it happens, and I know I can trust him to pass them to Cecil. And the Signor says I can put letters in with his and send them by his usual messenger. But I'm English, and I'm afraid that if there really are plots afoot, then my letters might be opened and read.'

'But about Ridolfi's messengers,' I said, wishing Kingham would keep to the point, and also feeling that initiative was not his main asset. Couriers could presumably be hired in Brussels as they could in any other big city. I was beginning to see why Cecil had so badly wanted me here. Kingham wasn't that effective. 'Who carries Ridolfi's letters for England?' I persisted.

'It's just one man, and he's the last one I'd entrust anything to. When he writes to England, Signor Ridolfi doesn't use one of his own employees. It's a man called Charles Baillie and he's really employed by – well, by the Holy Father himself! Giorgio Bruno knows all about it; he's very impressed by Charles Baillie. He's told me that Baillie was once part of Mary Stuart's household. Not now, of course; he wouldn't be allowed in and out of England the way he is if that were so. Nowadays he's a Vatican courier. He travels between Rome and England and he calls on Ridolfi to collect and deliver messages for him as well. He's Flanders-born, Bruno says, but Scottish by descent, speaks six languages, and he's a passionate Papist.' He said the last word with marked distaste.

'Bruno talks to you very freely,' I observed.

93

'Bruno talks freely all the time,' Timothy said. 'Too much for discretion, I sometimes think. But he thinks I'm a passionate Papist too.' He then startled me by spitting expressively on to the cobbles. 'I pretend,' he said. 'I cross myself whenever the Pope is mentioned, and when I was gossiping in the stables one day, I told the grooms a lying tale about a lazy stable-boy who took so long to saddle up one morning, I reckoned I could have recited thirty paternosters while he was doing it. I attend Mass most devoutly as well. No one doubts my beliefs, but many English Catholics are still loyal to Queen Elizabeth, and yes, I do suspect that I am being watched. I don't think I was at first, but I fancy I'm being eyed with some suspicion now. Probably because there *is* a plot under way. Perhaps it hadn't started properly when I first took up this post.'

'How did you get yourself taken into the Signor's employ in the first place?' I asked.

'There was a vacancy and I was sent along with a fine set of credentials, including a letter purporting to come from a Catholic priest in the north of England – there are quite a few of them there – extolling my regular attendance at Mass. But it didn't say whether or not I was loyal to the English queen. I think,' said Timothy, 'that the Signor does not always look far ahead. But now, perhaps, he has begun to wonder about me. Mistress Blanchard, I do know this. I still slip into his study when I can and look at his desk. Since arriving here in Brussels, he has

94

sent letters to England in cipher.'

'Timothy,' I said, 'what does this Charles Baillie look like?'

'So there we are,' Brockley said, when he and Dale and I were once more back in the house and had gathered in my room on the pretext of looking at purchases made on their behalf. I had bought white thread and linen for Dale so that she could make Brockley a new shirt. 'Signor Ridolfi is corresponding with England in cipher. With Ross perhaps, or Mary?'

'Ross is one of the few people allowed access to her,' I said thoughtfully. 'I do know that.'

'It might be worth trying to get a look at some of the Signor's letters,' said Brockley.

'No!' I spoke sharply. Several times in the past, I had been obliged to search other people's papers, and it was a task I detested. 'I'm always afraid of being caught and with reason,' I said. 'Remember Anne Percy, the delightful Countess of Northumberland, and what she did when she found me at it? And look what happened last year!'

The previous year, I had had good reason to examine someone else's document box but no means of doing so myself. Sybil Jester had tried to do it for me, with an outcome that nearly led to tragedy.

'I never want to do that particular task again or let anyone do it for me,' I said. 'I have nightmares sometimes, thinking what might have befallen Sybil. Look, I did find out what this man Baillie looks like. Short, stocky, non-descript colouring, very good clothes, usually black. I think Cecil's men would stand a fair chance of identifying him from those details. Dover's his likeliest port of entry. If the letters he's carrying are seized, then Cecil and Walsingham can get them decoded. Brockley, I can't leave for England while Margaret still needs me. I think you will have to carry the news of all we've learned – including Baillie's description – to England.'

'Young Kingham doesn't impress me,' said Brockley sourly. 'Most people would have dodged any possible watchers and found a messenger by now, privately.'

Dale had another of her perceptive moments. 'It's because he's frightened,' she said. 'He can't bring himself to take risks.'

'Maybe.' I looked apologetically at Brockley. 'Anyway, there seems to be no alternative to sending you. You'll take a letter for Sybil – instructions about the care of Hawkswood. That will seem quite natural. But you'll also have a letter for Cecil.' A further idea suddenly struck me. 'Brockley, yesterday, at the feast, there was one name I don't think either of us heard spoken. Did either Alva or Ridolfi mention the Duke of Norfolk?'

'I didn't catch it if so, madam.'

'Nor did I. It's a relief, knowing what the queen feels about him.' I gnawed my lip. 'All the same, when Ridolfi was in England and so busy plotting it's a wonder he had time to do any normal financial business, Norfolk was neck deep in those plots. He hoped to marry Mary Stuart, if I remember rightly.'

'Even though she's still married to the Earl of Bothwell as far as anyone knows,' Dale put in, making a disdainful grimace.

'She's probably decided that he's dead,' I said. 'Mary Stuart is the sort of woman who believes what she wants to believe. Norfolk had a bad fright that other time, and ended up begging for Queen Elizabeth's forgiveness. According to Cecil, the queen would be appalled to think that he was ungrateful enough to let himself be entangled in this latest web. And yet ... last time, I think Mary was depending on Norfolk to be her Trojan Horse for getting herself into English minds as a credible alternative to Elizabeth. He's an English duke, after all. If she has cast lures at him again...'

I made up my mind. 'I'll say in my letter to Cecil that we did not hear his name mentioned, but Ridolfi is definitely scheming. Cecil will have to decide whether to investigate Norfolk further or not. So there we are. Brockley, I'm afraid you will have to face the Channel again. Twice, since I'll want you to come back.'

'I'll leave as soon as you wish, madam,' Brockley said.

Dale, whose dislike of being parted from him seemed to increase with every year, looked miserable.

97

EIGHT

The Reluctant Ferret

'Margaret,' I said, intercepting her as she came out of the kitchen at van Weede's farm, and steering her into the parlour, 'we've been back here for over a week now.' I sat us down on a settle. 'I'd say you've become very much the mistress of the house! How are things otherwise?'

Margaret seemed reluctant to answer but at last, fiddling with the tassel of a cushion, she said: 'You mean that you want to go home.'

'Not until Brockley gets back from England,' I said. 'If he brings news that all is well at Hawkswood, I could stay a little longer. But in the nature of things, I shouldn't stay too long. Antonio won't want that and he's right. You know he is, Margaret.'

'Has he said so?'

'Not yet. He's too polite. But I can sense what he's thinking.'

'You were right to tell me that ... it ... wouldn't always be unpleasant,' Margaret said. 'I don't mind it now. There's no pain any more. And I do understand that it's a duty, part of being married and keeping one's husband contented. We all have to do our duty.'

I repressed a groan of sheer pity. It was so sad, I thought, that this likeable girl should experience no joy in what ought to be a glorious pleasure. I said: 'Men like to think that what they enjoy, we enjoy too. At least, try to make him think he is pleasing you. Very likely there will be a child on the way before long. That will be something to look forward to.'

'I shall be nervous about that, without you,' Margaret said frankly.

Here, I was on firm ground. 'You need not worry,' I said. 'Two of the women servants here are widows who have had children and I can tell that they're well disposed towards you. They will look after you. I think the elder one, Gertrud, likes you very much. I've seen her smiling at you. In fact, I think I shall go and talk to her now. Before I leave, I shall make sure that you are safe in kindly hands.'

I found Gertrud in the kitchen, slicing onions at a table beside the front window. The kitchen had windows looking both east and west, and although we had just had a week of wind and showers, this April morning was fine. Gertrud was about fifty, heavy in build, with a broad, amiable face and flat feet. Because of the feet, it hurt her to stand for long and her work was mostly concerned with getting food ready to be cooked, washing platters and glasses, and cleaning utensils, all of them jobs that she could do while perched on a stool. The other women

99

saw to cleaning the house and doing the laundry.

'Gertrud,' I said, joining her at her table and picking up a knife to help with the onions, 'one of these days, the young mistress will have a child, I expect – well, we all hope so – but I won't be here then. However, I am here to represent her mother and I want to be sure that Margaret will be looked after when the time comes, by someone knowledgeable.'

'Bless you, Madame. I've had six,' said Gertrud placidly. 'And reared them all, by the mercy of God and His mother. And Anna, that does all the polishing, she's had five and three are still living, grown up now. Madame Margaret will be as safe with us as with anyone. I'll tell her to let me know the first minute there's signs, yes, and warn her that when that happens, she's not to ride. The master's buying her a pony, did you know? He's a good, generous man. You don't need to be anxious about her. You're thinking you should be going back to England soon?'

'It's usually best for a newly married pair to be left to themselves,' I said. 'I need to wait until my Brockley returns, of course; it would be absurd if we passed each other in the middle of the Dover strait. I hope he comes back soon. Today is fine enough, but we've had some bad weather lately and the Channel...'

'Can't have caused too much trouble, Madame,' said Gertrud, and used her knife to point out of the window, towards the avenue of

100

poplars. A horseman was halfway along it, coming towards the house. 'I'd reckon that's Brockley.'

I greeted him when he arrived but then left him and Dale alone. Brockley would tell me his news when he was ready. Margaret had gone out to collect eggs from the poultry yard and I waited in the parlour, warmed by a sweetly scented fire of applewood. In less than an hour, Brockley and Dalc both appeared. Brockley, who wore no beard or moustache, had shaved, put on a fresh suit and donned clean indoor shoes, but his eyes were tired.

'You've made good time,' I said. 'You must have spent some long hours in the saddle!'

'I did,' Brockley said. 'But I didn't want to waste time and I was lucky. The horses I hired were good ones and there was a following wind for both the Channel crossings. But coming back it was mighty cold on deck and I stayed on deck because down below was as fetid as a midden. Most of the other passengers were seasick and I didn't want to join them. And then,' he added with feeling, 'the road from Ostend was mostly mud.'

'Oh, Brockley!' I said commiscratingly. 'Do sit down, both of you. You've had something to eat, I hope? Dale...?'

'Yes, ma'am. Gertrud made him something,' said Dale.

'Good. Well, Brockley? How did your errands go?'

'I saw Sir William Cecil, madam ... no, Lord

101

Burghley now. The queen has raised him up as he said she would. He gave me this for you.' He held out a thick letter bearing Cecil's seal. 'I also went to Hawkswood and can tell you that all is in order. Arthur Watts says he'll turn your mare Roundel out to grass if you're not back by May.'

'Thank you, Brockley. Tell me, did my lord Burghley say anything when he had read my letter?'

'Yes, madam. He admitted, with something like an apology, what we all thought – that he had placed you here, where you would be likely to meet Signor Ridolfi, on purpose, trusting you to realize – and to learn what you could.'

'I knew it,' I said.

'He also said that you had confirmed what he already suspected. His detailed answer is in the reply you're holding, madam.'

'Yes.' I fingered the thickness of it. There were several sheets inside. Cecil clearly had a good deal to say to me. 'I must read this,' I said, breaking the seal. 'But wait with me. I may want to talk the contents over with you both.'

It was a lengthy letter and I don't propose to quote it all. It exasperated me so much, indeed, that it's a wonder I didn't tear it into shreds then and there, or crumple it up forthwith and hurl it into the scented applewood fire.

It began by thanking me for telling him what Brockley and I had overheard at Margaret's wedding reception and for providing the name and description of Charles Baillie, for whom a watch would be kept at the port of Dover. As Brockley had said, I had confirmed suspicions that Cecil already had. There had been difficulty in confirming them before because it was not easy to get agents into place. He was glad that Timothy Kingham had made himself known to me. I might be able to help Kingham, as his means of communicating with Cecil had now failed. I read the next part aloud to the Brockleys:

I was appalled to hear that the agent who should have helped Kingham to keep in touch with me has been arrested. I urge you to take the greatest care. This is the second man we have lost. The first was a man named Robin Mayes, who had got himself into the service of the Duke of Alva. It was through him that we were first warned that Signor Ridolfi was probably trying to launch a new conspiracy and from England had written preliminary letters to the duke. Mayes sent letters to me by enclosing them with letters to his father. He was a skilled agent, better than Timothy Kingham, who has been hampered by his imperfect knowledge of Italian. He was the best I had available at the time but I knew even then that he was not ideal.

In the letter I had from Mayes, he said he feared that he had somehow incurred suspicion and that he would sooner open his veins than let the Inquisition Familiars take him. It is possible that one or two of his letters, ostensibly to his father, had been opened and read.

103

'That's the sort of thing you said Master Kingham fears, ma'am,' Dale said.

'He may be right,' I remarked, and continued to read aloud:

Mayes told me that he meant to escape to England, bringing any further news with him. He would need to pick a moment when his absence wouldn't be noticed for a while, so as to get a good start. I think he waited too long for he was found dead, floating in the Thames, just after landing in England. It is likely that he was followed and murdered to stop him from reaching me. There is no doubt that it was murder. I enclose a copy of the inquest report. As you will see, it appears to be a report on a man called Jacky Wickes. This was a name that Mayes used sometimes when he wished to cover his tracks. It seems that this time, it didn't cover them sufficiently.

With Roger Brockley's help, you have done better than either Mayes or Kingham. I may say that Her Majesty takes this whole situation very seriously and has temporarily recalled Walsingham from France, so he and I can work on it together.

It is now clear a conspiracy is afoot. One man has already lost his life because of it, and probably a second as well. Once more, I urge you to caution. I have described the fate of Robin Mayes in detail so that you fully understand the risks. If you have any reason to fear that you are under suspicion, get away as fast as you can.

104

I paused. Dale said: 'What are Familiars?'

Before setting out for the Netherlands, I had decided to find out how the Inquisition worked. Our local vicar, Dr Fletcher, was well informed. 'They collect evidence on behalf of the Inquisition,' I said. 'They carry out arrests and form the armed guard when victims are led to execution, to make sure they aren't rescued.' Dr Fletcher had added warningly, 'They are as fanatical as their masters, and thoroughly trained to work together.'

As I explained, watching the Brockleys' faces, Brockley merely nodded and I fancied that he too had made some enquiries beforehand. If so, he hadn't told Dale, who looked frightened, her pockmarks standing out as they always did when she was upset.

'I wonder they didn't just seize this Robin Mayes,' Brockley said.

'He may just have been chased by the Duke of Alva's men,' I said. 'Maybe things happened too fast for the Inquisition to be alerted. He evidently got aboard ship before he was caught – but someone who was hard on his heels managed to board a faster ship and got to England before him. Ships are sailing to England from Antwerp all the time. Poor fellow.'

I put the letter down, still half unread, in order to look at the report on the inquest, which I then passed to the Brockleys. It was a livelier document than Cecil's, since some of the witnesses had repeated, verbatim, the remarks they had made at the time. I wished I had been there to hear the skipper of the *Trusty* tell the coroner that on first catching sight of the body, he had shouted *Christ Almighty, there's a bloody corpse trying to get aboard!* I wondered if he had shouted it as he had presumably done originally, or repeated it in a flat voice, and whether those present had laughed. Even the worried Brockleys were amused.

All the same, the rest of it made grim reading. Robin Mayes – or Jacky Wickes – had been struck on the head from behind. Such an injury could have resulted if he had fallen into the river accidentally and been hit by the keel of a vessel, but his assailant had made doubly sure by stabbing him as well, again from behind. Also, there were signs that something, very likely a weight, had been tied to one ankle but had come off, allowing the body to surface. Murder by a person or persons unknown, that was the verdict, and Cecil clearly didn't dispute it.

While the Brockleys were reading the inquest report, I went back to Cecil's letter. He expected, of course, that I would wish to return home once Margaret was settled. However, he would be glad if I would do him one more favour. Could I, if the Ridolfis were still in Brussels, and given that it involved no further risk, arrange to make a further visit to them – to stay in their house for a little while, perhaps using my friendship with Donna Ridolfi as an excuse? Much remained doubtful. Even if Baillie were apprehended, there was no certainty that

106

he would be carrying questionable correspondence. As yet, there was no evidence that Signor Ridolfi had so far engaged in correspondence with Mary Stuart or her ambassador the Bishop of Ross, only that he had written cipher letters to somebody. During a stay in the Ridolfi household, perhaps I might find out. Cecil regretted that Timothy Kingham did lack certain useful skills.

Then came a reference to Thomas Howard, Duke of Norfolk. Cecil introduced it into the letter with an almost casual sentence to the effect that he was glad that Norfolk's name had not come up in the conversation I had overheard. The Duke, he said, had been living very quietly, and had shown every sign of loyalty to Her Majesty the queen.

But the following paragraph strongly suggested that Thomas Howard of Norfolk was the real or at least the most important reason why Cecil wanted me to go back to the Ridolfis.

I have spoken of this matter to her majesty. It seems to me that we need to know where Norfolk stands but the queen will not allow me to have him questioned or watched, or to have his house searched. She said she could not believe that Norfolk might be part of any new conspiracy and she does not wish to damage his loyalty by showing him that he is not trusted.

She also said that if he is plotting against her again, even though she graciously forgave him and spared his life after his past and most heinous disloyalty, then how can she trust

107

anyone at all? It is a sad prince, she said, who is betrayed twice over by her own kinsman, who is also one of the greatest in the land and who owes his life to her. The day after this conversation, she fell ill and was abed for two days. I fear for her majesty's health if Norfolk proves false, but I also fear for her safety. We need to know the truth, and her majesty needs to know that there are indeed those she can trust – including myself and including you, her sister. Please regard this as being of prime importance.

He trusted ... *dear God!* ... he trusted that I had my picklocks with me! I felt myself bristle and stiffen with determination to keep them safely in their pouch. I had brought them out of habit but now I wished I had left them behind.

And then came the coup de grace. Damn Cecil. Double, triple, damn him! He knew, said Cecil, that my loyalty to England and to my royal half-sister, Queen Elizabeth, would not fail. He was sorry to ask me to delay my return home, but so much was at stake that he must use whatever tools he had to hand. His thoughts and his prayers for my safety would be with me, however.

It had been written in his own hand; he hadn't dictated it even to his most reliable secretary. He had kept it private. But he had signed himself *Burghley.*

Well, naturally he was proud of his elevation to the baronage. Why not? It added to his status. It also gave strength to any orders that he gave to such tools as me. It made it that much harder for me to say no.

I thought: *He says he doesn't want me to take risks, but he has ordered me to do so, just the same. As he has done before.*

There was no escape. Cecil had called on my loyalty and I could not refuse him. I was the ferret that he was putting into the rat-run, and no matter how reluctant I felt, I must do my duty. I had to return to Brussels and once there, he evidently expected me to try to read my host's letters.

The idea made me cringe. Feverishly, I told myself that there were other things I could do ... I could listen, I could gossip with servants and grooms; I could encourage unwise confidences from Donna and Roberto alike. I would pick the locks of document boxes only as a last resort.

If it came to that, I thought glumly, I would also have to sit up all night struggling with ciphers by candlelight, and the last time I'd done that, I had learned that the former husband I believed to be dead, Matthew de la Roche, was still alive. The shock of that had been so bad that it had made me feel positively averse to the work of deciphering.

The letter had a postscript advising me to burn it. Very wise, I thought grimly. I didn't do it immediately, though, as I wanted to study it again. Nor did I at once tell Brockley and Dale what had been asked of me. I wanted to find the right words, words which would carry some re-assurance and a promise that we would still leave for home within a reasonable time. I sent them away and went to bed early.

I woke in the morning with a migraine.

I had suffered all my life from these occasional blinding headaches, usually at times of conflict or extreme stress. This one lasted all day, although Dale had with her the recipe for a herbal drink that usually relieved it, and Margaret, who had never seen me having an attack before, and was most alarmed, prepared the potion herself.

Towards evening, Brockley and Dale came to my room together.

'This is because of something in that letter, is it not, madam?' Brockley said. 'You told us what was in the first half, but then you read the rest and you said nothing about that. Will you tell us now?'

I peered miserably at them from under my fur coverlet. My head felt as though a crown of steel had been jammed over my brows, while an invisible demon with an invisible hammer was pounding the steel above my left eye. My stomach was nauseated but unable to come to the point.

'Ma'am,' said Dale, 'if there was anything in that letter that upset you, please tell us. Even if we can't help – could you not share it? It might make you feel better, just explaining, like.'

'Before we can go home,' I said wretchedly, 'I am ordered to pay another visit to the Ridolfis if they're still in Brussels and I dare say they are. Signor Ridolfi is probably still trying to persuade the Duke of Alva to lend him an army and Cecil wants to know if Norfolk is a party to this scheme or not. He also wants me, if I can, to find out at this end if Ridolfi has written to Mary Stuart or to Ross, in case Baillie slips the net or isn't carrying anything incriminating. He hopes I have my picklocks with me! Well, believe me, I shan't go opening document boxes if I can help it but all the same, we have to go back to Brussels.'

'Why can't Cecil have Norfolk watched, or his house searched?' demanded Brockley, while Dale was clearly on the verge of tears.

'The queen won't let him,' I said angrily. Then I sat up sharply, even though it made the invisible demon redouble his efforts, and made a wild gesture towards the basin that Dale had placed ready on the table beside me. She got it to me just in time.

I lay back, my mouth full of a vile taste, but my stomach empty, the grip of the steel crown already beginning to loosen and the demon's pounding less violent. Sharing the news was the cure I had needed.

The visit to the Ridolfis still lay ahead, a hateful obstacle between me and Hawkswood. I found however that while I had lain immobile, a decision had shaped itself. A little later, when the pain really had gone and I felt capable of getting out of bed and sitting in a chair, I told the Brockleys what it was.

'I've made up my mind. I'll do as I'm bid. We'll go back to Brussels – for three days, no more. If I can't find out anything useful in that time, then I'll admit failure and we leave for England. As for Signor Ridolfi's damned document box, I won't, I absolutely won't, attempt to broach it myself. Kingham is Cecil's agent as much as I am. He can't pick a lock, it seems. Well, he can learn. I'll teach him! He can undertake that and copy for me anything that looks suspicious. If he's willing to take the risk, that is. If he isn't, I shan't blame him, let alone argue. And that's final. Now, where's that letter? I'm supposed to burn it and I'm going to do that now.'

I tore it to pieces and cast them into my bedchamber fire. I meant to take Cecil's advice about one thing, for certain. I was going to take the greatest care, for all our sakes.

NINE

Sudden Death

Arranging to stay at the Ridolfi residence was as easy (and, I feared, as perilous) as slipping on ice. A brief message, asking if I might make a short stay to enjoy Donna's company before I left for England, brought a reply the same day, urging me to join her forthwith; she and her husband would be delighted to see me and I must stay as long as I wished.

'Damn!' I muttered. If the Ridolfis had said no, I would have been highly relieved. As things were, we set out for Brussels the next morning.

Donna, dear girl though she was, had always had a tendency to cling and she seemed to be as nervous in Brussels as she had been in London, even though in the Netherlands she had no worry about the language, because she spoke good French, which nearly everyone seemed to use.

Margaret was sorry to part with me but let me go without protest. Once or twice, when retiring late to bed and passing the bedchamber where Margaret and Antonio were, I had heard them

113

laughing together. It was high time to leave them. I felt far more anxious about Dale and Brockley.

For I knew very well that both of them, especially Dale, were longing to go home. Dale hated being in a Catholic country and having to pretend to be Catholic herself. When Signor Ridolfi, meeting us in his entrance vestibule when we arrived, told us that a Mass was being prepared and he hoped we would attend it, I heard her give a faint hiss.

'It is for such a sad purpose,' Ridolfi said. 'We would have put you off, except that in the confusion, no one thought of it and anyway, it was probably too late. Besides, I felt that Donna might be the better for your company, even though...'

We looked at him in surprise, wondering what in the world he was about to tell us, when Donna suddenly appeared and, just as she had done when we brought Margaret to the house, she rushed impulsively to embrace me. Only this time, it wasn't with a glad cry but with a sob.

'My dear Donna!' I said. 'Whatever is wrong?'

She raised a stricken face. 'It's so dreadful! It's Timothy Kingham! Last night! Why, it wasn't even after dark! It was only dusk. He went to see a girl in the Lower Town and we think he was coming home when...'

'Signor Kingham was stabbed by footpads yesterday, at twilight,' said Ridolfi heavily. 'He

114

was ... was free to go out in the afternoon. He didn't come back but no one was really anxious – and then, just after nightfall, a night watchman came here. His dog had smelt out something lying in an alley, and when the watchman went to see what it was and shone his lantern on it, he recognized Signor Kingham. They had met before, when Kingham was returning late from supping at his young lady's home. We had the body brought here at once, of course.'

Stabbed. Like Robin Mayes, I thought numbly.

'The wound was in the heart,' Ridolfi said. 'He must have died at once, which is one mercy. He is in the private chapel here and the Mass is for his soul. Now, Donna, stop weeping all over Madame Blanchard. This is no way to welcome a guest. Signor Kingham was helpful to you during your last visit, I believe, Madame. Would you like to see him?'

I had seen death before, oftener than I wished, but for me, the impact was always intense, and all the more so when the victim was young. Timothy Kingham was young.

He had been laid very respectfully on a table draped in a white cloth and there were candles at his head and feet. Father Fernando, Ridolfi's chaplain, whose plump pink face always reminded me of the painted cherubs on the ceiling of the great hall, had accompanied us. He drew back the covering sheet discreetly, presumably so that we should not see the damage done by the assailant.

115

'A coffin has been bespoken,' Ridolfi said, in appropriately hushed tones. 'There is no need of an inquest; he was clearly the victim of a violent theft. The purse he carried inside his doublet was missing.'

'The watchman told us it was very dark in the alley where he was found,' said Father Fernando. 'There are high walls to either side, apparently. No one knows why he should go into such a place when there is a direct way back here through well-populated main streets, but he may have thought it was a short cut. Poor boy.' Father Fernando sounded genuinely upset. 'And he was about to be dismissed! Somehow that makes it worse.'

'Dismissed?' I asked.

'I'm afraid so,' said Ridolfi with regret. 'And very publicly, too. Yesterday morning, I expected a business acquaintance to call on me and I instructed Bruno to place a flagon of wine and two glasses ready in my study. When he did so, he found Kingham in there, going through some papers I had placed on my desk, ready to be discussed with my visitor. They were of no great importance – they concerned the rental for this house and a mortgage on some land I own in Italy. It didn't matter who read them, but all the same, Kingham had no business to be looking at them. Bruno was outraged and created such a to-do, shouting at him, and dragging him to the hall where I was breakfasting, that most of the household must have heard him.'

'And of course, Signor Ridolfi had to dismiss

116

him, then and there,' said Fernando sadly. 'A great pity. And I fear that Bruno talked about it to the kitchen staff, afterwards. I have reproved him myself for his gossipy habits. Signor Kingham was not only ordered to leave this house by today, but had to be the subject of stares and whispers as well.'

'Worst of all,' said Ridolfi, 'when he went out yesterday, it was *because* I had dismissed him. He had not known her long but he was hoping to marry his young lady in the Lower Town. She is the daughter of a shoemaker. He went to see her, to tell her that he was leaving this household. This morning, Father Fernando took word of his death to the girl and her family. It seems that Kingham told them that he was obliged to go back to England unexpectedly and hoped she would come with him. She and her parents said they would have to consider the matter. They all came here to see his body and the poor bambina cried very much. She is only seventeen. Well, her parents will have to look elsewhere for a match for their Anna.'

'What a tragedy,' I said blankly. I saw Dale looking at me. We had both thought that Timothy Kingham was frightened. It looked as though his fears were justified.

A tragedy for Timothy and his Anna: also a disaster for me. I had been relying on Timothy's help in my dangerous assignment. Now I was cast back on my own resources.

During the Mass, I covertly watched Signor

117

Ridolfi, as he stood and knelt and prayed. He did it all with a humble mien and no expression whatsoever on his smooth olive countenance. I wondered what he was thinking.

In London, I had found that he was scheming against Queen Elizabeth, but I had not hated him for it. It was an absurd plot, too unwieldy to have any hope of success and I thought him foolish to believe in it. He inspired me more with sorrow than anger. No, I had not disliked him.

Now, I wasn't so sure. I had overheard him apparently trying to get the Duke of Alva to back him in a scheme which almost certainly involved the invasion of England. Timothy Kingham had been caught in Ridolfi's study, illicitly reading Ridolfi's papers. And that same evening, Timothy Kingham had been found stabbed in an alley where he wouldn't normally have gone.

A picture came into my mind. It was a picture of Timothy, making his way back to the Ridolfi house in the fading evening light, and meeting someone – a man – who belonged to this house. Someone he knew and did not distrust. Someone who suggested taking a short cut, or having a drink in a tavern; just through here, this is the way ... And I pictured Timothy, accompanying his acquaintance into a narrow alley where high walls to either side cut out the light so that dusk was darkness already. And then the glint of a blade; a cry, too brief and not loud enough to summon help; and a body slumping to the ground, and the assailant stooping over him to take the purse. Timothy carried it under his doublet, but the searching hands evidently found it.

Did the assailant know it was there? If he came from this house, he well might. Was his purpose truly theft, or did he just want to make the attack look like robbery? And if the latter – why? Was he acting under orders and if so, whose?

Signor Ridolfi?

I had the same room that I had had when we stayed in the house for Margaret's marriage, and the Brockleys once more had the small room adjoining. That night, in my chamber, I held a council with the Brockleys and described my suspicions about the death of Timothy Kingham. When I had finished, Brockley summed matters up.

'Let us think where we stand. We overheard Ridolfi asking the Duke of Alva for men and money. Alva refused. We have let Cecil – Lord Burghley – know of this. We think that a man called Charles Baillie may be carrying letters from Ridolfi to certain people in England and we have given his description to Lord Burghley. We know that Timothy Kingham was planted here as a spy, and that he was killed the very evening after he was caught prying in Ridolfi's study. So – what next?'

'I think this household is a dangerous place,' I said, 'and if you want to go back to England at once, the two of you, well, it might be wise.'

'But ma'am, you've got to have a maid!' said Dale bravely. 'And I don't want another woman in my place.' She added: 'I hate all this Popishness but I'll say the prayers and bend the knee to that statue of Our Lady in the vestibule and everything. I won't fail. I promise.'

'If I were to desert you in a time of danger, madam,' said Brockley, 'I think Master Stannard's ghost would haunt me.'

'You surely don't believe in ghosts, Brockley.'

'I might believe in this one,' Brockley said. 'We shall stay, madam. What do you propose to do next? The way to get firm evidence – details of what Ridolfi is up to – seems to lie in reading his letters, but...'

'Not if I can avoid it,' I said. 'For the time being, it's eyes and ears while we all look as innocent as we can. Talk to the grooms, Brockley. Oh, and cultivate the butler, Giorgio Bruno. He has a busy tongue. But arouse no suspicions! Dale, keep your ears open whenever you hear the women talking. We may learn all we need to know, just by keeping alert.'

'How long are we to stay, ma'am?' Dale asked, pleadingly.

'No longer than I can help,' I said, 'but I think we must forget the three-day limit. I'll need more than that if I'm to work without Kingham.'

TEN

Heart Failure

The Ridolfis' house had been let to them furnished, along with a small staff which included a cook who now acted as an assistant to Ridolfi's own chef (who regularly travelled with his master), and a big black tomcat whose job was to catch mice but whose favourite occupation was getting himself locked out at night and then yowling noisily to be let in.

There was a room exclusively for music, provided with a spinet, a dulcimer and a lute. This was one of Donna's favourite places. A week after my return to Brussels, just after breakfast, she drew me there so that we could practise a song that had caught her fancy.

She was playing the lute while I was seated at the spinet, when she suddenly broke off (causing me to strike a discord in confusion) and exclaimed: 'Dear Ursula! It is so good to have you here. Please stay at least until we leave Brussels. I am always homesick when I'm out of my own land, and Roberto travels so much. We spend half our lives away from Florence. A friendly companion is such a blessing.'

121

Ridolfi had, in fact, gone off on a solitary journey shortly after my return to Brussels, as soon as poor Timothy Kingham's funeral was over. I didn't know where he'd been and nor did Donna. He had come back two days earlier, just before supper. 'He has people to visit, business to do while we're in the Netherlands,' Donna had said vaguely.

I had wondered if that meant taking the opportunity to talk to the Duke of Alva again. I rather thought it had, for the day after his return, I chanced to step out of my bedchamber just as Ridolfi, down in the entrance vestibule, was greeting a messenger, and in tones so eager that my attention was caught.

'You have his reply?' The words came up clearly. 'Good!'

My bedchamber door opened on to a gallery with a banister overlooking the vestibule. Cautiously, I leant over it. Ridolfi was there below with another man, presumably a courier, breaking the seal on a letter. As I watched, he began to read. Then he cursed, loudly and un-inhibitedly, and threw the letter down on the floor. The messenger stepped backwards in alarm and I retreated hurriedly into my chamber.

I told the Brockleys what I had seen and we agreed that at a guess, though there was no proof, Ridolfi had indeed made another attempt to persuade the Duke of Alva into lending troops and money, and had once more been refused. A guess was all it was, of course. There

122

was no certainty.

I felt that I was wasting my time, and endangering myself and the Brockleys, by remaining here. For all her promises, Dale still, sometimes, failed to acknowledge the statue of Our Lady and sometimes didn't recite the responses during Mass. Eventually, someone would notice.

'It's kind of you to make me feel so much at home,' I now said to Donna. 'But you mustn't press me to stay too long. I have things to attend to in England. Come. Let's start the piece over again.'

I was turning my music back when there came an urgent tapping on the door, and I heard Dale calling my name. Donna tutted but I rose at once and opened the door, to reveal a pale and worried Dale outside.

'Ma'am! Oh, ma'am!'

'Dale, what is it? What's happened?'

'It's Roger, ma'am. He's had an accident. Oh, ma'am, can you come?'

'Excuse me, Donna,' I said. 'I'll come back as soon as I can.' I probably sounded perfunctory and Donna, who was too polite to protest but was in some ways oddly childish, pouted. I shut the door behind me and said tersely: 'Where is he?'

'On our bed, ma'am.' Dale had seized my elbow and was dragging me towards the stairs. 'He got himself indoors and up to our room and I fetched some hot water for him but oh dear, I can't abide to see him like this ... he said to

123

bring you at once; he wants to see you.'

I outdistanced her up the stairs. Brockley was seated on the bed with a steaming bowl of water on a table beside him. His jacket was off and his right shirtsleeve was rolled back. One shoe was off as well and he was alternately sponging his right ankle and a vicious graze on his right wrist and forearm. He looked round as we came in and said: 'No need for alarm, madam. Nothing's broken. I'm going to have a few fine bruises though.'

'Whatever happened?' I stepped aside to let Dale take over the business of sponging him.

'I was nearly ridden down,' Brockley said. 'Not on purpose. Simple accident.' He had obviously been shaken, however. 'I'd been out, on foot, down to the Lower Town to a saddlers there. I help the grooms when I can and there was a new bridle needed. I said I'd place the order and save someone else the trouble. So I did, and I was just coming back into the stable yard, walking in under that archway from the road, when a rider in the Signor's livery comes hurtling through in the other direction, going as if all the devils in hell were after him. The horse's shoulder caught me and threw me against the wall of the arch. And did the man pull up to see if I were hurt?' said Brockley, rhetorically and indignantly. 'No, he did not! He went straight off along the road, still galloping. I bashed an ankle and I've had a crack on the head as well...'

'What? Where? On the right side, like that

124

graze? Here?' I was already feeling his scalp. Dale, still sponging, said: 'There's a lump there, ma'am, but the skin's not broken.'

I had found it. Brockley winced as I pressed, but I was trying to find out if there was any damaged bone. As far as I could tell, there wasn't.

'You must rest,' I said. 'I've got a marigold ointment in my baggage, and another one with comfrey and golden seal in it. Gladys gave them to me before we left home. I'll get them. They'll help that graze.'

I picked up the jacket and found the torn cuff which had been scraped against the stone wall and pushed back so that his right wrist and forearm had had no protection beyond his shirt.

'My right shirtsleeve is ruined as well,' Brockley said ruefully. 'But there's something more – that's why I sent Fran to fetch you. I picked myself up, madam, and then a couple of the grooms – they'd seen what happened – came to help me. Well, I wasn't feeling so well but I was still capable of asking a question or two. What sort of horseman comes tearing straight out of the stable yard at a gallop as if he was leading a cavalry charge? Ruining his horse's legs, going at that speed on cobbles and paving stones! What did he think he was doing, I said to them – the grooms, I mean. Who was he and where was he going, careering off like that?'

'And?' I said.

'One of them said he was one of the Signor's

own couriers and he'd come rushing to the stables and ordered them to saddle a fast horse; He was taking an urgent letter to King Philip of Spain, from the Signor.'

'Spain!' Dale and I said it together.

'Spain.' Brockley looked better now. The warm water was easing his pain. 'Seems the fellow said he'd got to make the best speed he could. I don't know if you know it, but the Signor's got arrangements for remounts on main routes; all these bankers have. A lot of innkeepers get juicy sweeteners for having good horses always at the ready. You'd think bankers were royalty, the way they make life easy for themselves. Well, this fellow told the grooms his letter was so important, he'd been ordered to go as fast as he could and waste no time. The whole thing had the grooms gossiping and speculating. The Signor's had correspondence with King Philip before, it seems, but not like this.'

'Spain!' I said again. 'What do we make of that, I wonder?'

I broke off speculating to get the ointments for Brockley. They were in a leather bag in my clothes press. In the short time that it took me to step through to my own chamber and collect them, however, I did some swift thinking. Returning, I said: 'I wonder if this was the result of that letter from Alva?'

'I'm wondering the same thing,' said Brockley.

I opened the bag and began handing the

126

ointments to Dale. 'If we were right about Alva's letter, and if Ridolfi is writing to King Philip *because* of it ... then what is he saying?'

Brockley's graze, now that it had been cleaned, no longer looked so bad. Dale, spreading marigold salve gently over it, said: 'The Duke of Alva is King Philip's man, isn't he? I mean, doesn't he have to do what King Philip says?'

'If Ridolfi is writing to Philip to ask him to order Alva to lend those troops...' said Brockley.

'It's all *ifs*,' I said. 'We don't *know*. Maybe Alva's letter just said he couldn't accept some invitation or other and Ridolfi was upset because he likes to show off his high connections. And maybe your hell-for-leather messenger was being sent on business to do with finance. Ridolfi is a banker, after all.'

'There's only one way to find out,' said Brockley. He gave me a significant look.

'No,' I said. 'Look what happened to Kingham.'

'I know you don't like it, madam, but it's all I can think of. If we can get a glimpse of the Signor's correspondence, it could tell us a lot. He may keep copies of letters sent as well as the ones he receives. Men in his position mostly do.'

'Brockley, I can't. I think we should just send word to Lord Burghley, tell him what has happened and what we guess. He probably has someone in the Spanish court. Spying into correspondence always has been my nightmare

127

and after I was caught by Anne Percy, and then Sybil Jester nearly lost her life doing it for me, well, I took against it. *No,* Brockley.'

'I'm fairly sure I know where he keeps his private papers.' Brockley seemed determined to be obtuse. 'I showed a visitor into his study once when Bruno was off duty. There was what looked like a document box on the shelves to the left of the desk. It had a padlock. You could make the attempt at night. I would stand guard.'

'Brockley, you're behaving as though you were Lord Burghley, or the queen herself! Don't give me orders. *No!'* I said furiously and marched off through the connecting door, shutting it after me with a bang.

Next day, I woke with another migraine.

'All right, madam,' said Brockley, when he and Dale arrived at my bedside with Gladys' potion. 'I won't mention the matter of reading Ridolfi's documents again.'

'Thank you, Brockley.'

I drank the potion and turned over. Brockley's reassurance didn't help. The attack didn't climax until halfway through the afternoon, by which time the pain had made me feel as feeble as a newborn mouse.

Because I knew that like it or not, Brockley was right.

'As quietly as we can,' I whispered, as the Brockleys came through the connecting door. 'You're both coming?'

'I can help keep watch, ma'am, and I'd worry

128

myself to death, lying in bed, wondering what was happening,' Dale whispered back.

'You have your picklocks safe?' Brockley asked.

'Yes.' I patted my skirt, and felt the secret pouch and the outline of its contents beneath my palm. I glanced down and saw that in accordance with my instructions, the Brockleys were both wearing soft slippers, just as I was. I had a lantern, ready lit. I picked it up. 'Come along.'

It was past midnight, that same night. My shakiness had faded, once I had made up my mind. It was raining outside. Gusts of wind whined in chimneys and threw spatters of rain against the windows. I hoped that the sounds of the weather would mask any accidental noises we made.

Brockley led the way as we crept out on to the gallery and turned towards the stairs. These were a danger, because some of them creaked. We went down cautiously, stepping as gently as we could. Our descent, therefore, was slow. It felt as though a century had passed before we were all safely down in the vestibule.

Brockley turned to the left, and made towards the door of Ridolfi's study. He tried it, found it unlocked, and softly pushed it open. He looked inside, then turned to me and nodded. While Dale stayed on watch in the vestibule, he and I slipped into the room.

I put the lantern down on the floor in the shadow of the desk because to my alarm, the window wasn't shuttered. It looked out over the

129

garden and it was most unlikely that anyone would notice a light in Ridolfi's study, but I didn't like it, just the same. Going over to the window, I found that the inner leaded casement opened silently enough but when I reached out to close the shutters, the left-hand hinge squeaked. I withdrew and closed the window, afraid to try again. I would just have to take a chance.

Brockley touched my arm. He had picked up the lantern and was holding it to reveal the shelves beside the desk. 'There's the box, madam. Padlocked, as I said.'

I lifted the box, which wasn't heavy, and brought it to the desk. Brockley put the lantern down beside it. I reached for my picklocks.

And then stopped short with a gasp of fright as something moved outside the window, something that was not wind or rain. Standing rigid, I stared towards it. Two green, luminous eyes, stared in at me, and something yowled pathetically.

Evidently, the tomcat had been let out as usual after supper, set off on a hunting (or possibly courting) expedition, failed to come back before the servants' bedtime and had got himself locked out yet again, and in the rain, too. I had no wish to leave him out there on such a night and besides, now that he had found a human being who might let him in, he would demand admittance all too loudly. I knew very well how much noise he could make. It woke people up quite often. I went back to the window and opened it for him. He jumped over the sill, landed by my feet and rubbed my ankles in a polite if damp feline *thank you* before shooting out of the door. I heard a faint, startled exclamation from Dale as he sped past her, making no doubt for his basket in the kitchen. I shut the window with trembling hands, examined the sill with my lantern and used the hem of my skirt to wipe away a splash of rain and a couple of wet paw-prints.

Shakily, I began once more to feel for my picklocks. 'I'll go back to watch with Dale,' Brockley whispered. I nodded. My hands were not only shaking, but sweaty. If I – if we – were caught, what would happen to us?

Once again, that horrid vision of Timothy Kingham's last moments rose up in my mind. Timothy himself, unhappy after his dismissal, afraid of losing his girl, glad to see someone he knew and perhaps liked, someone – no doubt from the Ridolfi household – who perhaps said he was sorry Timothy was going, said he believed there had been a misunderstanding.

Come along to my favourite tavern. They have some fine ales there, and wine as well. Let me try and cheer you up. Through here's the quickest way; it's only a step...

And then, in the dark, narrow lane between the walls of tall houses, the sudden hard hand shoving Timothy back against one of those unyielding walls, and the swift thrust of a blade. He would have felt a pain in his heart and then he would have been falling, falling into a pit of darkness, his life ending, all in a moment. All because he had been found looking at Roberto Ridolfi's papers ... perfectly harmless ones. If I were found reading papers that were not harmless ... if the Brockleys were caught helping me...

My heart was racing and my sweat-soaked, quivering fingers were never going to manage those picklocks. I couldn't do it. I couldn't fiddle with the padlock, go through whatever was inside the box, perhaps have to make accurate copies of letters in cipher. I couldn't do that either by working here in the study or by taking the letters to my room, which meant three more journeys on those creaking stairs, up to my room, back to the study to replace the letters and back again to my room. I wouldn't have the tiniest excuse if I were caught. If *we* were caught. This expedition endangered the Brockleys as well as, as much as, myself.

I put the box back on its shelf, took my lantern and crept from the room, shutting the door softly behind me. I felt heavy, as though guilt and shame had actual weight, but I could not stay another moment in that room.

In the lantern light, Dale's face was white and frightened. Brockley's was bewildered. 'Madam?' he said.

'I'm sorry. My heart has failed me. I can't do it. I'm too afraid. I keep thinking of what happened to Timothy Kingham. I couldn't *do* it. I couldn't.'

He put a hand on my arm, a warm, kindly

hand. 'All right, madam. We understand. Now let's all go back to bed and hope to get there safely.'

ELEVEN

Calculations by Candlelight

I slept badly and picked at my breakfast next morning. Donna at once concluded that I was downhearted because I had been remembering Hugh, and that I needed distraction. Being Donna, she decided that the best way to distract me was to take me shopping at the Lower Town market. She always went shopping when she felt unhappy, she said.

'Are you often unhappy?' I asked her. 'I know you don't like travelling and having to stay in strange countries. Is it that?'

'Sometimes, but I could stay at home if I chose. I don't like to part from Roberto, so I don't choose,' Donna said. 'No, it's what happens every month. I would so like to have children, but there has never been a sign of one and Roberto is so good about it; it almost breaks my heart.'

'If you don't think about it too much, perhaps one day God will be kind to you,' I said, trying to comfort her.

'Father Fernando says that if it doesn't happen, it's God's will,' said Donna. 'For some

134

reason that we poor mortals wouldn't understand.'

Father Fernando was good at pious platitudes. I suspected that this saved him from having to think too deeply. If someone brought him a problem, he just trotted out the conventional answer. This time, clearly, the conventional answer hadn't satisfied Donna. 'I think we should have the chance to understand,' she said now.

I agreed with her, and said so. She smiled at me and said she had always liked me because I was easy to talk to. I wanted to maintain these friendly relations and in any case, I felt genuinely sorry for her. Therefore, I also agreed to go shopping.

Donna's current maid, Giulia, who was a sallow and silent widow in her forties, came with us, and so did Dale, and one of Ridolfi's menservants, wearing a sword, to protect us from attempts to snatch our jewellery or grab new purchases from us. Brockley, still sore after his accident, had asked to be excused.

Very soon, I found myself wishing that I too had made an excuse to stay indoors, for the weather hadn't improved. It was very cold and raining steadily. Everywhere underfoot seemed to be mud and puddles. We had hooded cloaks and gloves and sturdy footwear but the chill penetrated my garments as though they were made of tissue paper.

Understandably, the market wasn't crowded. But the stallholders were there just the same, with protective awnings over their wares, so we

135

wandered about, examining the bolts of fabric, the dyed leather bags and belts, the hats and cloaks, and the patterned earthenware dishes on sale.

I bought a length of black velvet to make new sleeves for one of my gowns, and some silvery silk thread with which to embroider them. Donna gazed a little forlornly at a stall selling little ready-made kirtles and jackets for children, but let me persuade her into buying a russet velvet hat. She then sneezed loudly and Dale said that all this dawdling in the damp was giving her the shivers. A moment later, I sneezed as well and declared that we had better go home before somebody caught cold. Donna, who really loved shopping, would still have liked to linger, but I overrode her.

'I've already got one foot soaked above the ankle and the hems of my skirts are drenched,' I said. 'You're mud-splashed, too!'

She was. We all were. Giulia backed me up, insisting that her mistress ought to get home out of the wet. With Giulia and Dale carrying the packages, we hurried back to the Upper Town, trying to keep warm by rapid movement. Our manservant marched just behind us, hand on sword hilt, but no one tried to molest us. I think the weather had depressed even the criminal element. Once indoors, Donna called for mulled wine and I asked that mine and Dale's should be brought to my room. I was cold to the bone and the wet skirts of my black wool gown were like freezing fingers round my legs. I wanted to get warm and dry and then rest.

At the top of the stairs, we encountered Brockley, who must have been listening for our return, for he stepped out to meet us the moment she and I set foot on the gallery. In a voice that was barely above a whisper, he said: 'Madam! I have something to show you that will interest you.'

I felt too tired to be interested in anything but, not wishing to disappoint him, I said: 'Of course,' and led the way into my room, hoping that whatever it was could be dealt with quickly.

In my chamber, Brockley, whose grazed right wrist didn't seem to affect the use of his right hand, slipped it inside his jacket and pulled out some papers.

'The Signor's gone to dine with some fellow bankers,' he said, 'and he's taken Bruno with him. Bruno said they wouldn't be back till nightfall. The house was very quiet after they left. All the servants seem to be keeping warm in the kitchens. So I went to Signor Ridolfi's study and collected that box of his.'

'You...?' I stood staring at him, while Dale lifted my wet cloak off my shoulders.

'I managed the padlock,' said Brockley. 'Back in Hawkswood, the moment we suspected that Cecil was up to something, I decided to put one of your spare sets of picklocks in my luggage. Last year, you taught Mistress Jester how to use them and I tried my hand as well, if you recall. I'm slower than you are but it didn't matter

137

because I didn't linger in the study. I had an old cloak with me. I wrapped the box up in that and brought it to our room. If anyone saw me, I just had a cloak bundled under my arm. But no one did see me,' said Brockley, with his rare grin. 'I tackled the padlock behind a safely bolted bedchamber door. It was an easy lock, as it happened.'

'*Brockley!*'

'There were quite a few papers in the box,' Brockley said. 'Most were to do with loans and investments, but there were three that were just lines of figures, like those cipher letters you once decoded.'

'Are you saying...?'

'I took the liberty, madam, of helping myself to some of the writing paper you carry. I copied all three sheets of cipher and I have them here.'

With the pleased air of a conjuror who has just discovered a rabbit in his hat, he handed me the papers. 'I was as accurate with the copying as I could, though I admit I did it in some haste,' he said. 'After that, I put everything back, snapped the padlock shut again, wrapped the box in the cloak, and slipped downstairs and there was still no one about, so I stepped into the study, put the box back on its shelf and was out in the vestibule in seconds, strolling harmlessly across it, and this time what I had under my arm really was only a rolled-up cloak.'

Horrified, I stared at the papers he had given me. 'Brockley, after what nearly happened to Sybil, I'd never never have asked you to do such a thing. Dale wouldn't have forgiven me if I had! Would you, Dale?'

'I wouldn't put it so strongly, ma'am,' Dale said. 'But believe me, if I'd known what he was planning, I'd have tried to stop him. You took such a risk, Roger! I shudder to think of it!'

'So do I,' I said feelingly. 'Even doing the copying in your room, you had to brave the study twice, once to take the box and again to get it back. Someone could have come in at any moment while you were there – a maidservant to dust, someone to leave a note on the desk – anyone! If you'd been caught with that box, how would you have explained yourself?'

'The vestibule floor is stone,' said Brockley calmly. 'One can hear footsteps easily. If I'd heard anyone coming, I'd have had time to put the box on its shelf and then walk straight out to meet whoever it was and ask, all innocently, where the Signor was. As things were, I never saw a soul.'

'Well, you got away with it, thank God, and I suppose I'm grateful but I'm still so appalled...' Words failed me.

'It had to be done,' Brockley said. 'But it would have been cruelty to press you, madam. Only now, the rest is up to you. Can you remember the key of the cipher you decoded last year?'

'I think so, but what if the code's been changed? The key won't work then, and anyway, even if it's the same code, we need an abacus!'

'Quite so, madam. I thought of that. When I

139

was taking precautions against whatever Sir William Cecil might have in mind, and deciding to bring a set of picklocks, it struck me that if we found ourselves opening document boxes again, we might find ourselves decoding letters again, too. Better be ready for anything, I thought. So I packed the abacus from Master Stannard's study desk, as well.'

'I see,' I said faintly and sat down heavily on the bed. I was trembling. 'You did it because I was too afraid,' I said. 'I'm sorry. I should have seen to it myself.' I couldn't meet Dale's eyes. If Brockley had been caught, he might well have gone the way of Timothy Kingham, leaving her to grieve and it would have been my fault.

'I was careful. No need to fret, madam,' Brockley said, with a glint of satisfaction in his eyes. He had carried out a dangerous and necessary task which I hadn't dared to do. He was pleased with himself. 'I just hope that the code *is* the one the Signor used in London.'

'If he has any sense at all,' I said, 'it won't be. *Surely* he must have guessed that the one he used two years ago had been broken? Even if he didn't know who broke it. Changing it would be a basic precaution.'

'I don't think he's all that intelligent,' said Brockley seriously. 'Clever enough with finance, no doubt, but not in other ways. Didn't you find out, in London, that he was simply using a code he had been shown, even though he could have refined it quite easily, to make it

140

harder to break? If you ask me,' said Brockley, 'he likes to invent magnificent schemes but he doesn't pay much heed to details. He locks his important documents in a box but then he puts the box on a shelf in a study that's never locked at all! If these letters are what we think – about Mary Stuart, thrones and invasions – then I can only say that if they were mine, they'd be in a safe behind a sliding panel that no one could see unless they knew it was there, or else under a floorboard, with a hefty piece of furniture on top!'

I remembered Timothy Kingham saying that the Signor didn't seem to look far ahead. 'I can only try,' I said. 'But not during the day. Donna could come tapping at my door at any moment. I'll have to work by night.'

'We'll watch with you tonight,' Brockley promised.

He left us then, saying that he could see I needed to change my muddied dress and shoes. I folded the papers small. 'I want to rest, Dale,' I said. 'I need more sleep. Get out a fresh gown and kirtle for me. I'm going to put these in the overgown's pouch. I think they would be safest there.'

Silently, Dale helped me out of my damp garments, put a wrap round me and fetched fresh clothing from the press. She did not speak and I saw that her lips were tight.

'Dale,' I said, 'I did *not* expect Brockley to investigate the Signor's study for me, and I meant it when I said I would never have asked it of him.'

'I half wondered if he'd do it, ma'am.' Dale gave me the overgown and I put the papers away before laying the gown across the bed and getting under the moleskin coverlet myself. 'I feared that he might,' she said. 'If he'd told me outright, I would have begged him not to. But I couldn't plead against it *unless* he'd told me first, because I didn't want to put ideas into his head.' She paused. And then said: 'He wouldn't have done it for anyone but you.'

The time had come to speak, to make an effort to put this right. I mustn't let this moment pass.

'Dale,' I said, 'there is a very real regard between me and Brockley but there is nothing in it that threatens you or can harm what is between you and him. Do please believe me.'

'I know you mean what you say, ma'am.' Dale became very busy, rearranging things in the press, her face turned away from me. 'But if he dies in your service, taking risks for you, will that be harming us, or not?'

To that, I had no answer. Dale gathered up my muddied garments and said she would dry and brush them. I told her to change her own clothes first.

'As you say, ma'am,' she said politely, and left me.

I lay miserably thinking that she had understood the situation better than I had. I was a danger to her and to Brockley, every moment that they stayed with me. Brockley didn't seem to mind. But Dale would always mind. For both their sakes, I ought to send them away from me.

Well, I had tried once, and they had refused to go. I could have insisted, I supposed. Only, the thought of doing without them was frightening. I had lost Hugh; was it now my duty to cast away my best friends as well? Who would replace them? I needed someone! All the more, if Cecil meant to go on making use of me.

And now, I must try to decipher those damned letters and hope that if I succeeded, I wouldn't find anything as shocking as last time, when I learned that my former husband Matthew de la Roche, was still alive. I almost hoped that Ridolfi had altered the code. To break it then, I would need a miracle and fortunately, miracles are rare.

It was deep in the night. We had shuttered the window and Brockley had pushed a rug against the foot of my door, to make sure that no line of candlelight would show, if anyone chanced to be prowling. I had asked for our wood basket to be filled, saying that I still felt chilled after our damp morning expedition, and might want warmth in my room during the night.

Dale, still dressed, was curled up on my bed under my coverlet. Brockley and I were seated by the hearth, on opposite sides of a small table. He was tending the fire from time to time. I was equipped with paper, quill and ink. I was decoding the three letters.

None of them, mercifully, was long, but it was still a slow business. To my regret, coherent

143

words had emerged as soon as I applied the key that I had used before and (also to my regret) had found that I remembered perfectly well.

It involved numbering each letter according to its place in the alphabet, using number one for A, number two for B and so on, setting out one's text in numeric form, and then multiplying each number in turn, not by the same figure, but in a short, repeated sequence of them. The result was that in the final document, letters weren't always represented by the same number. For example, the letter B, number two in the alphabet, might be multiplied by three in one place and would appear in the final version as six, but in another place might be multiplied by five, and so would appear as ten. To decode, one had to divide the cipher numbers in the agreed sequence.

I toiled steadily, working with the abacus. Brockley did not try to talk to me. When at last I finished, I sat back, uncurling my fingers from my pen and Brockley leant down to put another piece of wood on the fire. Then he too sat back and observed: 'I fear I may have made a few mistakes when I was copying, madam. I was nervous, I expect.'

'I'm not surprised!' I said with feeling. 'You must have been as jittery as a cat in a dog kennel. Yes, I did find some oddities. Did you know, for instance, that Mary Stuart is a truly rebel lady?'

'A what?'

'I think, judging from the rest of the sentence,

that the Bishop of Ross meant that she was a truly regal lady, but the word came out as *rebel.'*

Brockley grinned. 'And,' I said, 'the good bishop recommends that all Catholics should if necessary revolve to die for the honour of Cod.'

This time, Brockley let out a half-stifled snort of laughter. 'I'm sorry, madam.'

'No need.' I said. I looked at the results of my work. 'Both of you,' I said, 'come and look at these. They're not copies of any letters sent by Signor Ridolfi. We still don't know what was in the one he sent to King Philip. These all seem to be replies – but they come from the Bishop of Ross, and clearly they're answers to letters he's had from Ridolfi. It seems that they communicated in writing even while Ridolfi was still in England, rather than meeting. Perhaps they didn't want to be seen to meet. The letters certainly are interesting.'

Dale emerged from the bedcovers, picked up a stool, and joined us. Together, we read the decoded versions, which I had spread out for inspection. There was a silence, the silence of sheer, staggered amazement.

Then Dale said: 'But ... but...'

And Brockley, in awed tones, said: 'Good God! Is Signor Ridolfi in his right mind, do you think?'

'I'm beginning to wonder,' I said. 'And the same applies to the Bishop of Ross, since he seems to be taking all this quite seriously. Though Alva obviously didn't. I feel almost

145

sorry for the man, confronted with this sort of request! Ridolfi has such a wild imagination that if this wasn't so frightening, it would be funny.'

'If he thinks he could make this work, he's like a man trying to play chess in a blindfold,' Brockley said. 'How on earth – how on *earth* – would one get armies from as far apart as the Netherlands and Spain to work as partners? How could the commander of one, for instance, let the other know if the wind is keeping him trapped in port so that he can't reach England on the chosen date – or tell him anything else that might cause a change of plan? He couldn't!'

'I know,' I said. 'It's impossible. And the Bishop doesn't seem to have noticed that it's impossible. He's obligingly repeated the details, as he says, *to make sure that he has them correctly!* Are they both living in dreamland? If the scheme did work, it would only be through luck.'

'I think,' said Dale, 'that they believe God is on their side.'

We looked at each other. 'And that, of course, is the heart of the matter,' I said. 'That's exactly what they do believe. Though, the last time Ridolfi indulged in plotting, God let him be arrested, and the whole conspiracy was destroyed. God is his captain and that's enough for him. If a real captain of a real ship made such a havoc of a voyage, a sensible crew would probably mutiny! But Signor Ridolfi isn't sensible.'

146

There was another silence, until Brockley said: 'Well, we now know what Ridolfi wanted Alva's men and money for.'

'Quite. And it isn't what we thought. Oh, it's ridiculous!' I was on the verge of hysterical laughter. 'He wants Alva's men to invade *Ireland*, so as to draw Elizabeth's army out of England. Then a Spanish army, which would have to reach our shores by an agreed time – as if contrary winds didn't exist – can march in, collect supporters among the English Catholics, and release Mary. And presumably put her on the English throne though that isn't said in so many words. Of all the crazy, cumbersome schemes!'

'Ridolfi seems to have a *few* doubts,' Brockley said. He picked up one of the letters. 'This one is evidently a reply to one where he's asked the Bishop of Ross to find out how many English Catholics really would rise in revolt against Elizabeth if they had enough encouragement – such as an army from Spain, while most of Elizabeth's soldiers are away in Ireland. Hm. Ross says he can't be sure of extensive support within England, in spite of that Papal Bull last year.'

'Absolving them,' I said sourly, 'from any loyalty to the queen and virtually threatening them with excommunication if they give her their allegiance. He all but promised to canonize anyone who assassinated her!'

'This one,' said Dale, pointing, 'seems to be about money. The bishop's asking how the

Signor's efforts to raise funds are prospering. He says a great deal of money is needed. I should think so!'

Brockley studied the letter in question. 'He suggests approaching the Duke of Alva and says he will provide a letter of introduction. The last paragraph seems to answer an enquiry about whether Mary Stuart has been informed of the plot. Apparently she has been told something but not every detail.'

'Francis Walsingham hoped that Ridolfi would get up to more mischief,' I said. 'Well, it seems he has his wish.'

'There's no mention,' Brockley observed, 'of the Duke of Norfolk.'

'No,' I agreed regretfully. 'There, we're no further on. Even so, there's enough here to be very valuable indeed to Cecil and I think that considering his past record, there's enough to justify investigating Norfolk, whether Ross spoke of him or not. Just in case. This scheme is insane, but it's also big and Norfolk is an important man.'

Dale said anxiously: 'Signor Ridolfi is addled in his brains, if you ask me. All the same, however mad this plot seems, just suppose someone – King Philip perhaps – thinks of ways to make it not so mad? Think how dangerous that could be! What if that rider who nearly knocked Roger down, rushing off headlong to the king of Spain, *was* carrying a letter that's something to do with this? I don't like it.'

'I know,' I said. 'Crazy or not, Ridolfi is

obviously persuasive. Ross takes him seriously enough. If King Philip were to agree with Ross ... we have to get back to England and take these papers with us. At once.'

TWELVE

Encounter with a Ghost

We have to get back to England and take these papers with us. At once.

It was easy enough to say. I slept heavily through the remaining hours of the night, and woke next morning cold and shivering despite my warm bed-coverings, with aching limbs and a throat so sore that I felt as though a brick had been thrust down my gullet. There was no question whatsoever of travelling anywhere. I couldn't even get myself downstairs, let alone set out for England. The damp outing while I was still weak from the migraine, and my soaked shoes and wet skirts, had done their worst.

'Ma'am!' Dale said, discovering me huddled miserably in the bed with my teeth chattering, 'you have a fever!'

'I feel half dead,' I croaked. 'Fetch Brockley.'

When he came, I said hoarsely: 'I'm ill. Can't travel. Take those papers to England, Brockley. The cipher copies you made, and my deciphered ones. Then Cecil can check our work. Get them to him. I can't.'

Dale, of course, at once looked miserable but

dispatching those letters to Cecil could not be hindered by vapours. Brockley knew that too. He was on his way before the morning was half done. He came to say goodbye and explained that he had excused his hurried departure by telling the Ridolfis that there was business to be attended to at Hawkswood, and that it was worrying me.

'I said I hoped that by going to see to it, I would put your mind at rest and help you to recover.'

I croaked: 'Thank you, Brockley. That was clever.' I could only just take in what he was saying. In my whole life, I had rarely felt so ill.

I was sick for ten days. The Ridolfis called a physician, and on his instructions, Dale dosed me with warmed honey and horehound and mulled wine and an infusion of willow bark that was supposed to ease my pains, although if it did, it wasn't by much. I ached all over. My head and my nostrils seemed to be clogged with thick wool and then I developed an awful grating cough. It was as though an iron bar were being run across my ribs, and my chest felt as though it were filling up with a viscous fluid. I seriously considered dying.

It was Dale, in the end, who turned the tide. On the seventh evening, she brought me another honey and horehound drink and I resisted, though feebly. I only wanted to be let alone, to slide down into warmth and darkness and never again emerge. But Dale lifted me up, propped me on my pillows, held the beaker to my lips

151

and said firmly: 'Swallow this, ma'am. You have to get better, ma'am; you *have* to. Your daughter Meg will give you a grandchild in August. Girls always want their mothers by them when they have their first babies and you'll want to hold the child. And Meg will want *you*.'

She was right. Meg would need me. I had worried over leaving Margaret to the care of others and Meg I couldn't and wouldn't so leave. I had to recover, for Meg.

I drank the warm potion. I fell asleep, still thinking about Meg. When I woke, in the morning, the fever was almost gone and my throat and chest were easier. Dale brought me soup, and some bread cubes in hot milk, with more honey.

On the eleventh day, I got shakily out of bed, washed my face, let Dale do my hair, and then sat by the window. April was passing and in the garden, flowers were opening and there was sunshine and birdsong.

That day, Brockley came back. When Dale brought him to me, I was touched by the relief in his face, as he saw that I was up.

'Fran has told me how ill you've been, madam. I am thankful to see you out of bed. Though you must take care not to overdo things; not to have a setback.'

'Sitting in a shaft of sunlight won't set me back, Brockley. Dale has taken wonderful care of me. What news have you brought? Look, sit down.'

Brockley settled himself on a stool. 'I've quite a packet of news, madam. Cecil was exceedingly pleased with the letters. Baillie was seized at Dover on twelfth April and taken to the Tower, but it seems that the letters he was carrying were harmless – they were to a fellow banker about an investment in a voyage to the New World, and a civil enquiry to the Bishop of Ross about some relative of Ross, who's been ill. All the same, Baillie was taken to the Tower for questioning and I gather that a few things were wrung out of him. He admitted the existence of the conspiracy against England and the fact that Ross, Mary Stuart's ambassador to Elizabeth, is part of it all. The letters you deciphered confirm all the details and he added a few more. Before you ask, he didn't mention Norfolk.'

'Perhaps this time he's not involved,' I said. 'Cecil and the queen would be thankful for that but I wish we could be sure. Has Ross been questioned?'

'Francis Walsingham ordered it,' said Brockley. 'But I gather that the bishop stuck his nose in the air and said that as an official ambassador, he couldn't be interrogated. He said he wouldn't answer questions and can't legally be racked. He's been put into a kind of house arrest, in the custody of the Bishop of Ely.'

'How did you find all that out?'

'I was able to have a few words with Walsingham and also with some of his staff – it's his business now as much as Cecil's. He's still the

153

Ambassador to France, but since he's been recalled to England because of this emergency he's Acting Secretary of State. Cecil's been made Lord Treasurer now, though he still takes a very immediate interest in anything concerning the queen's safety. I'd rather have talked to him than to Walsingham,' Brockley said. 'Walsingham is a very ... how shall I put it – a very stark figure compared to Cecil and some of his staff are similar. There's a new fellow working with him now, a tough-looking young man called Roland Wyse. He's said to be a marvel at decoding ciphers. From the look of him, I'd say he'd also be a marvel as an assassin. I know the type. I met quite a number when I was a soldier, long ago.'

'You sound as if you didn't like him!'

'Two of Walsingham's other aides told me he was ambitious and would probably elbow them out of his way if he could. I don't think they like him, either. I wonder how long he'll last,' said Brockley musingly. 'Walsingham's no fool; he won't want to keep a troublemaker on his staff, however clever he is with ciphers. Truth is, I can't like either Walsingham, or his choice of staff. I prefer to deal with Lord Burghley.'

'I'd agree there,' I said. I had not met Walsingham very often, but I knew I would never be at ease with him. I was far more at ease with Cecil even though he had sent me into danger and lied to me by telling me that Matthew de la Roche was dead. He had had his reasons and I

154

understood them, if grudgingly.

'Well, that's most of my news,' Brockley said, 'though ... there is one more item...' he sounded uncertain. 'I'm not sure...'

'Out with it, Brockley. If you're afraid that I'm not well enough to withstand something upsetting, well, I'll be even more upset if I'm left to imagine horrors instead of being told the facts. What is it?'

'It's Mistress Jester, madam. Sybil. I made time to go to Hawkswood and she wanted to know why I'd made this second journey back to England. Everything is going well at Hawkswood, and also at Withysham by the way – Adam Wilder has visited it lately. I told Mistress Jester what we'd overheard and how we'd found incriminating correspondence, and I explained the anxiety about Norfolk.'

I thought about Sybil, visualizing her. She had a striking face; it looked a little as though it had been compressed between crown and chin, so that all her features were just a little splayed, yet the result was not unpleasant but rather attractive. And behind those long eyes and eyebrows, there was an intelligent brain.

'Go on,' I said.

'She said that two years ago, she had the impression that Norfolk was actually in love with Mary Stuart, even though he'd never met her, and she also told me that she didn't have a high opinion of his common sense.'

'Neither have I, Brockley.'

'Madam, when I left, she was packing for a

155

journey to London. She said she wished to visit some merchants there, buy materials for new gowns, and call on some old acquaintances, including Mistress Dalton, the housekeeper at the Duke of Norfolk's London home. Mistress Jester says she got to know her quite well, two years back. She thought she might pick up some gossip about the Norfolk household; who's been visiting and who the duke is writing to, for instance. She said that she would try to find out whether he's been in touch with the Bishop of Ross, and whether Charles Baillie ever brought him any letters.'

'She's doing all this on her own?' I said.

'Yes, madam. I certainly didn't suggest it.' Brockley looked worried. 'It's as it was last year. You didn't ask her to search for dangerous letters in the Ferris household. She insisted on doing it, and said she'd do it even if you forbade her!'

'Sybil is grateful to me because I give her a comfortable home,' I said. 'But she seems to think she must show her gratitude by sharing my work and my dangers. I wish she hadn't done this, Brockley. God's Teeth, she was terrified when she was caught last year. I can hardly believe that she's throwing herself into the arena again!'

'I doubt if she will do anything dangerous, madam. Can she really come to much harm, just gossiping with Mistress Dalton?'

'I sincerely hope not. I'll worry until I hear she's safely back at Hawkswood, though. Oh,

156

Brockley, the sooner we're *all* safely back at Hawkswood, the better!'

'Amen to that,' said Dale.

My recovery was rapid. Five days later, I was walking in the garden, eating good meals, my health and strength returning swiftly.

I liked the garden. It had a small scythed lawn and a knot garden, where little beds, edged with smooth pebbles that looked as though they had been brought from a shingle beach, had been planted with flowers and attractive herbs. A vegetable plot lay to one side, screened by a box hedge, and at the very end of the garden was a grassy bank where there were primroses and cowslips and some unusual and very beautiful red and yellow, cup-shaped flowers that I had never seen before. They were past their best now but some were still in bloom.

Signor Ridolfi said they were called tulips, and that they had been recently introduced from Turkey. 'Someone in Antwerp has taken to importing the bulbs and the previous tenant of this house bought some. Not many people have them as yet.'

There was a bench where one could sit to admire them and that was where I was on the fifth morning after Brockley's return. The sunshine was warm and I had a book of Thomas Wyatt's poems with me, but I hadn't opened it; preferring to gaze at the garden. I felt peaceful. My illness was over. A few days more, and I would say goodbye to Donna and her husband,

and with Brockley and Dale, who would be only too thankful, I would at last turn towards home.

It would be a kindly gesture to call in on Margaret and Antonio van Weede just for one night, and to make sure, finally, that all was well with my erstwhile ward. Then we would ride for the coast and take the first boat to Dover, and oh, how good it would be, to stand in the bows and see those white cliffs appear on the horizon and grow as the vessel came nearer.

I closed my eyes for a moment to think about it, and only when the sunshine ceased to warm my face did I open them to find Donna in front of me, casting a shadow.

'I am disturbing you! I'm so sorry. But Roberto says that a guest of some importance will be joining us for dinner, and so the ladies are to dress in their best. Ursula, will you wear that lavender and silver gown you had on for the wedding? Black doesn't suit you, you know.'

'If you wish,' I said, smiling. 'Black doesn't seem quite right on a sunny spring day.' Indeed, I couldn't imagine Hugh approving of it. 'Who is the guest?' I asked.

'I don't know. Roberto was going to tell me, but he was called away just then, and I haven't seen him again since. I went to the kitchens to give instructions about dinner. Our guest has six or seven men with him, apparently. Then I thought, I must tell Ursula.'

I stood up. 'Let's go and get the lavender

gown out of the press.'

I went upstairs with Donna, and found Dale already brushing the gown in question. Donna must have found a moment to drop a hint to her.

'Your amethyst pendant and the matching earrings will look well with this, ma'am,' Dale told me. 'You've worn no jewellery of late, except for Margaret's wedding.'

'I haven't had the heart, Dale.'

'It will be good for you,' said Dale firmly.

'Very well,' I said. Dear Dale. She hated travelling, but throughout our association, I had dragged her ruthlessly about from place to place and even country to country. I had endangered her, made friends with her husband to an extent which was greater than it ought to be; and lately, I had terrified her by threatening to die on her hands. The least I could do was let her tell me what to wear when there was a special guest at dinner.

Donna called for me when dinner time came, looking very charming in rose pink and pale green. Her pretty, kittenish face lit up in an immense smile when she saw me, duly arrayed in lavender silk, silver embroidery and amethyst jewellery. 'Oh, Ursula, you look so elegant. We both do. We shall decorate the dining room better than any flowers. Let's go down.'

We did so, skirts whispering on the treads of the main stairs. There was a murmur of masculine voices from the small ante-room that led to the dining room. A page on duty at the door, opened it for us and we went in.

'Ah,' said Ridolfi, turning as the door creaked. 'Here are the ladies. Donna, my dear, and Madame Blanchard, let me present...'

The world tilted. It was as if up and down, left and right had become confused. My breath stopped, started, then baulked a second time.

It was fortunate that I already knew he was alive. If I had still believed him dead, I think I might actually have fainted. As it was, I somehow willed the world to stop reeling, forced my breath to become even once more, and made the obligatory curtsy. Dark eyes, glittering with amusement, looked into mine. A strong brown hand reached out to draw me to my feet. 'Up you come, Madame Blanchard. What a joy to see you again. It has been many years.'

He was completely in command of himself. Had he too known that he had been lied to and that I still lived? If so, I wondered when he had learned it. The last I had heard of him was that he had married again and presumably, then, he still thought I was dead. But now he showed no signs of being shocked, whereas I, for a moment, had felt that I was looking at a ghost. Indeed, in one sense, I was. It was the ghost of a dead marriage, a vanished past.

I stood there, my hand still in his, face to face with my second husband, the man that Cecil had told me had died of plague, the man I had once loved to desperation point and then almost hated because he was Queen Elizabeth's enemy. The man I had cut out of my heart because when it came to the point, I preferred the peace

160

and order of life with Hugh.

Matthew de la Roche.

'Have the two of you met before?' Ridolfi was saying, slightly puzzled.

I had no idea what to answer, but Matthew did it for me. 'Yes, a long time ago. I was once at the court of Queen Elizabeth of England and I met Madame Blanchard there. After dinner, I would like a little private talk with her, in the garden, to ask after mutual friends. You will not object?'

'No, why should I? Donna, Madame, will you take wine? Dinner will be served in a few minutes. My chef has prepared a new dish...'

He went on talking but I took none of it in. My pulses were jumping so hard that they almost choked me. Matthew always had that effect on me. I never understood why; I still don't. He was tall and moderately handsome though his chin was too long for perfection and his shoulders too wide and bony. He had diamond-shaped dark eyes under dramatic black eyebrows, dark hair, and a skin that tanned if it as much as saw the sun. For me, to be near him, was to feel my head swim and my bones melt with something that I had once thought was love but now knew was unvarnished lust, which had nothing to do with any genuine feeling on either side, or any compatible quality of our minds.

And I had no idea what to do about it.

The door to the dining room opened and Bruno appeared. Dinner was served.

161

* * *

Dinner was over and our private conversation had begun, except that at first, neither of us spoke at all. We had walked the length of the garden, side by side, before I finally broke the silence by saying: 'Did you know I was still alive? You didn't seem surprised to see me.'

'Yes, I knew.' I struggled not to let that deep, dear voice do such alarming things to my nervous system. 'Though I haven't known for long. I married again, you know. I have a little boy, Jacques, a lively lad, nearly three years old now. You'd like him.'

'So you have a wife?'

'Not now. Marie was very sweet, but not very strong. She died last year, of an illness very like the one that Roberto says you have just had. Come. Let us sit down,' said Matthew, leading me to the bench where I had sat in the morning,

Some irrational part of me was wondering where Hugh was and why he hadn't come to help me out of this uncomfortable situation. Seated beside Matthew, I could feel the warmth of him, the strength, as though I were sitting by a fire. And yet I still wanted Hugh.

'Did you know *I* was alive?' Matthew enquired. 'If not, I must have given you a shock. I'm sorry. I should have asked Roberto to warn you.'

'You know Signor Ridolfi well?'

'Fairly well, yes. *Did* you know?'

'Yes.' I hesitated and then said: 'I have been at court from time to time. Many visitors come from abroad; one hears all kinds of things. I think it was someone in an ambassador's suite, who mentioned coming across you in France. I asked a question or two, and learned that the Matthew de la Roche this man had met, lived in the chateau of Blanchepierre. Then I knew I had been lied to. Sir William Cecil admitted it when I challenged him.'

I hoped that Matthew wouldn't ask for details of my imaginary ambassador or the gossipy member of his suite. Inventing details for them at such short notice might be difficult. But I couldn't tell him I had learned of his survival while decoding treasonable correspondence filched from a messenger's saddlebag, in order to outwit a plot against Elizabeth, whom he would not acknowledge as a queen.

I hurried on. 'But by the time I found out that you weren't dead, I had married Hugh Stannard. You know about that?' He nodded. 'I was happy with him.' I said. 'When I found that you ... were still alive, I told him. He asked what I meant to do, to stay with him or come to you. I chose him. I chose *him*, Matthew. Not you.'

'Even though I am your lawful husband?'

'Are you? I am English. The queen of England annulled our marriage, because I took the vows under duress, and because the priest was not an Anglican.'

'I take it,' Matthew said, 'that you were told the same lie that I was: that your spouse had died of plague?'

'Yes.'

163

'Someone was determined to keep you in England, it seems. I have also learned of a rumour that you are related to Queen Elizabeth. That you are her sister. Is that true?'

'Half-sister,' I said. 'My mother served Queen Anne Boleyn – and King Henry the Eighth ... took a fancy to her. She left the court when she knew she was with child, and went home. As far as I know, King Henry never even learned that she was pregnant. My mother wouldn't say who my father was. She never said, to the day she died. Sir William Cecil told me, in the end. A maid who had served her at court, knew the truth and wrote a memorandum that came to light after she too had died.'

'We were deceived, I imagine, by orders of your queen,' said Matthew dryly. 'No doubt she has sisterly feelings for you.'

'And I for her, as well as the loyalty of a subject,' I said, and made my voice sound sharp. I steeled myself, and added: 'Matthew, our marriage is dead. Please don't cling to its ghost.'

'Ghost? Oh, surely not. Roberto tells me that you have now embraced the true faith, though for safety's sake you pretend otherwise when you are in England, which I can well understand. If you are a Catholic, my darling Ursula, then you know that our marriage was valid, and stands, and you know too that your half-sister, whatever she may be to you as a sister, is not and can never be, your queen. She was not born of a legal marriage. The true queen, of Scotland and England alike, is Mary Stuart.'

'Mary Stuart,' I said (and didn't have to steel myself this time), 'is a beautiful, charming and dangerous woman whose husband was murdered, and there are good reasons to suppose that she knew of the plan to put gunpowder under his bed, even if she didn't actually order it. She then married the man who almost certainly organized it. Such a woman shouldn't sit on any throne, Scottish or English. She has never cleared her name, probably because she can't.'

'Ursula, why do you trouble your head about such matters? They are not for women.'

'Elizabeth and Mary *are* women!'

'Royalty is different. But you are free to be just a woman. Come back to me, Ursula. What keeps you in England now? Master Stannard is dead and I believe your daughter is now married – that's so, isn't it?'

'Yes,' I said waspishly. 'And how do you know *that*? Are spies of yours among the visitors to my sister's court?'

'Saltspoon,' said Matthew.

It was his old nickname for me. He had always said I had a salty tongue. My insides wobbled. He was laughing at me. 'I have no spies in the court of Elizabeth. I wish I had. No, Donna told me, this very afternoon. Darling, your Meg no longer needs you but my son needs a mother and I would like more sons.'

I had nearly died once, trying to bear him one. I found myself shrinking away from him. But he drew closer and put his arm about me. 'Please come back to me, Ursula. I came here

165

on purpose to ask you.'

His arm was heavy and warm. He turned me to face him and his other hand began to caress my back, with long, sweeping male caresses, something I had missed more than I knew, until now. The melting in my bones began again.

But I still had questions to ask. I drew myself away. 'Who told you I wasn't dead? *How* did you find out?'

'I am as ever trying to raise money for Mary Stuart,' said Matthew. 'I am constantly moving from country to country, calling on people who might be glad to contribute.'

Such as Ridolfi? I thought.

'I was in Bruges,' Matthew was saying, 'visiting an exiled Catholic lady there – the former Countess of Northumberland...'

'Anne Percy!' I gasped.

He didn't notice my horror. 'Yes, the lady Anne Percy. Alas, it seems she hasn't much to spare. She is living in a cramped house in Bruges, with a handful of servants and the little daughter – Mary, her name is – who was born after Lady Anne fled from her English home. The lady has a pension from King Philip. The daughter's a pretty infant,' he added. 'Going to be fair, like her mother, I'd say, though she's still not a year old.'

'How sweet,' I said sardonically.

'The Countess has no coach these days,' he said, 'though there's a pony to pull a little cart so that the nursemaid and the baby can take the air. It must be hard for Lady Anne to endure

166

such straitened means. She told me that she thinks of moving to Liege, where there are a number of Catholic exiles from England, and she has been told she can find better accommodation. Bruges smells of canals, she says. She thought I might do well to approach the exiles in Liege myself and I intend to do so. However, she gave me a pendant, an emerald cross edged with small diamonds. It's valuable and will help. But all that's by the way. While I was there, Roberto Ridolfi came visiting as well. They move in the same circles. They are both acquaintances of the Duke of Alva.'

Distracted for a moment from the matter of who had told Matthew I was still alive, I wondered if Ridolfi had wanted her to use her influence with the Duke of Alva. If so, I didn't think she'd had much success.

If Matthew was raising money for Mary Stuart, I thought, working it out, it was a fair bet that he knew all about Ridolfi's latest plot on her behalf and expected any funds he obtained to be used to further it. I compressed my lips. Matthew must never suspect that I had been spying on my host, or that I knew anything at all of his schemes. I must watch every word I said.

'Anyway,' Matthew continued, 'Roberto mentioned you over dinner one day. He was describing the wedding of your – ward, is it? Margaret Emory, now Margaret van Weede.'

'Yes. I escorted her to the Netherlands and represented her mother at the wedding.'

'Roberto referred to you as Madame Ursula Blanchard. He said that you were a widow and that after your ward's marriage, you were making a stay in his house in Brussels, to visit his wife. I was puzzled. He described you, a little, and I thought: but that, surely, is *my* Ursula! You were once called Blanchard. Could there be two, the same age from what Roberto said, both dark, both with a daughter called Meg? He mentioned her, though not her marriage. I learned that from Donna, as I said. But when Roberto spoke of someone who sounded so much like you, I asked, very carefully, whether you had brought your own servants and Roberto said yes, and that you had an excellent manservant by the name of Roger Brockley. Then I knew.'

'I see. And Signor Ridolfi does not know that we were once married?'

'No, I wanted to see you before I talked about that to anyone. Ursula, I would have come here at once, to see you, but I had appointments to keep and it was some time before I reached Brussels, and when I did, I learned that you were ill and...'

'It's a good thing you haven't told the Signor. I haven't, either. It would sound so complicated. The poor man would be confused.'

Ridolfi struck me as a man who lived in a state of confusion, mainly on account of his own grandiose imaginings. There was no need to muddle him still more. Trying not to sound too fearful, I said: 'You said you knew I had married Hugh Stannard. I suppose it was

168

Roberto who told you that. Was that at the same dinner? Did Anne of Northumberland hear?'

'Does it matter? Yes, it was all part of our dinner conversation,' said Matthew cheerfully. 'Roberto told us about your return to the true faith and your doubts about the legality of your marriage to Master Stannard, which was why, since he had now died, you had given up using his name.'

'Dear God!' I said faintly.

'But surely it's of no importance. Ursula, how real is your conversion? Is it just a pretence for safety, in a country under Spanish rule? Or have you, at last, let yourself be led from error into the light of truth?'

I ignored this. 'Let us be plain,' I said. 'Do I have it correctly? Does Anne of Northumberland *now know that a woman once called Ursula Stannard is here in Brussels?*'

'Yes, of course. Ursula, I don't understand...'

In short, angry sentences, I explained to him that the lady was in her impoverished exile partly because of me, and that she had done her best, the previous year, to get me discredited and executed in my own country. I didn't suppose for a moment that her rage against me had abated.

'And now,' I said furiously, 'you have told her where to find me. Thank you, Matthew. Thank you so much!'

'But, Ursula...! Ursula, I am sorry. I would never put you in danger deliberately!'

'Did you really come here to this house in

169

search of me?'

'Yes, my love. That exactly.'

'Matthew, I am not your love.'

'Listen, darling Ursula, darling Saltspoon, *please* come back to me. I have people to see in Brussels, so I must stay here for a while, but if Roberto understands the situation, he will protect you. I can explain to him about our marriage, and that you are in danger from Countess Anne – because of something you did out of loyalty to your queen. He will understand that. Then, when I've finished my tasks here, I'll take you home to France, to Blanchepierre. You will be safe there from a thousand Countesses.'

His hand was stroking me again, raising my pulse rate, warming my whole body, calling to me to yield. If I lingered here, I feared I would.

I summoned up my memories of Hugh and Hawkswood, but now they seemed like something seen through a mist; colourless and insubstantial. If I let Matthew raise our marriage from its grave, then Hugh and Hawkswood would become my ghosts. In time they might even cease to walk.

'Let me go!' I shouted. Wrenching myself free, I ran headlong across the garden, into the house, up the stairs, into the sanctuary of my own room.

I threw myself down on the bed and would have liked to cry but the tears wouldn't come. I felt only an emptiness, and, once more, an overwhelming longing to go home.

THIRTEEN

A Cry for Help

'We start for home tomorrow,' I said. 'I can't stay under the same roof as Matthew, and in any case...'

'Anne Percy now knows you are here,' said Brockley succinctly.

'Dangerous!' said Dale. 'It's all dreadful. Why, seeing Matthew de la Roche again, with no warning and so soon after losing poor Master Stannard, too – a shock like that could have made you ill again!'

I had pulled myself together, summoned the Brockleys and explained the circumstances. They were both worried already, since both had recognized Matthew.

'I shall have to invent an excuse for the Ridolfis,' I said, 'but I mustn't mention the Countess. I'll say I'm still anxious about something to do with Hawkswood.'

However, as it turned out, I had no need. Five minutes later, Donna came to tell me that a messenger had arrived for me. 'I sent him into the hall to wait. He's from van Weede's, he says.'

'From Margaret?' Well, I had better deal with that before I told the Ridolfis about my intended departure, as Donna would probably argue and it would take time. I made my way down to the hall.

The messenger was a rustic-looking young man, with ingenuous blue eyes in a rosy, weathered face, a loose, open-necked linen shirt under a hairy woollen jacket, patched hose and grimy boots. He was pacing about in the hall, hat in hand. He turned at once as I came in, looked at me a trifle shyly and then said: 'Madame Blanchard!' in tones of recognition.

'You know me?' I said.

'I've seen you, Madame, though not close to. You mightn't recall me.' He spoke French, but with a bucolic accent. Its English equivalent would have been along the lines of *Oi've seen 'ee, mum, but not near to; you moightn't mind on I.* 'I work on the land at van Weede's,' he explained. 'I've word for you from Madame Margaret.'

'You have a letter from her? Do sit down, Master ... er...'

'No letter, Madame. It was the woman Gertrud that spoke to me, not Madame Margaret herself. Gertrud's fond of her; all of us like the new young mistress. Gertrud said Madame Margaret couldn't write you a letter – said something about all the writing things are in her husband's study and he locks it when he's not there.'

'Gertrud said ... *what*?' I was instantly alert,

172

and spoke so sharply that he recoiled. 'What do you mean?'

'That's what she said Madame Margaret had told her to say, Madame. She gave me some money and said I was to take Madame Margaret's pony, and if anyone asked, to say I'd been told to exercise it for her. I was to come to you here, as fast as I could. Gertrud says Madame wants you, and it's urgent.'

'But...'

This made no sense. Antonio had seemed such an amiable man; Gertrud herself had said he was kind and generous. He had evidently bought Margaret the pony that Gertrud had mentioned. The messenger was looking at me pleadingly. 'Madame, Gertrud said, Madame Margaret says, *please.*'

The day was wearing on. It wouldn't be possible to reach van Weede's before dark. 'We leave at first light,' I said.

'If van Weede is ill-using Margaret in any way,' I said to Brockley and Dale as we started out, in the chill of early morning, 'we'll take her straight home to Hawkswood, and we'll petition the Pope to get the marriage annulled.'

'On what grounds, madam?' Brockley asked.

'We'll think of something,' I told him. 'Or persuade the queen to think of something. She's the head of the church in England.'

'It was a Catholic marriage, ma'am,' said Dale, who was bouncing unhappily on Brockley's pillion.

173

'Margaret is still an English subject,' I said.

Brockley, riding at my side, gave me a warning glance and nodded towards the back view of the young messenger, who was leading the way. We were talking somewhat freely, and not as Catholics would be likely to speak. But the messenger, who was clearly eager to hurry our journey, was riding well ahead, even though his mount was a stolid pony mare with much shorter legs than either of our own mounts. 'He can't overhear,' I said.

'Better be careful, just the same,' Brockley said.

We rode on in silence. The day had dawned coldly, with a silvery haze in the air, but as we journeyed on, it gradually began to soften towards mildness and colour. By the time the morning was half over, the sky had changed to a gentle blue and the sun was growing warm. It would have been a pleasant morning for riding, if I hadn't felt so worried.

Donna had been predictably upset at our hasty departure. 'Of course you must go; Margaret obviously needs you. But you'll come back, won't you?' she said pleadingly. 'When you've done whatever you can for your young friend – or ward, or whatever she is?'

'I may have to take her home,' I said. 'And in that case, we'll leave for England at once.'

'But you can't just take Margaret away from her husband, whatever has gone wrong between them!' Donna was shocked. 'She's his wife, and van Weede's is her home now.'

174

'Can't I?' I said grimly. 'Donna, my dear, you'd be surprised.'

But I too was surprised. The message was incomprehensible. The implication was that Antonio van Weede had suddenly turned into some kind of bully, and Gertrud, who liked Margaret, had sent for help – presumably because Margaret could not send for it herself. It sounded as though Antonio was preventing her. He had apparently put writing materials out of her reach. Why? What did he fear she would say? Yet van Weede hadn't struck me as a man with a sinister side to him and I couldn't imagine Margaret provoking him so much that he would turn on her like this.

When I left her, Margaret, a level-headed young woman if ever there was one, had accepted her duty as a wife, was recovering from her homesickness and growing used to the love-making that she had at first disliked. I remembered how I had heard her and Antonio laughing together in their room. This cry for help bewildered me. Was this the Antonio I had met, the amenable man who was so impressed by great men that he proposed marriage to Margaret just because Walsingham and Cecil had suggested it? Or did that matter? Bullies were sometimes like that: humble in the presence of powerful men, but harsh to those beneath them.

And, yes, I remembered him saying, the day we first met him, that he did not want a wife who couldn't face what he called the realities of

175

life. Had her dislike, her fear, of love-making, surfaced again and caused trouble? That was just believable. Oh dear God, what had I done? What had Walsingham and Cecil done? How dare they make poor defenceless Margaret a sacrifice to their political schemes?

Well, if they had, I would find out soon enough.

I found out a good deal sooner than I expected. We had been riding through open country with fields and heathland, but ahead the track ran into a belt of woodland. The messenger slowed down as he neared the wood, to let us catch up. We urged our horses into a canter to do so but once more slowed to a walk as the track beneath the trees received us. The trees were heavy with leaf now and under them was a greenish underwater light with deep shadows on either side, making the path narrow and dim. Brockley fell back, since we could no longer ride two abreast.

Then the world exploded into uproar and violence. Birds flew up; a jay shrieked a warning. The messenger pulled his horse aside and three horsemen, who had been waiting motionless among the tree trunks, suddenly appeared in our path. Dale screamed and Brockley swore and their brown gelding whinnied in fright. The foremost of the three horsemen seized my rein in a gauntleted hand. 'Mistress Stannard, I believe,' he said, in English.

I knew him. He had a face like a stone outcrop and I wasn't likely ever to forget it. I recognized

his north-country voice and even that gauntleted hand of his seemed familiar. Once it had
tried to drag me from the back of a horse I was
riding. He had a scar at the corner of his mouth
and I knew how he got it. I had met the gentleman during our unpleasant encounter with
Countess Anne, a year and a half ago. He had
been her butler. He had also been among those
who pursued us when we escaped. Then, the
injury to his mouth was bleeding. I had given it
to him. He hated me.

'Ulverdale!' I said, furiously. Behind me,
Brockley had drawn his sword and was fending
off an assailant who was attempting to grab his
horse's bridle. It is difficult to manage reins,
whip and dagger all at once but I thrust my
whip under my right knee as I groped for my
dagger and I was quick enough to get my blade
out and brandish it in Ulverdale's face, so that
he released my rein and swung his horse away.
He collided with the third rider, knocking man
and horse aside, and from the edge of the track,
I heard the messenger, who had taken no part in
the onslaught, let out a laugh.

Whereupon Ulverdale leant angrily from his
saddle to cuff the young man across the face.
He was still blocking the way ahead but his
brief moment of distraction gave me time to
yank my mount round to face Brockley and
shout: 'Back the way we came! Go!'

It was no use. The man who had been fighting
Brockley had been wounded in the shoulder,
lost his stirrups and been thrown. He was now

177

sitting beside the track, clutching at his injury, the blood oozing between his fingers, while the horse, apparently bored by the insanity of the human race, was grazing on a patch of grass under the trees. But Ulverdale and the third rider came up one on either side of me and Ulverdale had seized my rein once more. I tried again to use my dagger but this time he caught hold of my wrist and twisted it. The dagger fell.

'Go, Brockley!' I shrieked. 'Get away! *Go!*'

'Damned if I will!' said Brockley, but his horse, sensibly wishing to escape from the uproar and unable to go forward because we were in the way, spun on its hocks, so violently that Dale screamed again and clutched desperately at Brockley to keep herself from falling, and I lost my temper.

'Brockley, will you bloody well do as I tell you, for once!' His mount was at least facing back towards Brussels. *'Go!'* I shouted again and snatching my whip out from under my knee, I used it to send the gelding into a gallop. It fled, taking the Brockleys with it, willy-nilly. The messenger, resentfully rubbing his face where Ulverdale had hit him, showed no disposition to give chase.

'We are so sorry for the apparent discourtesy,' said Ulverdale, smiling disagreeably. 'But my lady of Northumberland is so very anxious to see you, madam. She was overjoyed to hear that you were in the Netherlands. It is a pity you have dismissed your servants, as you will have to make do with hers, who may not be so devoted as your own, and I would have liked to renew my acquaintance with Roger Brockley. That was Roger who was with you, I think? Yes, I am *very* sorry to miss the chance of knowing him better. However, we have you. Please come this way.'

FOURTEEN

The Third Wine Cellar

Anne Percy had once been – indeed, theoretically still was – the Countess of Northumberland. She was accustomed to houses with great halls approached through ante-rooms, long galleries and a choice of parlours according to the weather or the importance or otherwise of visitors. She was used to private chapels, warren-like kitchens full of cooks and scullions on whom she never set eyes, and deer parks in which to ride and hunt.

The furnished house she had rented in the town of Bruges must have felt to her like a hovel.

It did have an arched street entrance leading into a small courtyard, but this was so very small that plain *yard* described it better and it was overlooked by taller houses opposite and to either side. I was pulled off my horse at the foot of the steps to the front door proper, and marched inside, to find myself in what most people would call an ordinary-sized house, though I didn't think Lady Anne of Northumberland would agree with them.

Through a half-open door I glimpsed a cramped and sparsely furnished parlour, though the small hearth had a cheerful fire and I caught sight of a spinet. I couldn't see where the kitchen was but I smelt onions cooking and bread baking. Somewhere, a child was crying and I thought I heard a girl's voice soothing it. A maidservant scurried down a flight of stairs and crossed our path, giving me a quick, furtive glance on the way and I saw a couple of faces peering inquisitively over a gallery at the top of the stairs. My arrival had been expected, of course. The young messenger, whose name I never heard, had ridden on ahead during the last stage, to announce that we were coming.

Ulverdale was my escort as we went through the house, gripping my left arm in strong and unkind fingers. My bonds had been removed at the front door but I had been roped during the ride to Bruges, elbows bound to sides and feet tied to stirrups. We changed horses twice, in order to keep up our speed, Ulverdale said, and then I was lifted down outside the gate and kept out of sight of inn and stable staff. I told Ulverdale that my original horse was Ridolfi's property. 'It will be returned to him. I am not a horse thief,' said Ulverdale curtly.

It was over fifty miles to Bruges and it took us seven hours. The man that Brockley had wounded managed to ride with us for some distance but was left at the inn where we first changed mounts. Ulverdale, his undamaged colleague and the young messenger snatched some food and drink at the inns but they didn't give me any, and once, when it was imperative that I should dismount and be private for a few minutes, I had to argue with them before, reluctantly, they helped me down and undid my bonds while I withdrew behind a tree. They were waiting, ropes in hand, when I emerged.

Most of the journey took place in a grim silence. I knew they were angry that Brockley and Dale had escaped, and probably they were worried in case my fleeing servants summoned help for me. It was to precisely that hope that I silently clung as my throbbing, hungry, thirsty, furious and frightened self was propelled through the house and into a small, dusty study. There were bookshelves but they looked forlorn, with empty spaces between a very few books and some ledgers and boxes. The onyx writing set on the desk was expensive, though. No doubt Lady Anne had brought it with her.

I had time to absorb all this because when Ulverdale thrust me into the room, and I found myself facing the woman who sat at the desk, she did not at first speak to me. She merely told Ulverdale to shut the door and remain in the room. Then she leant against the oaken back of her chair, and stared at me. I waited silently, mostly because I could think of nothing to say. The skin of my arms and ankles burned where the ropes had rasped me and my mouth was intolerably dry. My legs felt weak. My illness was not so very far behind me, after all.

The erstwhile Countess of Northumberland

still answered to a description of her that I had been given long ago. *Tall, ash-pale hair, well-dressed, commanding manner.* She still took care of her appearance. The pale blonde hair was carefully crimped in front of a blue velvet hood; her ruff and her blue velvet dress were edged and embroidered with silver; the high-bridged nose was as lofty as I remembered, the expression in her light eyes as haughty.

I had seen her when she didn't look so impressive, though. I had seen her when she had just fallen victim to a booby trap laid in the kitchen through which she, Ulverdale and others were pursuing Brockley and myself. She had slipped in a pool of spilt olive oil, was spattered with pottage and had an upturned colander on her head. I found the memory heartening.

At last, she spoke.

'I believe you are calling yourself Mistress Blanchard these days, are you not? Is that correct?'

'Yes – my lady.'

'I was with child,' said Anne Percy reminiscently, 'when you and that odious manservant of yours caused me to fall so heavily, that night nearly two years ago. I might have miscarried.'

'We were running for our lives,' I said. Or rather, croaked. My mouth was so dry that I was hoarse.

'Are you unwell?' Her eyebrows had been darkened, and plucked, to create two thin, aristocratic crescents. They rose, enquiringly.

'I'm a little thirsty,' I explained. I was more than that, since my stomach was an aching hollow and my legs now felt so shaky that I thought I might well be about to faint. I wished I could sit down. 'I was not offered any refreshment on the way here,' I said.

'You are complaining about your treatment? My dear, you will complain much more before I'm done with you.'

She wasn't quite as good-looking as she had been, I thought. There were silver strands in the crimped hair and new lines round the chilly eyes. No doubt she had suffered; separated from her husband, driven from her home, compelled to live in what to her must be appallingly restricted conditions, and obliged to subsist on the charity of King Philip.

'But I don't wish you to collapse just yet,' said Lady Anne. 'The young man who fetched you from Brussels, and rode ahead just now to tell me you were nearly here, said that when he was in Ridolfi's house, someone told him you had lately been ill. I don't want you to relapse. That wouldn't do at all. I intend a far less pleasant fate for you than a mere inflammation of the lung. Indeed, you don't look well. Ulverdale, bring a seat for our guest and fetch some food and white wine. And a jug of water. Wine revives the weary but it doesn't quench thirst. And I think the – er – spare room we have prepared for her may need a few extra luxuries after all. See that a bed and blankets are put there.'

184

Ulverdale grunted, in a way which made me feel that he disliked these instructions, even though he knew that they were nowhere near as considerate as they sounded. However, he obediently departed to carry them out and as soon as he had gone, Lady Anne said: 'I hear from Signor Ridolfi that you have adopted the Catholic faith and are calling yourself Blanchard because you arc not sure that your marriage to Master Stannard was entirely legal because it was by the Lutheran rite. Why do you think that? Your first marriage to a Master Blanchard was the same, was it not?'

'I was very young and gave no thought to such matters,' I said, inventing the best excuse I could at such short notice. 'But by the time I married Master Stannard, I had changed. I had come to ... to take matters of religion seriously. It makes a diffcrence.'

'I don't believe in your conversion,' said Lady Anne. 'It's a political ploy. You are Elizabeth's half-sister and one of her most devoted servants. I know that much about you. I am sorry that my attempt to deal with you last year came to nothing. It's difficult, working at a distance and through other people. It won't be so difficult now, however. Do you admit that your conversion is a pretence?'

'No, my lady. Because it isn't.'

'You now support the claim of Mary Stuart to the throne of England?'

'No, my lady. It is possible to be a Catholic and still be loyal to our anointed queen.'

185

'The Pope says otherwise.'

'I think he is wrong.'

'You call yourself a Catholic and yet have the impertinence to say that the Holy Father can be wrong?'

'Yes, I suppose I have,' I said wearily and wondered where Ulverdale had got to. If someone didn't offer me something to sit on very soon, and provide me with something to eat and drink, I really would faint.

Ulverdale, however, appeared at that moment, carrying a tray and followed by a lad with a stool. Lady Anne invited me to sit down and put the tray on my knees. Ulverdale and the boy withdrew.

I said: 'You set a clever trap for me, my lady. You must know a great deal about Antonio and Margaret van Weede and their farm.'

'Signor Ridolfi was here not long ago and talked at length of Antonio's wedding, and yes, about his kinsman's farm. Laying my plans was simple enough. Now, eat and drink, and listen. I will do the talking. I will tell you what lies before you.'

She watched in silence, though, as I filled a tumbler with water and drank it all, before pouring in some wine, and taking a bite of what proved to be a slice of meat pie. Chicken and bacon, I thought. My stomach wrapped itself gratefully round the offering and the wine warmed my blood. Lady Anne was watching me.

'You will soon feel stronger, I hope. Then you

186

will be better able to take in what I intend for you. I do not believe in your conversion and I propose to hand you to the Inquisition in this country. The Duke of Alva has been severe, in the past, when there was a Lutheran rising. I shall let it be known that you are here to learn if another rising is likely; indeed, to encourage it. I shall state that your return to the true faith is assuredly false, that you are still a heretic. The Inquisition particularly dislikes pretended conversions. That alone, my dear Ursula, can bring you to the stake.'

My stomach heaved. Somehow, I concealed it and went on eating and drinking though the wine now tasted poisonous and the pie was like dust in my mouth. I needed the strength they could give for all vitality seemed to be leaking out of my muscles. I had never witnessed that horrible form of execution but my guardians, Uncle Herbert and Aunt Tabitha, had done so and they had described it to me in monstrous detail. I had never forgotten.

'I shall of course not hand you over at once,' said Lady Anne. 'I would like you to have time to think of your future – and perhaps to repent of your past. The Inquisition will persuade you to confess. You will be soft clay in the hands of their Familiars.'

I stared down into my wine glass and said nothing.

'By the way,' said Lady Anne, 'I understand that your wretched manservant, Roger Brockley, escaped capture. No doubt you hope he will find a way to rescue you. He will not. Signor Ridolfi is too anxious to coax soldiers and money out of the Duke of Alva to irritate him by championing a spy and agitator such as yourself. Once he knows the truth about you, you can be sure that he will have no interest in pleading for you.'

I made myself take another mouthful of pie, hating it.

'I'll let you finish your repast,' said Lady Anne. 'It's the last good food or drink you will taste for a long time, if ever.'

She sat back and watched me but now my appetite did fail and I pushed the rest of the pie aside. Then she shouted for Ulverdale, who must have been hovering close at hand, so quickly did he come. 'Take her to the wine cellar,' said Lady Anne. She added to me: 'There isn't any wine there. I can't afford to buy it in quantity any more. Thanks, very largely, to you.'

This was the third time in my life that I had been imprisoned in a wine cellar, though the others had contained wine. Here, not even the scent of it lingered. In this cellar there was only the dank smell of stone walls. Instead of wine barrels, it held a bucket and a narrow bed with a straw mattress, some hairy blankets and a moth-eaten cushion for a pillow, Lady Anne's concession to my recent malady. The air was cold, though ventilated, for there was a grating in the door and another, quite sizeable, high in

188

one wall. It let in some light as the walls evidently reached above ground level. But the night would be very dark. I had no lantern, no candle.

I huddled on to the bed and then had to get up again and use the bucket because fear had sent my guts into spasm. When it was over, I cleaned myself as best I could with my handkerchief. I pushed the soiled thing under the mattress. I still had my hat and cloak. I spread the cloak above the blankets and cowered beneath them, pulling my hat down over my ears. I could keep warm, more or less.

It was nearly dark when Lady Anne and Ulverdale reappeared, bringing wine, a water jug, a chunk of rye bread and a bowl of hot stew. 'We must keep your strength up, must we not?' said Lady Anne sweetly. 'If not with luxurious viands.' She then dismissed Ulverdale, and said: 'I am a Christian woman and also fastidious and I will not impose total squalor on you. I have a question to ask.' She asked it.

'Not for two and a half weeks,' I said.

'Good. By then, the Inquisition will have you and they will be responsible for the way you are treated. Eat your stew while it's hot.'

With a whisk of velvet skirts, she was gone. I took up the spoon that had been provided and began forcing myself to swallow the stew. I *must* maintain my strength. I was not without hope. There was Brockley, after all. Lady Anne was right to say that Signor Ridolfi wasn't likely to help but did she know of my marriage

189

to Matthew? I thought not. Surely, Brockley would go to Matthew!

Since I had refused to return to Matthew, turning to him now, trading on his feeling for me, was hardly in good taste, but just now, mere good taste had shrunk into nothingness. To get out of the clutches of Anne Percy and the Inquisition, I would make a deal with Satan himself.

Matthew couldn't ride through Bruges with his men and attack the lady's front door. Half the citizenry would come out to interfere. But the difference between this house and the mansions Lady Anne had known in England, had given me an idea. Matthew was wealthy. If he couldn't use force, he might be able to buy her off.

My last and most desperate resort, was in its sheath, close against my body, under my buckram stomacher. If I was not rescued from Anne Percy, if the Inquisition came to claim me, I still had that tiny knife. I would use it.

FIFTEEN

An Air of Disturbance

It was a wonder that in such dire circumstances, I could have slept, but exhaustion finally overtook me and sleep I did, curled under the blankets, with my cloak spread on top. In the morning, Ulverdale and another man brought me more bread, and a bowl of salted porridge, along with a jug of small ale and another of water. I asked for washing water and a comb but neither answered. Neither, in fact, spoke at all.

When I was alone again, I ate and drank, and huddled once more under the blankets. I understood my plight all too well. Anne Percy meant me to have enough food and warmth to keep me alive, not from humanity but to keep me in reasonable health so that I would suffer all the more in the hands of the Netherlands Inquisition. She would hold me, probably, for days, even weeks, to give me ample time to imagine my fate. She wanted my terror to grow and grow. She called herself a Christian woman. I wondered what Christ would have thought of her.

Sunlight crept through the grating in the wall. I studied my surroundings. I had not been searched and I still had my picklocks but I had heard bolts slammed home on the other side of the door. I could not escape that way. Nor would either of the gratings, in door or wall, be of any use. Both were too high up and neither was big enough for a human being to squeeze through.

There was an adventurous streak in my nature which had helped me through other frightening times, but I had never before been so helpless and alone, and facing so much horror. I tried my best to think hopeful thoughts. I might evade the Inquisition if I swore convincingly enough that my return to the fold was genuine. Or could I use my relationship to Elizabeth, hint at reprisals from England if harm came to me? King Philip couldn't afford a war with England. Keeping hold of the Netherlands was expensive enough, as Alva's refusal of Ridolfi's appeal made clear. I could...

The Duke of Alva would be hard to deceive. I reckoned he had seen through Ridolfi. He would probably see through my pretended conversion and no doubt he also knew that Elizabeth didn't want war any more than Philip did. She was known to regard it as wasteful. She wasn't likely to squander men and money on the gesture of avenging just one person, even her own sister. Her bastard sister. And if she did, it would only be a gesture. I would be dead – hideously dead – before she even knew I was in danger; Lady Anne, the Duke of Alva and his lackeys in the Inquisition would make sure of that.

There was still Matthew. Would Lady Anne be tempted if he tried to ransom me? Or did she hate me so much that she would reject a fortune so as to have her revenge and could he afford a fortune anyway? How much ready gold could he find? Much of his wealth had probably been dedicated to the cause of Mary Stuart already. He had land and a fine chateau but would he surrender those for me? I doubted it.

I crouched deeper under the blankets, shivering, and felt the outline of my little knife. Could I really use it? Could I slash my wrists, drive the blade into my own heart? *Could* I? But if I were thrown to the Inquisition, I might have to. It would be the easier alternative. Easier! My God!

Dimly, I was aware of sounds and smells, of the daily life of the house, going on as usual overhead. The gratings let in the smell of bread baking, and a distant tinkling; someone was surely playing the spinet I had seen the day before. Presently I heard hooves and the rumble of wheels on cobbles. The pony and cart that Matthew had mentioned? Yes, there was a child's voice, laughing this time. Lady Anne's pretty daughter Mary, who was going to be as fair as her mother, was being taken out for a ride in the sunshine. That was the normal world up there; the world of cooking and music and outings for children. I thought of Meg and the grandchild that now I might never see. I gave way then to grief and terror, lying face down on my pallet, weeping, shuddering. Despair is supposed to be a sin but I doubted if whoever decreed that, had experienced it.

My useless tears dried up in the end. At midday, food was brought to me again; bread and stew and small ale and a jug of water. The bread wasn't fresh and the stew had little meat in it but was mostly made of carrots and onions and some kind of cereal. However, it was hot. I repeated my request for a comb and washing water but once more, Ulverdale and his companion, a sullen-looking youth, remained silent.

Could I possibly, somehow, exploit the moment when the door was next opened? Could I pretend to be ill, cause a distraction, fling my blankets over my enemies' heads, rush out and bolt the door behind me?

I doubted it. If I did get out of the cellar, how would I get out of the house without being caught? I would just be overpowered, possibly injured and certainly hurt, and I'd been hurt enough already. I'd been recently ill; my back and thighs still ached from that interminable ride and my rope burns were sore. I was not as young, as resilient as once I was.

The day passed. Supper was reheated stew though the bread was fresher. I remained unwashed and uncombed. Night fell.

Exhaustion had made me sleep on the previous night but I had been sitting on my bed all day. Now, sleep eluded me. The hours of

194

darkness crawled past and in the small hours, fears always multiply. Once again, I sank into hopelessness and useless tears.

Another daybreak. Another tray. Bread, a very tiny omelette, small ale, water. The water jug wasn't big but I thought I could spare just a little. I tipped some over a corner of my cloak and wiped my face and hands with it. Then I took off my hat and used my fingers as best I could to tidy my hair.

The day followed the pattern of the previous one. Bread was baked, spinet music tinkled, and again there was the sound of a pony's hooves and wheels on the cobbles, and once again a small child giggled. My solitude had become a torment. I wanted someone to talk to. I wanted to get *out*. I wanted to beat on the door and shout for help and batter the walls with my fists. I sat on the bed and bit my knuckles to keep from stupidly hammering the timber and stone. I didn't want the enemy to laugh.

At midday and evening, I was given more bread, some pottage, and the usual ale and water. My bucket was taken away and replaced by an empty one. Once more I tried to sleep, and this time dozed uneasily.

Another day dragged by, following the same pattern. I don't like to remember it. My best hope had lain in Matthew but hope needs encouragement, just as a living body needs food, and mine was failing now for want of sustenance. My fears grew and grew, gathering round me like grey wraiths. Almost, I could see them.

The fourth morning of my solitary imprisonment began like the rest. Weary from another troubled night, I ate another depressing breakfast and then lay down again on my bed, curling up with my knees close to my chest, trying to shut out my thoughts. It was about noon when I became aware that the sounds of the household had changed.

The awareness began when I heard Lady Anne's voice, quite close to the grating above me and a man's voice replying. I couldn't make out any words, but Anne Percy sounded both angry and alarmed, and the man who was answering her sounded worried. I sat up to listen. Finally, I heard her footsteps, sharp and quick, going away.

I lay down again but not for long, for presently, a noisy disturbance broke out in the house overhead. Through the grating in the door, I could hear raised voices and someone crying, and then, surely, a girl was screaming. Feet were running about, doors were banging. Like a pervasive smell, agitation filtered down to my prison.

It was surely near dinner time and I wondered uneasily whether whatever the trouble was, would cause me to be forgotten. However, the food did appear, brought this time by two women, a heavily built one who wheezed, and a younger one, who seemed upset, for she had reddened eyes, as though she had been weeping. I was encouraged to try once more to talk.

'What's the matter?' I said, using a low voice.

196

'Something is – there's upset in the house. I can hear it. What's wrong?'

They looked at me in a confused way as though they hadn't thought I was capable of speech. 'I *know* something's wrong!' I said. 'What is it? Surely there's no harm in telling me.'

'It's so awful!' The younger one burst out with it and her hefty companion didn't try to stop her. She just let out a sound halfway between a sigh and a groan. It suddenly struck me that the confusion upstairs had been so bad that no one had remembered to tell them not to talk to me.

'The nursemaid!' said the young one. She spoke in French; presumably she was not one of the household that Anne Percy had brought from England. 'Suzanne – the nursemaid – took my lady's daughter, little Mary, out in the pony cart this morning like always on nice days and they didn't come back, and then Suzanne did, frightened out of her wits!'

'That's right,' said her companion, also in French. 'Some way from here, she said, two men got into the cart when it stopped to let a big wagon pass. They had a dagger and said they'd kill her if she screamed. She said they drove out of Bruges to a wood, and then one of them dragged her out of the cart and the other one went off into the wood with the child.'

'You mean, my lady's daughter has been kidnapped?' I whispered.

'Yes!' The big woman's eyes were wide and
197

shocked. 'Someone was waiting in the wood, with a horse. The man who got hold of Suzanne brought her back on it, holding her in front of him, saying he'd knife her if she made a noise. When they got here, he gave her a message for my lady, and then pushed her off the horse and told her to deliver the message and be quick about it. We don't know what it was but the mistress is beside herself!'

'She's beaten poor Suzanne, as if it was her fault,' said the young one. 'Poor Suzanne, she's crying on her bed, crying something awful!'

'What are you two doing down there?' Someone was shouting from upstairs.

'We mustn't stop! We'll be in trouble!' The big woman grabbed her assistant's elbow and they fled. I heard the bolts slide home.

I ate my meal: yesterday's bread and luke-warm pottage. As I finished, a new sound made me stiffen. Someone, somewhere was pounding on a door, and voices were being raised in a confused babble. Then rapid footsteps were descending to the cellar. The bolts were shot back and there stood Ulverdale and Lady Anne. Lady Anne was white with rage and Ulverdale was scarlet with it. They looked at me with such hatred that I sprang up in alarm, wondering if they meant to murder me forthwith.

'Your husband is here. Your real husband, apparently,' said Lady Anne, through her teeth. 'It seems that when you were calling yourself Mistress Stannard, you were actually living in sin. According to Matthew de la Roche, you are

198

married to him, and he has come for you. He is a man I have heard of, whose reputation I respected, and at our one meeting, I respected him even more. Until now. *Now,* I would happily drive a dagger into the bastard. He has kidnapped my daughter and....'

At this point, her anger overcame her to such an extent that her words dissolved, literally, into a snarl. Ulverdale took up the tale.

'He is at the main door, bold as Lucifer! If we bring you to the door, he will send a messenger to fetch little Mary and the exchange can be made. If we do not, or if you have been harmed...'

Ulverdale too seemed on the verge of being strangled by his own wrath. He didn't finish the sentence, but strode into the cellar, seized my right arm in a grip so bruising that I thought it might amount to doing me harm, all by itself, and marched me out. Lady Anne, after giving me one more look of loathing, spun round and led the way up the steps. Once at the top, I was hustled through the house towards the front door. As we reached it, she stepped aside so that I could see beyond her. 'Here she is, de la Roche. Undamaged, as you see. Take her forward, Ulverdale. But not too close.'

And there, on the threshold, stood Matthew.

'Ursula! Are you all right? Have they ill-used you?'

'No, we have not.' Ulverdale answered for me. 'She has been a prisoner, but she has been warm and properly fed.' His grip on my arm

199

continued to be savage. 'But we don't hand her over until Mary is here. In fact' – he turned to look at Lady Anne – 'even now, can't we seize him and make him talk? I can make him tell us where Mary is! He frightened you by saying that if we raised a hue and cry, you'd never see your child again, but if I get my hands on him, I'll frighten him much more! Madam, just give me the chance.'

'If you seize me, you will be seen to do it,' said Matthew calmly. 'I thought it unwise to create a public disturbance by using the short and obvious method of bringing armed men here and rescuing my wife by force. But I have a dozen men at hand. I am being watched at this moment.' He glanced up at the tall houses that overlooked the little front courtyard. 'So are you. I will not enter your house unless you drag me, and then my friends will come to my aid at once, even if it does start a riot.'

According to Donna, Matthew had been travelling with an escort of six or seven. I wondered where the rest had come from.

Matthew was still talking. 'I repeat the message I sent by the nursemaid. If Ursula is not returned to me, at once, then you will never see Mary again.'

I tried not to gape. I could not imagine Matthew harming a tiny child, a little girl less than a year old, but the threat clearly terrified Anne Percy. Her glance at me was still full of hatred, but she was shaking: body, hands, mouth.

'I shall not, of course, murder her,' Matthew

said smoothly. 'Many nunneries take in found-
lings. If you have to search Europe for the one
on whose doorstep Mary has been left, it may
take you a long time. If you ever do chance on
the right one, she may well, by then, have
changed beyond recognition. You may not
recognize each other.'

'I won't hand Madame Bl— Madame de la
Roche over to you until Mary is here!' Lady
Anne said fiercely.

'Of course not,' said Matthew. He put two
fingers into his mouth, turned to face the courtyard, and whistled. 'She'll be here in a few
minutes. You'll find the cart abandoned by the
roadside to the south, just outside Bruges, by
the way. I wouldn't wish to be accused of theft.
Ah.' He turned to look towards the gate. 'Here
is Mary.'

A rider had just come through the arch from
the road. He was a big man with a cloak drawn
round him. He halted, loosened the cloak and
revealed that part of his bulk was a small girl
who had been held against his chest. She seemed to be drowsy, and nestled quite trustfully
against him.

'She's a trifle sleepy,' Matthew said. 'We
gave her a poppy juice drink. It hasn't harmed
her; she'll wake up properly before long. Now,
let us conduct this business in a proper, formal
manner. I will step aside. Master – Ulverdale, I
believe is your name, sir? – can lead my wife
down the steps and to the middle of the courtyard where my man Francois is waiting with

Mary. The exchange can then take place. Only Ulverdale is to come with Ursula. But he must not try any tricks. Remember, we are being watched. Now, shall we proceed?'

He retreated down the steps and withdrew to one side. Ulverdale pulled me forward. I stumbled on the steps and he jerked me upright with a wrench that nearly dislocated my elbow. I decided that I hated him even more than I hated Lady Anne. I had harmed her much more, after all, than I had harmed Ulverdale.

The big man called Francois was talking quietly to Mary, who continued to snuggle against him, holding on to his jacket. For a moment, I understood Anne Percy. Because of me, this child had never seen her father, probably never would see him, might never enjoy her birthright of lands and wealth and marriage to a powerful husband. Because of me, this child had nearly been deprived of her mother and her home as well. Anne had every right to be furious, every right to detest me.

But here we were in the middle of the court-yard and the two parties were face to face. Francois gently detached Mary from his jacket and lowered her towards Ulverdale. Ulverdale emitted a growl like an angry panther, but Matthew had stepped forward and his arm was already round me. Ulverdale let me go and Francois handed Mary down to him. It was done.

'Out of here,' Matthew said tersely. I caught one brief glimpse of Lady Anne running down

202

the steps to meet Ulverdale and snatch her daughter from him, and I thought that she was weeping, but I couldn't be sure because Matthew was already sweeping me through the archway to the street, and his mounted friend was following. Outside in the street, another man awaited us, also mounted, and holding the reins of two more animals, both laden with bulging saddlebags.

'Thank you, Raoul,' Matthew said, and heaved me on to one of the horses before getting astride his own. I too would have to ride astride, I found and I heard my skirt tear as I scrambled for the stirrups, all in a muddle of haste and tangled clothing and knees that banged against the saddlebags. And then we were away. Weak from hunger, fear and sleeplessness, I stayed on by clinging to my saddle pommel. I was also aware, so very much aware, of those few moments in Matthew's grasp, of his strength and the familiar, spicy smell of him: like a mixture of leather and cinnamon.

We were side by side as we clattered along the street. Breathlessly I said: 'Was it Brockley? He told you what had happened when he got back to Brussels, I take it. Where is he now?'

'Still in Brussels. I told him to stay there. He was so angry he might have done something rash. His wife didn't want him to come either, because she said that the Countess hated him as much as she hated you and would be only too glad to get her hands on him. When we join up with the rest of my men, I'll send one hotfoot to

Brussels ahead of us, with the good news.'

The street had narrowed and I had to fall back. It was reassuring to hear the hooves of Francois' horse just behind me. But a few moments later I was able to come alongside Matthew again and without being prompted, he said: 'I got to Brussels the evening after you were captured. To start with, I tried to bribe the Countess. God knows, we're supposed to be on the same side, both supporters of Mary Stuart, but there's no denying, the Countess is a bitch. She laughed in my face though my offer was good – I was ready to sell land to save you. She said she didn't care. That paying what she owed you was more important to her than a fortune.'

I could believe it. 'So then you thought of Mary?' I said.

'Yes. I knew what her routine was – I saw it when I visited the Countess before I came on to Brussels. I spent a day making plans. Then, today, I and Francois – because he's big and strong – seized Mary and her nursemaid, and took them out of Bruges. I had Raoul hidden in a wood, with our horses. Mary was bewildered, Ursula, but she's too small to understand and be frightened. I sent the nursemaid back with Francois to deliver my message to Anne Percy and I gave Mary a drink with a little opium in it. After I reckoned Anne Percy had had time to hear my threat and get into a thorough panic, Raoul and I mounted and came back into Bruges. Francois was waiting in a tavern, on watch by a window, with his horse tethered

204

outside. He mounted, I handed Mary to him, told him to bring her in when I whistled and then I got down and marched to the Countess's front door. You know the rest.'

'Matthew,' I said, 'would you really have ... have left Mary on a nunnery doorstep as a foundling if – well, if I'd been already in the hands of the Inquisition? That's what she planned for me.'

'Yes, she told me.' I heard the anger in his voice. 'But no, of course I wouldn't victimize a child. What do you take me for? I was bluffing. I'd have returned Mary to her. But I think *she* might be capable of doing such a thing and people often assume that others resemble themselves. I hoped she would believe I meant what I said – and she did!'

We were leaving Bruges. 'Are we going far?' I asked. I was still keeping a shaky hand on my pommel.

'Two hours' steady riding and then there's an inn where we can rest. Don't be afraid. Lady Anne has the manpower to ambush you and Brockley but she hasn't the wherewithal to take on me and my men.'

'Have you really got twelve of them?' I asked. 'And how did you get the people in those houses next to Anne's, to let your men watch her courtyard from their upper windows?'

'I have seven men. Raoul and Francois are with us now. I left the others hidden in the wood where Raoul waited for me to bring Mary. They'll join us there. No one was watching from the upper windows of the houses overlooking that courtyard. I'm a convincing liar, that's all,' said Matthew.

'You ... you mean that was bluff as well?'

'Precisely.'

I burst out laughing.

SIXTEEN

Vortex

Matthew's other five men joined us, as he had said they would, when we were passing a small wood. They rode out of the trees, grinning, and exchanged greetings with us all. Matthew sent one of them off at a gallop, ordering him to make haste to Brussels with the news of my rescue. The rest fell in behind us. Every man had a sword. We had become a well-protected party. Let the ex-Countess of Northumberland try to tackle us now!

We rode steadily on. I managed to disentangle my skirts, and took to looking about me. 'This isn't the road to Brussels,' I said. 'Where are we going?'

'Towards Antwerp,' said Matthew. 'Just in case your delightful hostess does try sending someone after us. We'd be a match for them if she did but I'd rather avoid a fight. She'll expect us to make for Brussels, so we won't.'

I was grateful for the precautions but I was very tired and aching badly before we reached the inn that Matthew had in mind. 'I've never been there myself,' Matthew told me, 'but

Raoul has kinsfolk hereabouts and has dined there. He recommends it. Don't you, Raoul?'

'The food is good,' said Raoul. 'The inn is called Le Martelets Trois.'

'The Three Martlets?'

'It stands on land owned by a knight whose shield blazon is argent, three martlets sable,' said Raoul.

'We should be safe enough there,' Matthew said. 'However, just as a precaution, I shan't use my own name.' He gave me a wicked grin. 'I have occasionally, and illicitly, been in England since last we met, and there, I used the name of Jean FitzAlan. I was posing as the employee of various vineyards in France, sent to obtain orders for their wines.'

'Weren't people annoyed when the wines didn't arrive?' I asked.

'The wines did arrive. The vineyards were real and their owners are my friends. My commission, though, was dedicated to the cause of Mary Stuart.'

I said nothing. This was no time to argue over the rights and wrongs of Mary's claim to Elizabeth's throne.

Matthew, more concerned with concealing our identities, was saying: 'We had better give you a new name as well, Ursula. What do you suggest? It had better be an English name, as you have an English accent. I can say that I am escorting my English cousin to a family gathering in Antwerp.'

'Smith is a common surname in England and

Katherine a favourite Christian name. I can call myself Katherine Smith.'

'Very good. You are Madame Katherine Smith.' In a quiet voice, he added: 'You made it clear enough, in Signor Ridolfi's garden, that you do not wish to resume life as my wife. I also recognize that you lived as the wife of Hugh Stannard, whoever he was, for some years and that you are now mourning for him. I shall make no demands on you. I certainly don't want payment in kind. I came to your rescue because I love you and I ask no reward. I wish you would change your mind, but I shall do nothing more towards persuading you. Tomorrow, we shall alter our route and begin the journey back to Brussels by a roundabout way. We will take it easily. You have had a bad time.' He added: 'We'll be at the inn very soon now.'

It was indeed a good inn. Dinner time was past and supper still well ahead but we were all shown to a public room where there was a hearth, a long table and benches, and a servant brought us wine and cold chicken pie. Supper would be in four hours' time, he said, and then there would be roasted capons and hot stew, new bread and syllabubs.

After the meal, our escort withdrew to the stables to tend our horses (like Brockley, they distrusted strange grooms) but Matthew and I, at his request, were shown to small separate bedchambers and supplied with washing water. Matthew's preparations for my rescue proved remarkably efficient. He had brought me a brush and comb, soap and a towel, clean stockings and linen and a fresh gown complete with sleeves and kirtle, though no ruff or farthingale.

'Some things don't fit well into saddlebags,' Matthew said. 'Dale chose and packed the clothes.'

A wash, a sleep, and clean garments helped me. By the time we all met again for the inn's excellent supper, I felt much stronger. Matthew and I ate with other guests in the main dining room, while our escort supped elsewhere, among the servants of our fellow guests. After the meal, Matthew went to see them and came back laughing.

'They've made friends with their table-mates and they're all playing cards or backgammon.' He glanced round and noticed that some of our own table companions were settling down to the same amusements, mostly with tumblers or tankards to hand.

'Do you want a game of any kind, Ur— Kate?' Matthew said. 'Or are you tired?'

'I don't feel as tired as I did, but I think I need some more rest, all the same,' I said. 'I'd like to go upstairs.' I added in a whisper: 'You nearly called me Ursula just now.'

'Hush. So I did. Sorry. We'll quietly withdraw.'

The upstairs rooms opened on to a gallery that overlooked the inn yard and as we stepped on to it, we paused to look over the balustrade. It was still light and in the cobbled yard below, pigeons were pecking. As we watched, a maid-servant came out and threw some bits of bread to them. And then became indignant as a groom appeared to sweep the yard, and would have swept the bread up too, but for her protests and her wagging finger.

'Normal life,' I said. 'When I was shut in that horrible cellar, I kept hearing the sounds of the house and the stable yard, just everyday noises and oh, those ordinary things are so precious! Matthew, thank you for rescuing me.'

I turned to look into his face. His eyes seemed to widen. On impulse, I put my arms round him and kissed him. It was the least I could do, I thought, to show that I truly appreciated what he had done; that I was as grateful as I ought to be.

He seemed to hold back for a moment, and then his arms encircled me and I felt his heart pounding. His mouth blended with mine and our bodies exchanged their warmth, and all the sensations which I had fought against back in the Ridolfi garden, returned, more powerful than ever, to overwhelm me. I was losing my-self, ceasing to think or remember. Once again, I tried to recall Hugh, to summon up a vision of Hawkswood but the pictures they made in my mind were tiny, far away ... and then they were gone. I seemed to have no mind, no will of my own. I was a vortex, spinning, seeking to draw Matthew into me...

I heard him say: 'Come. This way.' I was aware of being guided through a door and lifted

211

off my feet. Matthew's face was above me. 'You are glad? You want this? You want me?'

'Yes, I want you.' I couldn't have said anything else. He had always had this physical power over me. I could not be near him, ever, and not feel it. I needed him. I felt as if I had been hungry for him for a thousand years.

All my weariness was gone and my aches seemed unimportant. That night, it was long before either of us slept.

SEVENTEEN

Matters of Loyalty

'How much does Signor Ridolfi know?' I asked Matthew, when we were breaking our fast. 'What did Brockley tell him?'

'What he told me, and what I at first believed, until Anne Percy herself informed me otherwise.' Matthew grinned. 'He is so dignified, that manservant of yours. He looks as though he is full of integrity...'

'He is,' I said.

'...but he's not above adapting the truth on occasion. He found me and the Signor together and he said that you had been kidnapped by men in the pay of the former Countess of Northumberland, who had a grudge against you. He said that you are truly a Catholic and always have been, but that in the lifetime of Master Stannard you kept the religious laws of England, and that you are loyal to Queen Elizabeth. Ridolfi said he could respect that. Then Brockley explained that some time ago, by chance, when you were travelling in the north of England, you found that the Countess, who was thought to have fled to Scotland after a

213

failed rising, was still secretly in England, hoping to renew the rising. As an honest citizen, you informed the authorities, causing the countess to be thrust into exile.'

'That's more or less the case,' I said carefully.

'There was a little more to it, according to Anne Percy. It seems that you committed some kind of personal offence against her, though she wouldn't give me any details.'

'That's true,' I said, 'but I'd rather not give you the details either. I injured her dignity. Best leave it at that.'

'As you wish. Anyway, I knew nothing of that at the time when Brockley came back. He declared that the countess had seized you and sent him back to raise a ransom for you, the money to be put to the cause of Mary Stuart. The Signor and I believed him. It wasn't till I reached Brussels that I found out that the lady's plans for you didn't involve a ransom at all. She tried to snatch Brockley too, it seems, but he escaped. However, back in Brussels, Signor Ridolfi and I accepted Brockley's tale and the Signor contributed generously to the ransom. It was included in the bribe I offered the lady. I shall have to return it to the Signor.'

I said nothing. Bleakness had been gathering in me ever since we woke at daybreak, side by side. Ecstasy lay only a few hours behind, back beyond a deep, satisfied sleep in Matthew's arms. But now, safely out of Anne Percy's grasp, I must consider the future and the choices before me were all unhappy.

214

We were breakfasting a little late and most of the other guests had finished already. We had the public dining room to ourselves. He smiled at me across the table, narrowing his dark eyes, and as ever, my heart turned somersaults. I said something trivial, about the route we would take that morning. I could not yet face the moment of decision.

The road we took led back towards Brussels in a circuitous fashion, but we made good time. I wasn't talkative and Matthew didn't press me. However, when we paused at midday to eat at a small tavern, and were sitting on a terrace over-looking the road, he said: 'We will have to spend one night on the way but we'll get to Brussels tomorrow.' He took a mouthful of fish and then said, casually: 'How did you come to be staying with the Ridolfis? You were there for your ward's wedding, and went away with her – but why did you go back? Roberto said you were paying them a farewell call and for some reason I never asked why. But it does seem strange. You hardly know them.'

'But I do,' I said. 'I met them in London two years ago. Hugh and I were visiting the Duke of Norfolk, who knew the Signor. Donna and I made friends. It's for Donna that I'm staying in Brussels now. She is always nervous in countries not her own. She wanted me with her for a while.'

'I see. Ursula, when we talked in the garden in Brussels, you ran away from me without answering a question I had asked you. Is your

215

conversion real – or not? I promise that if it isn't, I won't give you away. But I must *know.*'

'I could swear to you that I was a genuine convert,' I said. 'But would you believe me? Obviously, saying I'm a Catholic would be wise in any country under Spanish rule. In my place, what would you do?'

Matthew nodded. 'I suppose that's as good an answer as any. But, my dear, surely we are now husband and wife once more. We can have a second marriage ceremony if you wish it. We can live at Blanchepierre, and if you are sharing the Ridolfi way of worship while you are in their house, then I hope you will do the same for me. You did once before. If you are not yet a true believer, belief will come to you, in time. I promise.'

'Why is it,' I asked him, 'that you are in Spanish territory to raise funds for Mary? Spain and France have never been friends.'

'I am not interested in politics in that sense. I serve the Catholic church and the cause of Mary Stuart,' said Matthew.

There was a clatter of hooves from somewhere on our left, round the corner of the tavern building. I heard Raoul's voice, soothing a restive animal. Our horses were being brought out of the stable where they had been having rub-downs, mangers and a rest. I stood up. 'I think it's time we were on our way again.'

Matthew gave me a shrewd look, but he too rose, and the topic of religion and Mary Stuart

216

was dropped. 'Yes, we have a good few miles to do before the evening,' he said.

The inn we found that night was a miserable place, with only a couple of proper guest chambers. Most overnight customers were expected to sleep in communal fashion on pallets on a half-floor above the entrance hall. Matthew obtained a room for us by bullying the landlord and outbidding a fat, red-faced and wealthy wayfarer who thought he had snatched one of the two bedrooms for himself. Ousted, he was obliged to share the half-floor with our escort and several other people. Next morning, he complained bitterly about bedbugs.

So did we. As far as comfort went, our sleeping arrangements weren't much better than his. Except, of course, that we had privacy.

And we used it, bedbugs or not. This time, though, our love-making was gentler. That first raging hunger had been slaked and now we could exchange caresses in a more tender fashion, and fall asleep by midnight.

But some time in the deep of the night, I woke. Matthew lay beside me, breathing evenly, fathoms down in contented slumber. I lay still, listening to him, and it was then that Hugh came back to me.

Last night, I had not been able to imagine his face or properly remember our home. Now I saw them so plainly that it was hard to believe they were not real. I could see every feature of Hugh's dear countenance; I could walk through

Hawkswood House from room to room, pace through the hall and the two pleasingly furnished parlours, climb the stairs to our bedchamber, gaze from its window at the terrace below and Hugh's rose garden beyond. In my mind, I sauntered through that garden, holding his arm, and it seemed to me that I could feel his muscle and bone, firm and reassuring under my hand.

I turned to look into Hugh's eyes, and I asked him what to do, and he replied.

Then he was gone, to be replaced by Sir William Cecil, his bearded face long and anxious, with the line that was always there between his eyes, and beside him was my sister, Elizabeth, red hair crimped in front of a spectacularly jewelled headdress; stiffened lace ruff, open, spreading behind her head like the uplifted tail of a peacock. Her amber eyes watched me from her pale, shield-shaped face, a face that was indeed a shield, since it forever hid the true thoughts and feelings of the woman behind it.

Those two had used me but paid me well for my services; they had lied to me and yet protected me; loved me, I think, in their fashion; demanded my loyalty, as a right. And it was a right. They were the bulwark that kept the throne out of the hands of Mary Stuart, with her questionable past and her dangerous religion. They were the defenders who kept the Inquisition away from English soil.

Ridolfi wanted to raise an army to take England, to destroy Elizabeth, to open the ports to the Inquisitors, and from the moment that I realized that Matthew knew Ridolfi well, I had not doubted that he knew about Ridolfi's plot. He said he was here to raise money for Mary Stuart. Presumably, he expected Ridolfi to be the user.

I turned on my side, away from Matthew. I didn't want the dawn to break. I didn't want to face the next day. For tomorrow, I must declare my choice. *How would Hugh want me to decide?* I had asked that question in the night and known at once what his answer would be. Clear, loving, and uncompromising. And besides...

Matthew had probably saved my life and it was shameful ingratitude to have twinges of conscience about the methods he had used. Mary had come to no harm and according to Matthew, would never have done so. She hadn't even been frightened and he would have returned her to her mother anyway. Yet something in me still recoiled from using a child in such a way. And therefore, something in me recoiled from Matthew himself.

I feared the dawn, for next day, I must tear my heart and Matthew's heart, out of our bodies, and throw them down and stamp on them.

Next day, we made conversation as we rode, about ordinary things: the bright May weather and the temperaments of our mounts (Matthew's was inclined to bite horses he didn't know). Then we were riding into Brussels and there was the Ridolfi house and here came Brockley and Dale, hastening out to greet us, their faces full of thankfulness. I dismounted quickly to embrace them both.

Then the Ridolfis were there, exclaiming.

'I had no idea that the Countess had a grudge against you! Dear Madame Blanchard, I would never have mentioned you to her, had I known!'

'Ursula, Ursula, you're safe!' Donna was almost crying. 'We were horrified when Brockley told us what had happened. I begged Roberto to ask the Duke of Alva to intervene but he is one of the Countess's friends and we feared it might do more harm than good ... oh, *Ursula*, we've been so worried...!'

I embraced the Ridolfis too. And then, because I had now realized that delay would only drag the agony out, I said: 'Signor de la Roche and I need a few private moments. One can't talk properly on horseback or among other people in inns. Might we use one of your parlours, Signor Ridolfi?'

'Of course. But wouldn't you rather wash and change and take some wine first? You've had a dreadful experience. I hope the Countess didn't treat you too badly, at least...'

'It's important,' I said, cutting Ridolfi short. 'I can wash and change afterwards.'

'Then use the front parlour, by all means. I'll send a tray of wine in.'

'There's no need. I don't think we shall be long.'

Somehow, I extricated Matthew and myself

from all this anxious fuss. He accompanied me to the front parlour without protest; in fact without saying anything whatsoever. But once we were in the small, prettily furnished room and had closed the door behind us, he found his voice.

'You are going to tell me, aren't you, that you're not coming back to Blanchepierre with me after all.'

It wasn't a question but a statement.

'Yes,' I said. A wave of exhaustion broke over me and I sank on to the nearest settle. I sat there, looking up at him. It was grievous to see the pain on his face, in those dark eyes that I thought so beautiful. 'I can't,' I said. 'In spite of what has happened between us these past two nights, in spite of what you did to bring me safely out of danger, I can't. I'm sorry.'

Matthew also sat down, facing me. 'Why can't you?' he said. 'I am entitled to an explanation, aren't I? I told you, we can go through another marriage ceremony if you wish, if you doubt that our original one was valid.'

'It isn't that. It's Mary Stuart. You know that as well as I do, Matthew. You want her to be queen of England...'

'She *is* queen of England.'

'You see? The gulf between us is too great. I am sister to Elizabeth and I uphold her right to the throne. I am on her side. How can you and I ever live in peace together?'

'Ursula, darling Saltspoon, *why* do you trouble yourself with such things? Elizabeth has

221

plenty of supporters and advisers – too many for my liking! – she can do without you easily enough. I am your husband. Cleave to me. Come and help me rear my son, and give him brothers and sisters. He'd like that, and so would you.'

He half rose to come to me but I raised a hand and said: 'No, don't, please. *Please*,' and my tone warned him not to touch me.

He sat back and said: 'There was a time when we lived happily together in Blanchepierre, until you had to go back to England because your daughter needed you. And then, of course, Elizabeth kept you there. But why can't we live happily together now? What's so different?'

'Things were not well between us, even then,' I said. 'Don't you remember? We quarrelled before we parted.'

'You were ill after that stillbirth. It would have come right in time, if you had stayed.'

'Perhaps,' I said. 'Or perhaps not. But other things have changed. I didn't then know that the queen was my sister. That makes a huge difference. It also makes me, potentially, a useful hostage for any nation that wants to bend Elizabeth to its will.'

'I doubt it. She'd sacrifice you,' said Matthew bluntly. 'And you know it. Ursula...'

Again I cut him short.

'That isn't all,' I said.

Hugh's body lay sleeping in the churchyard at Hawkswood but in that Brussels parlour, he seemed once again to be beside me, advising

222

me, as he had done in the night just gone by. Dear Hugh, sensible, reliable Hugh, had shown me the worth of a peaceful married life, full of pleasant, everyday concerns and without conflicts. Life with Matthew would be all conflict. I didn't want such a life. Not even leavened by the passion that Matthew and I had shared these past two nights.

'Matthew,' I said, 'in your blind devotion to Mary Stuart and to what you call the cause of the true faith, you are liable at any time to become involved in schemes to bring Mary – and her faith – into power in England. That is what you want, isn't it? Not just to reinstate Mary on the Scottish throne but to put her on the English one as well. Do you deny it?'

'No of course not. I said, she *is* England's rightful queen.'

'Well, then. If we are living in Blanchepierre and I should find out that you are involved in a plot to – well – to put her in Elizabeth's place, then it would be my duty to interfere if I could. To spoil the plot. To warn Elizabeth. You would have an enemy in your house.'

'Ursula, I am sure that in time, you would come to see...'

'I would *not* come to see. Dear God, you've just saved me from being thrown to the Inquisition! Put the Catholics in power in England and we'd have that horror there!'

'Mary, when she has been able to communicate with us, has said that she doesn't want that.'

223

'Bah!' I said inelegantly. 'What I see and you don't, or won't, is that Mary can only be put into power in England with the help of a Spanish army. Do you think I want Spanish soldiers tramping all over the soil of *my* country? And I tell you, if Philip of Spain were to be her backer, then if he wanted to introduce the Inquisition, and he probably would, then he'd do it with or without her consent.'

'Ursula...'

'*No*, Matthew!'

He had gone so white that I was frightened, though whether of him or for him, I didn't know. Was it the pallor of misery or the pallor of rage? But I had gone too far to turn back.

'There's more. You said, just now, that before I left Blanchepierre, we were at odds because I had been ill after a stillbirth. Can't you understand that I am terrified of another such disaster? Hugh had been married before but he never had children. I don't know why. Some doctors say that some childhood illnesses can destroy fertility when the child grows up. Perhaps that was the case with him. Anyway, with him, I felt safe. I wouldn't have that safety with you.'

'But that's absurd. Women are born to have children. You would see. Once a child was on the way ... indeed, one may already be on the way! We have had two nights.'

'I *pray* it hasn't happened.' In fact, the fear that it might have done so had already begun to haunt me. '*I cannot come back to you, Matthew.*

224

I am Hugh Stannard's widow. I am not, and cannot be, your wife. Thank you for saving me from Countess Anne. Thank you a thousand times. You know I mean it – but we have to say goodbye. Please go, Matthew. It would be best if you left this house soon, best if we never meet again.'

He was so white now that I thought he might either faint or attack me. I had heard people use the words *his eyes burned*, and thought it just a conventional phrase. Now I saw it in reality.

Love, I thought confusedly, can be a dreadful thing. It's too powerful. It's powerful enough to create new living things, and powerful enough to break them in pieces.

I sprang up and ran from the room. I had to get out of his presence.

I could only pray that he would do as I had asked him, and go.

I didn't so much enter my bedchamber as burst into it headlong. I almost collided with Dale, who was just crossing the room to put something away in the press. I collapsed on the bed and she came to me.

'Ma'am ... what is it? Can't I help? Did you have a very bad time in the hands of that Countess woman? I'll get some wine...'

'I had a terrible time in Anne Percy's hands,' I said. 'But that isn't all. I owe my rescue to Matthew de la Roche, but he wants me to go back to France with him and I can't. I want to go home to Hawkswood and Withysham – I've neglected Withysham, these last few years. And

I can't ask you and Brockley to come to Blanchepierre. You both detested it, I know you did. I'd *have* to send you home, and I'd rather go home as well.'

'You've told him no, then, ma'am?'

'Yes. He's hurt and angry. But I want my own life back, and Hawkswood, and you and Brockley ... Brockley's like an anchor. He's always tried to keep me out of danger. But oh, dear God...'

The memory of that wild night at the Three Martlets suddenly returned to me. Words abandoned me.

'There have been letters for you, ma'am,' Dale said. 'Two couriers came while you were away. One from Margaret van Weede – a real one this time, it's directed in her handwriting – and one from England, from Mistress Jester. The courier who brought that one said he couldn't stop; that he had other deliveries to make, but I know you'd have liked to see him. He was...'

'Later, Dale. Not now.'

'As you wish, ma'am.'

EIGHTEEN

The Velvet Gauntlet

I have heard that animals like foxes and stoats, if caught in a trap, sometimes free themselves by gnawing the trapped paw off. In severing myself from Matthew, I had done something similar and like a wounded animal I yearned for solitude, in which to suffer and, perhaps, begin to heal. But Dale had hardly been gone for half an hour before Donna arrived in my bed-chamber.

'So here you are, Ursula. Oh, I *am* so glad you're safe. Master de la Roche has left – he's ridden off with his men just this minute. He left me a note for you. Here it is. I asked why he was leaving in such a hurry and he told me that he had asked you to marry him but you had said no! Really,' said Donna, out of the depths of her innocence, 'he should have taken his time more. He's only known you a few days! What a way to go about a courtship! But I'd better go away and let you read his note in private.'

She laid it on the bed beside me and left. I sat up and looked at it miserably, not wanting to read it yet knowing that I must. I broke the seal.

Ursula, I am leaving at once, because it would embarrass us both if I stayed longer. I have appointments in Brussels which I hope to finish by the end of tomorrow and then I will set out for Blanchepierre.

On the way from Bruges, you confided various things to me. I have not repeated them to anyone and will not do so. I will keep your counsel.

You have hurt me, but my feelings for you are as ever. If you change your mind, then come to Blanchepierre. You will be welcome.

I have to tell you, however, that since Marie died, more than one good French family has sought me as a husband for one of their daughters. If a year goes by and you have not come, I will accept that our marriage is void, and make a new one for myself. My chateau needs a mistress and my little son needs a mother.

I wish with all my heart that you would come to me and fill those places. All my love. Matthew.

He had told me, wording it very carefully, that he had not suggested to Ridolfi or anyone else that my conversion might be false. If the letter should after all be seen by other eyes than mine, *various things* would mean nothing, or anything. If questioned, I could tell whatever tale I wished.

He had also offered me a further chance to join him, and he had assured me of his enduring love.

But it was not enough. We would be happy for a while and then the happiness would shatter, as though a stone had been flung through a glass window. He was still holding out a hand to me, but I must refuse it. I must reject him all over again.

I threw myself down, burying my face in the moleskin coverlet, and the wounded animal howled.

But sooner or later, of course, however grief-stricken one may be, the time comes when one must sit up, get up, pull oneself together, wash one's blotchy face, remove one's headdress, which is all askew, comb one's hair, resume the headdress at a civilized angle, paste a smile on one's face, and return to the world of people.

There was a small fire in my room. I burned the note and then went to find Dale. She and Brockley were in their room. They eyed me with anxiety and I knew that they had guessed more than I had told them. Briskly, I said: 'I think there are letters for me?'

We all sat together while I opened the one from Margaret first. It was cheerful.

I was foolish to make such a to-do at first. It was just that everything was so strange to me, and I was far away from England and there was no going back. I feel quite different now and Antonio is the kindest of men. And I have other news!

She had reason to hope that a child was on the way. Gertrud was going to look after her when the time came. She and Gertrud were the best of friends. Margaret needed me no longer.

Sybil's missive was bulky and when I opened it, I found two enclosures. One had a superscription in a hand I knew; that of the steward at my Sussex house, Withysham. The other had a seal, that I also knew. It was that of Lord Burghley. Sir William Cecil, in fact.

'Dale,' I said, 'you started to tell me who the courier was who brought Mistress Jester's package. I cut you short. Who was it?'

'John Ryder, ma'am. Cecil's man.'

'And my old friend,' Brockley said. 'He's doing courier work for Cecil these days, it seems, and he was in a hurry. I'm sorry you missed him, though, and he would have liked to see you.'

I was sorry too. John Ryder, greying, solid, fatherly, had been one of our companions in time gone by. He and Brockley had known each other long ago, when they were both in the army, and Cecil had sometimes lent him to us. He was getting on in years, though, I thought, and a courier's work is anything but restful. I hoped he wasn't being driven too hard.

But he had not been able to wait, and that was that. I looked at Sybil's package, and opened her letter first.

As Brockley had said, she had gone to London, taken lodgings and was in touch with Mistress Dalton, the housekeeper in the Duke

230

of Norfolk's London house.

I see her quite often – I have had gossips with her in her sitting room and been marketing with her. As yet I have learned nothing to the point and I am careful what questions I ask. But something may yet transpire and I will stay in London for the time being.

Her letter continued with news about Hawkswood, which Adam Wilder, the Hawkswood steward, had sent to her. All was well and the farm was prospering. I turned to the Withysham enclosure. It was a straightforward report on events there. Young stock were flourishing except that a few lambs had been lost, that were born early, during a cold spell. New plum trees had been planted...

I had chosen to read the Cecil's enclosure last because I was nervous of it. I broke the Burghley seal with great reluctance.

It was as though I had known in advance what the contents would be. I had been right to be afraid of them.

Ursula: destroy this letter when you have read it. One of my agents recently succeeded in entering the Duke of Alva's household, just as Robin Mayes did. He too had reason to fear discovery but succeeded in getting safely back to England, with worthwhile news. It is known to the Duke that Signor Ridolfi, because the Duke will not back his insane scheme of invading England, intends this summer to visit the Pope in Rome and then King Philip in Spain, to appeal for support from them. Ridolfi is said to have written to King Philip already; to prepare the ground. I have no agents in positions where they can learn the outcome of those appeals but I and your royal sister, Queen Elizabeth, need this information so that we can act for the safety of this realm. If possible, can you go with the Ridolfi family on this journey?

Also, although the man Charles Baillie is now in custody here, the letters he was carrying told us little. No doubt Brockley has said as much to you. We suspect that he somehow passed them to someone else, who substituted innocent documents before we laid hands on him. We still lack certainty concerning the Duke of Norfolk, and this is a question that must be answered, even if the answer causes pain to her majesty. Your gentlewoman Mistress Jester has called on me and I understand that she is in touch with his household, but she had nothing useful to tell me. Perhaps you can find out more at your end. I am sorry to ask this of you but there is no one else. Be wary. God go with you.

Burghley's signature followed.

He had put a horrifying suggestion in the form of a question. *If possible, can you go...?* But it wasn't a question. It was an order. He was sorry to be sending me into danger, but he was doing so all the same.

'He's commanding me to stay with the Ridol-
232

fis,' I said. 'It isn't worded that way but all the same, a command is what it is. Burghley has thrown a velvet-covered gauntlet at me.'

I handed Cecil's letter to the Brockleys. They read it, and then two horrified pairs of eyes stared into mine. 'Command or not, madam,' Brockley said, 'you mustn't. It's too dangerous. To travel as a spy, into Rome and into Spain! It would only need one moment of bad luck – a careless word – madam, please!'

'I know,' I said. 'But...'

Matthew's farewell message had done me harm. He would wait a year, he said. Throughout all that year, I could, if I wished, return to him. My wound was being kept open instead of being allowed to mend and it was now an injury so severe that it seemed to have cut me off from life. I could not get back to reality.

I must not go to Blanchepierre. But what I was to do with the rest of my life was beyond imagining. So I might as well obey the veiled command in Cecil's letter, and do what I could for him, for my sister, for my quiet green England, which if I had any say in the matter should not, *should not* be trampled by a foreign army, or thrown into the hands of Mary Stuart, who had almost certainly connived at the murder of her young husband, and would in all probability be the conduit through which Philip of Spain's loathsome Inquisition could snake its way into my country.

But to the two people who were now staring at me with such appalled expressions, I had a

233

responsibility.

'I don't expect you to come with me,' I said to them. 'This is my task and I will do it, but I refuse to endanger you. There has been too much of that in the past. I am sending the two of you home to England. That's a command, as well.'

I might have known. Brockley was never one to obey orders if he didn't approve of them. 'I can't let you take such a risk on your own, madam,' he said. 'I think Master Stannard really would rise up from his grave and haunt me if I did any such thing. I shall come with you, with or without your permission.'

'Brockley, really! I want you to take Dale home to England.' I didn't want to drag Dale into the Catholic heartlands. She would be terrified. She could also be a liability. She had failed again to acknowledge the statue of Our Lady as we came in from the courtyard when I arrived. But Brockley's face was implacable. 'Please do as I ask,' I said, appealingly this time.

'I am coming with you, madam, and that's that.'

'I could dismiss you for this!'

'Do so. I shall still come with you. I have enough money to support myself for quite a long time. I am of a saving disposition.'

Dale's prominent eyes were bulging with alarm, the pocks of her long-ago attack of smallpox all too noticeable. 'I don't want to go to Rome, or Spain! They're Papist places and they're dangerous!'

'You mustn't come,' Brockley said at once. 'Madam is right. You must go home. I'll find someone to escort you – perhaps Madame van Weede could lend you a man to go with you. I suppose there'll be time to pay a quick visit to van Weede's?'

But Dale's eyes were flashing. 'Where you go, I go! Even if it is dangerous! And I can't leave the mistress! I'm not having some other maid taking my place. If you go with her, then so do I. None of us ought to go at all! It's not safe! Ma'am, please ma'am, don't do this. Let's all go home!'

It was clear that which of the Brockleys was going where, wasn't to be settled by me. Perhaps I ought to take us all home. But this assignment was important. I would have had to undertake it, even if Matthew had not overset me, however great my affection for Dale and Brockley. I must do as I was bid and look after my two obstinate adherents as best I could.

Firmly, I said: 'I am staying with the Ridolfis, that is if Donna wants me.' I knew she would. Rome, of course, was in Italy, which was her home country, but Spain was no doubt as foreign to her as England or the Netherlands. 'You two can decide for yourselves what to do. I shall leave you to make up your minds. Mine *is* made up. Don't try to change it.'

I left the Brockleys and went to find Donna. It would be best, I thought, to get my own decision made and ratified as quickly as possible, so that there would be no turning back.

As I expected, Donna was only too glad to keep me as her companion for the foreseeable future. Remembering that I wasn't supposed to know about her husband's plans, I began by simply asking if I could prolong my stay but Donna interrupted me.

'Ursula, Roberto told me, just last night, that we are to leave Brussels very soon. We are to go to Rome and then Madrid! I meant to tell you this evening, when you had rested. If you are willing to come with us, I would be so pleased. My husband would let you if I asked him, I'm sure he would!'

The idea of more long hours on horseback made exhaustion pour over me but I ignored it. I would love to see Rome and Madrid, I said untruthfully, and if I could be of help to her, Donna...

'I shall love to have you with me,' said Donna, giving me a hug, and then dragged me off to Signor Ridolfi's study, to get his consent.

I told Dale and Brockley about it after supper. They listened silently and then Brockley said: 'Did you say that we would be coming too?'

'Yes. Ridolfi expects that anyway. He travels well attended, it seems. You can still go home if you choose. The choice is yours, not mine.'

'And we have made it, madam,' Brockley said. 'You need us both.'

That night, as I lay restlessly tossing, unable to sleep, I heard raised voices in the adjoining room. Concerned, I slipped out of bed, pulled

236

my dressing robe round me and stepped over to the wall. I put my ear to it.

'...you just want to be with *her*. It isn't just that it's your duty to protect her, you know it isn't. You just want to be with *her* and you'd rather be with *her* than with me, if it comes to it! When we were attacked in that wood and the mistress shouted at you to get me away, you didn't want to go! *Damned if I will!* That's what you said! You wanted to stay and be taken prisoner with *her*!'

It was Dale, crying, and only just coherent. Brockley was saying something in reply, in a low voice. I couldn't hear the words. Then Dale burst out again.

'...she calls you her anchor. That's what she said to me. She wants you with her too. She'd send me home and never think twice about it, but she'd keep you by her.'

'She tried to send me back to England as well!'

'She knew you wouldn't go! Oh, if you cared a straw for me, you'd take me back to England but you just want to be with *her*...'

'Stop this, Fran!' Brockley raised his voice. He was angry now. 'Come to bed. You're getting hysterical and I won't have it!'

Dale began to cry again. Brockley spoke to her once more, his voice fallen to just a murmur. I hoped that he was comforting her, had put his arms round her and was trying to reassure her. Presently, the sobbing stopped.

I went back to my own bed. I don't think I

237

slept at all that night. It seemed that no matter how hard I tried, I could not cast out Dale's suspicions, and it wasn't surprising. It was not just that Brockley and I had shared adventures in which she was not involved. Once, though it was long ago, we had very nearly become more than friends and colleagues, and two winters ago, when Brockley and I had gone on a journey without her and fallen into the hands of Anne Percy, we had during our escape formed an extraordinary partnership, as if for a while, our minds had blended. It had left a mark.

Poor Dale. I could only hope that I could carry out my mission, and get all three of us safely home again.

NINETEEN

The Long Way Round

We left Brussels on the twelfth of May, and arrived in Madrid on the twenty-second day of June, having gone round by way of Rome. Signor Ridolfi arranged the route; much of the time, I had no idea where we were. Ridolfi was in haste and we travelled light. He arranged for his household's bulkier possessions to be sent off to his home in Florence, and we took with us only essential changes of clothing and toiletries, stuffed into saddlebags and satchels.

Donna protested that she and Ridolfi could hardly visit such great cities as Rome and Madrid with only such changes of clothing as could be carried on horseback but Ridolfi merely said: 'We can buy new clothes, and all the ruffs and farthingales we need when we get to Rome and have them sent after us when we go on to Madrid. We'll do better without them on the road,' and that was that.

I asked Donna why she wanted to make such a long journey when I supposed she could if she wished go home to Florence. I rather hoped she would as I could hardly travel to Madrid except

239

as her companion and at heart I didn't want to travel at all. 'But I want to be with Roberto,' she said. 'I always want to be with Roberto.' There was no escape for me that way.

We went most of the way on horseback but travelled from Italy to Spain by sea. Dale had to ride a horse herself because Ridolfi said that pillion riders slowed a party down. She promised me that she wouldn't complain, but every day, we heard of something that she couldn't abide and she was noticeably stiff every time she dismounted.

Because of the need for haste, we changed horses regularly. Brockley had been right when he said that on major routes, bankers of Ridolfi's status had regular arrangements for re-mounts. However, the Signor noticed Dale's discomfort and tried to ease it by hiring amblers for her when they were available, since the ambling pace is smooth. She was grateful and I had sympathy for her for I too had my troubles. The inns we used weren't all ideal. I have particularly vivid memories of a curiously flavoured stew that gave Dale indigestion but caused me, half an hour after the meal, to throw it all up again.

But why go on? I wondered, often, if the journey would ever end.

We were a party of twelve. Most of the servants at the Brussels house had been hired with the house and were not part of the Ridolfi ménage. Our cavalcade consisted of Signor Ridolfi, Donna, Giulia, Giorgio Bruno, Father

Fernando, the Brockleys and myself plus four menservants who acted as grooms and also as an armed escort, since they all carried swords. Brockley kept an eye on Bruno and took every chance he could of riding beside him and talking to him.

'He talks much more than a confidential secretary should,' Brockley told me. 'But so far he hasn't said anything useful. Norfolk's name hasn't been mentioned. Though I've been careful not to ask many questions. That might be unwise.'

I agreed. Asking questions, I thought, could be very dangerous. I was becoming more and more afraid, as we went further from home and closer to Elizabeth's enemies.

Our visit to Rome was brief and without excitement. I took the chance of seeing a few sights. It was interesting, if a little unnerving, to behold the ruinous walls of what had once been the Coliseum where so many of the early Christians had died by Nero's orders. I wondered what they would think of the divisions that now racked their faith – and the things that the two halves of Christianity were prepared to do to each other. The Inquisition was at least as bad as Nero and possibly outclassed him.

Ridolfi had an audience with the Pope and told us afterwards that the Pope had approved his plan to place Mary Stuart on the throne of England and thus return England to the true faith, but how Ridolfi went about it was clearly being left to Ridolfi. Money had not been

offered. We were now to start for Madrid and King Philip, taking ship from the port of Ostia.

The weather was good and the sea was calm, but I hated the voyage because, to my surprise, I was seasick all the way.

I didn't like Spain, or Madrid.

I don't mean that they weren't beautiful, for they were. We rode to Madrid through a country that was clearly arid by nature, but was being skilfully cared for and irrigated, with good use made of the warm valleys. There were flourishing orange and olive groves, almond orchards, well tended crops, cattle grazing in carefully nurtured pastures. Once in Madrid, we saw bustling markets, elegant churches and houses, and glancing between them, caught glimpses of a great palace and its surrounding parkland, full of greenery and vivid flowers. Everywhere, there was much to delight and intrigue.

I recalled as a girl, learning from my cousins' tutor, something about the history of Spain and I knew that Madrid had been won from the Moslems back in the eleventh century. Traces of its former occupants remained. I saw churches that still resembled mosques and secretive houses walled against the eyes of the outside world – except that once in while, through an open gate, I would glimpse an interior courtyard overlooked by many windows. In those houses, it seemed, life was turned inwards, not towards the street.

242

The climate was hot, naturally, but there was a light wind, which was pleasant. Ridolfi mentioned that he had heard that Madrid stood higher than almost any other city in Europe, and that snow fell there in winter.

But I was uneasy, troubled by that elusive thing called atmosphere, which doesn't make itself felt through any of the five senses, but can still be palpable. Mingled with all the beauty and stateliness was a sense of oppression. And then, just before we arrived at the hostelry that Ridolfi, who knew the city, had already chosen for us and arranged by sending two of his men ahead to see to it, there came a warning which did manifest itself physically, by way of one's nostrils.

It was a smell, a stench from which one recoiled by instinct. Some of our horses snorted in disapproval, tossing their heads and showing the whites of their eyes. Then Brockley, who had been riding beside Bruno, came up alongside me, caught my eye and pointed.

In the distance, rising above the buildings to our left, were columns of smoke and the wind was blowing from that direction. It was carrying the smell. 'Have you noticed, madam,' said Brockley softly, 'how few people are about?'

'I don't understand,' I said. My nostrils were wrinkling.

'I think I do,' said Brockley grimly. 'I've been talking to Bruno, and when we entered the city, he had a few words with the gate guards. Most of the population has gone to see the spectacle.'

243

'Spectacle?'

'King Philip wishes to purge Spain of heresy. According to Bruno, when heretics are to burn, it's done at a ceremony called an auto de fe, and people think it is wise to attend. Churchmen watch to see how many of their flock put in an appearance. Those who absent themselves too often, may be suspected of heresy themselves.'

'Roger, are you saying there's an auto de fe going on now?' said Dale, her voice high with fright.

'Luckily,' said Brockley, 'we're too far away to hear anything. The smell is bad enough.'

'Brockley! Don't!'

'I sometimes wonder,' said Brockley in a low voice, 'what Christ himself would have thought of it.'

I was trembling. 'Brockley, Dale, we must be very very careful. I don't think we should talk about such things, even among ourselves in private. We're in danger here.'

'I know,' Brockley said. 'I wish to God we were somewhere else.'

The reek had faded by the time we reached the hostelry that Signor Ridolfi had in mind. It was a big place, accustomed to large parties and designed for hot weather, with arches rather than doors between its public rooms and floors of smooth stone. 'They put rugs on the floor and curtains in the doorways in winter,' Ridolfi told us.

For the moment, the coolness was pleasant.

244

The menservants, except for Brockley, had their own accommodation but the rest of us shared a spacious first floor suite, with sufficient bed-chambers and a parlour with latticed windows that excluded the June sun. Its ceiling held a lurid painting of Judgement Day but after all, one need not look at ceilings very much.

We also had the use of an inner courtyard laid out as a small garden with a fountain, and there was a veranda looking towards the palace and its parkland, and canopied from the sun by a thick, tangled vine. We foregathered there when we had all washed and changed: the Ridolfis, Father Fernando, Giorgio Bruno, myself and the Brockleys, to drink the local wine and take our ease as evening drew on. It was there that John Ryder found me.

I could hardly believe my eyes at first. I had assumed that after leaving Brussels, Ryder had discharged whatever other errands he had, gone back to England and stayed there. But here he was, hat in hand, stepping out through the shadowy arch from our parlour: John Ryder, dressed in the soldierly buff clothing he preferred, looking just as I remembered him, though his stiff hair had grown still greyer than before and his fatherly face was more lined.

'Ryder!' I said in astonishment.

'Your servant, Mistress Blanchard, Signora Ridolfi, Signor Ridolfi, everyone. It is good to see you again, Brockley.' He bowed to us all, meeting everyone's eyes in turn, but his gaze returned to me. 'Mistress Blanchard, I have

245

letters from England for you. I wonder if we might have a brief private conversation.'

'Of course,' I said. 'But first, won't you sit down and have some wine?'

'I can have that while we talk. As soon as the landlord here assured me that I was in the right place, I arranged a private room. My Spanish is fairly adequate.'

'Excuse me,' I said to the rest of the company, giving them all a bright and apologetic smile but not inviting comments or questions. Without delay, I followed Ryder through the parlour, out of our suite and into a little chamber where there were chairs and a settle, and a small table on which glasses and a flagon of the local red wine had already been placed. The room had a door with an inside bolt, which Ryder promptly used.

'I hope your Florentine companions won't think all this secrecy is suspicious,' he said. 'But I need to talk to you and Ridolfi shouldn't overhear the conversation. The moment I got back to England, I was sent off again with more letters for you and I've had a hell of a task, catching you up! I went to Brussels, of course, and found that Ridolfi and all the rest of you had left for Madrid, via Rome, over ten days before! Ridolfi left word there, about the places he might stay in, in both cities, in case any messages had to be sent after him. I decided to come to Madrid direct rather than chase you round via Italy but what a journey! I only got here two days ago. I feel as if I've travelled across most of bloody Europe.'

I poured him a glass of wine. 'You've found me now, anyway. What are these letters?'

'Sybil Jester,' said Ryder, 'has – as I think you know – been in London, cultivating the Duke of Norfolk's housekeeper. She has also been in touch with my lord Burghley. She has written to you. I know what is in the letters. Here they are.'

He pulled a package out of his doublet and handed it to me. The Burghley seal, as ever, gave me a jab of disquiet. I broke the seal nervously.

But for once, I was not being sent into peril. This was merely a covering letter to tell me that I would probably find Sybil Jester's message of interest. It repeated Cecil's hopes that I would succeed in learning what kind of reception Signor Ridolfi got from the Pope and King Philip, and how serious was the danger that Spain would back an attack on England on Mary Stuart's behalf. But I must take no risks and return to England at the slightest sign of danger.

Take no risks. That made me smile grimly. I imagined that Robin Mayes and Timothy Kingham had had similar orders. But both were dead, and every time I looked at Signor Ridolfi's smooth olive complexion and pleasant smile, I thought of Timothy, walking into a dark alley, almost certainly in the company of someone he believed he could trust, and...

He had a strangely confused character, had

Ridolfi. He had been kind about arranging amblers for Dale. He seemed to be kind by nature, but he was hopelessly in thrall to his religion, unable to recognize its cruelty, unable to tell the difference between dream and reality. It remained to be seen whether King Philip could.

'I wish I could get myself and the Brockleys out of this place at once,' I said. 'When we arrived, there was an auto de fe in progress somewhere. We saw the smoke. We smelt it.'

'If I had had the power,' said Ryder, 'I would have kept you from being sent on this mission. My lord Burghley hesitated, you know but necessity – and Francis Walsingham – tipped the balance. Walsingham insisted that we *must* know what happened in Rome and here. In my opinion, you should leave at once and simply say that your mission was impossible. I have orders to stay with you and help to escort you home, once you do decide to leave. I think it should be now.'

'I am not in immediate danger,' I said, though I had felt as though I were, from almost the moment I set foot in Spain and it was hard to push the words out. 'I must wait,' I said, 'until Signor Ridolfi has seen King Philip. I must try to learn the result of that. That's what I'm here for.'

'I see. Very well.' Ryder spoke soberly. 'But if any threat does arise, then I insist that we all leave instantly. I know the shortest route through Spain to reach Portugal and the coast. I

248

have friends in Portugal. We can get away by ship from Oporto.'

'I'll be glad of your help, if it comes to it,' I said.

'I'll give you one piece of advice now,' said Ryder. 'Never stay in any house or inn without making sure that if there is a pounding on the front door in the small hours of the morning, there is a back way out. There are several back and side doors on these premises, I'm glad to say. I pretended to get lost while looking for the way out to the stable yard, saying that I wanted to make sure that my horse had been well-housed.'

'You sound just like Brockley,' I said, and we both laughed. I was glad of Ryder's presence. It was a relief to have another friend at hand, someone with whom I need not watch my words. 'Now,' I said, 'what about this letter from Mistress Jester?'

I opened it but here, as I have done before while enlivening my old age by writing an account of my adventurous life, I prefer to let others speak for themselves, about events that occurred to them and not to me. This time I will just tell it as a story, rather than in her own words, because Sybil Jester was never very good at putting flesh on the bare bones of a tale.

TWENTY

Conversation in a Courtyard

Her hopes of learning anything from the gossip of Howard House were fading, Sybil told herself as she made her way yet again from her lodgings to the London residence of the Duke of Norfolk. Resuming her mild former friendship with the housekeeper, Mistress Dalton, had seemed like a good idea but if Norfolk were involved in anything questionable, she had not discovered it, and was becoming hard put to it to pass the time between meetings with Mistress Dalton.

These had to be carefully spaced out, so as not to look, well, odd. Her enquiries had to be made with caution, too. Sybil had adopted an attitude of sycophantic interest in court affairs. Conversations with Norfolk's housekeeper were larded with naive enquiries.

His Grace the Duke of Norfolk often attends on the queen, I suppose. Do you hear the court gossip? How exciting!

Has it yet been announced where the queen is going for her Summer Progress? Will the Duke be accompanying the court on the Progress?

250

What a striking new gown, Mistress Dalton! Is that neckline the newest court fashion? I suppose the ladies of the court often have a chance to see fashions from abroad, when visitors come from France and other countries? I envy you. You must hear so much of events outside England, quite apart from changes in fashion! My life is dull by comparison.

So far, the most exhilarating piece of gossip that Mistress Dalton had vouchsafed, concerned a minor accident to an ambassador from Sweden, who had been finishing his journey to the English court by barge and had the misfortune to lose a roll of valuable tapestries in the Thames, after a collision with a ferry. The tapestries had been a gift for Elizabeth and the ambassador was now engaged in an acrimonious argument, likely to proceed to litigation, with the ferryman. 'He says the man should pay compensation,' explained Mistress Dalton, 'but the ferryman says that if his passengers weren't hurt, they were frightened, and it was all the fault of the barge captain.'

It was hardly the sort of information that Ursula Stannard needed. Trying to find out anything useful through Mistress Dalton was like fishing in a drainage ditch in the hope of catching a salmon. Thomas Howard, Duke of Norfolk, was in residence at Howard House, but if he was conspiring against the queen, he hadn't told his housekeeper.

In between visits, Sybil went to markets and warehouses, made purchases, took boat trips on

251

the Thames to admire the royal palaces from the river, and hoped her two companions weren't as bored as she was.

A lady would attract notice if she came to London and took lodgings on her own, so Sybil had come accompanied by Tessie, the youngest of the Hawkswood maids, and Joseph, the junior groom, who drove the cart in which they had all travelled, and looked after the horse, which was currently stabled at an inn not far from the very respectable house where Sybil and Tessie had taken rooms. Joseph was at the inn with the horse.

Tessie knew, of course, that there was more behind this excursion to the City than a desire on Sybil's part for a change of scene but fifteen-year-old Tessie had accompanied Sybil on a mysterious errand before and understood that she shouldn't ask awkward questions. She was too timid to ask them, in any case. Sybil had chosen Joseph as her groom because he really did need a change of scene. The previous year, a girl he had been in love with had died, and he still hadn't got over it. A visit to London would give him new things to think about.

One or both of them would attend her on her meanderings through London, and this time it was Tessie. She looked tired. It was still the month of May, but the south of England was having an early heatwave and London was sweltering. The drainage ditches were sluggish and in the streets, the debris underfoot was smelly. Old cabbage stalks and horse droppings were the least offensive items. The streets were a menace to the hem of Sybil's elegant gown but she always had to dress well for these visits as Mistress Dalton dressed like a duchess. But farthingales and kirtles and wide starched ruffs, even open ones, were a nuisance on hot days. Sybil's ruff was pricking her neck and the starch was surely wilting. Heat meant the risk of plague too.

They turned in at the gate of Howard House with relief, for once there, it was hard to believe that the place was actually in the City. A wide courtyard swallowed up the noise of traffic and at the back, the garden that swept down to the river was as quiet and secluded as though it were a hundred miles from a town. Mistress Dalton met them in the servants' entrance hall at the side of the building, and led them to the rooms that she occupied as befitted her house-keeper's status. They consisted of parlour, bed-chamber and office, all small, but providing their tenant with privacy.

'Dear Mistress Jester, how pleasant to see you again. And Tessie too – I do believe you've grown since I last saw you, my dear. It must be five days, surely – we went round some ware-houses to choose lengths of linen, did we not? How hot you both look! Sit down, do.' She had steered them into her parlour, and was gesturing for Sybil to join her on a comfortable settle. Tessie took a padded stool at a little distance.

Mistress Dalton picked up a small bell from the window sill and rang it. 'I have some cooled

253

small ale waiting for you. Ah, here it is. Yes, Kitty, put it down on the little table. We'll pour for ourselves.' The maidservant who had brought it, bobbed and withdrew. Mistress Dalton picked up the flagon and began to fill the glasses. 'So – tell me your news,' she said to Sybil.

'I have very little,' Sybil said. 'There is no word yet of Mistress Stannard's return.'

'No doubt she wishes to be sure that Margaret is well settled in her new home, before leaving her.'

Sybil had told Mistress Dalton that Ursula had escorted Margaret Emory to her wedding but nothing more. The Ridolfis had not been mentioned. 'And what has been going on here?' Sybil asked, letting herself, as usual, sound faintly roguish.

This time, there was a response of some interest. 'Oh, we have had quite a time of it! I even wondered if I should send to put you off, we have all been so busy. A high-up cleric came to dine today – I believe he is chaplain to the Bishop of Ross. Father Andrew, that's his name. The bishop has upset the queen somehow and is under – I think they call it house arrest – with the Bishop of Ely, but his chaplains seem able to come and go. My lord duke was as particular about the food provided today, as though the man were the bishop himself! I have spent two days giving orders in the kitchen about the specialities that had to be served. There is a shellfish sauce to which the chaplain is especi-

254

ally partial.'

'What a responsibility!' said Sybil.

'Indeed. Well, the dinner is now over and was a success, I think, but Father Andrew is still with the duke, no doubt discussing matters of state.' Mistress Dalton lowered her voice and mouthed the last three words as though they tasted of gold leaf. 'My lord and the bishop are old acquaintances, of course.'

'Of course,' said Sybil, nerve endings twitching. John Leslie, Bishop of Ross was indeed one of Thomas Howard's old acquaintances. He was also Mary Stuart's ambassador to Elizabeth's court.

Ross's servants were still free to come and go. Sybil considered this. Ursula had told her that Francis Walsingham had a reputation for cunning. Was he baiting a trap for the bishop? Or for Norfolk? Or both? Had she now discovered signs that the ducal and ecclesiastical mice were nibbling the cheese?

'I am not as young as I was,' Mistress Dalton was saying. 'I'm glad of the chance to sit down for a gossip this afternoon. I seem to have been on my feet for a century ... oh, *now* what is it?'

Someone had knocked on the door. A head came round it. 'Mrs Dalton!'

'Mr Barker? What brings you here? You have a message?'

William Barker, the younger of the duke's two secretaries. Sybil had immediately recognized the round dark head with its black velvet cap. She knew him well enough by sight, as she

255

also knew the senior secretary, Robert Higford. Two or three times, when visiting Mistress Dalton, she had encountered one or other of them and said good day. She would have liked to talk to them, to see if they would let anything slip about their lord's affairs, but my lord of Norfolk's grave-faced secretaries in their dark clerkly gowns, simply did not hobnob with his housekeeper or her women friends, and by the secret rules of society, such women would not try to strike up an acquaintance with them. Barker now acknowledged Sybil with a polite bob of his head but nothing more.

'I'm on my way to my lord's study to take down some letters,' he said to Mistress Dalton. 'He and Father Andrew are having a business session. The page who summoned me, said that they wanted some wine and gingerbread and comfits. I've informed the kitchen. The page should have done so but he is young and new and was flustered because of having two errands at once. I said I would take his message. I thought I'd better mention it to you.'

'After the dinner they've had, I wonder they can bear the thought of sugared nuts and gingerbread,' said Mistress Dalton with asperity. 'You did quite right, of course, but the page should have completed his task properly. Who was it? Harry Grey? He's the youngest.'

'Yes, ma'am. It was Harry.'

'I shall speak to him. However, there's no harm done. As long as I know what's going on. Away with you. We're having a ladies' afternoon, discussing the new fashions.'

'I shall have a busy afternoon, I think,' said Barker. 'It's Higford's day off. Good day, ladies.'

He favoured them with the slightly patronizing smile of the hard-working professional man confronted by a pair of women who had nothing better to do than talk about fashion or problems with servants (such as Harry Grey), and disappeared.

'Always something,' said Mistress Dalton. 'Even an hour or two of peaceful chit-chat never goes undisturbed. I shall have to wag a finger at Harry Grey. He really mustn't go asking my lord's secretaries to take messages to the kitchen! But that can come later. Now, I know how interested you always are in fashions. I believe that there is a new style of hat that is becoming popular at court. I understand...'

The rest of the visit passed in a detailed and serious discussion of sartorial trivialities.

At the end of the afternoon, the visit was over. As usual, Mistress Dalton came with Sybil and Tessie to see them out of the gate. They found themselves crossing the outer courtyard in the wake of a group of gentlemen. My lord of Norfolk and his secretary were seeing Father Andrew to his coach, which could be seen waiting in the street beyond the arched gateway. Father Andrew had not, of course, come unattended but had a junior chaplain and a clerk with him. They were going slowly, all deep in conversation. Mistress Dalton slowed down in turn, so as not to tread on their heels. Tessie began to say something but Sybil nipped her elbow in warning, taking care that Mistress Dalton didn't see. The bishop's chaplain and his clerk were talking to each other and a few words had reached her. Had she or had she not heard the name Baillie?

She let herself go on ahead of her companions, only by a few unobtrusive steps, but it gave her a chance of hearing more.

'...I am sorry for the man. I hoped that because of the help his grace of Ross gave him, he would not be put in the Tower. The Tower is a name to make one shudder,' the junior chaplain was saying. The clerk nodded agreement and said something in reply, which was lost because just then, Norfolk made a quip that made his secretaries laugh. But as the laughter died, Sybil heard the junior chaplain observe, '...I'm thankful I managed to meet Baillie in time. It was by a very narrow margin but still, I did it. Things might have been even worse for him if I hadn't!'

The bishop's party were quickening pace as they neared the gate. Sybil dropped back, not daring to look as though she wanted to overhear their conversation.

At the gate, while Father Andrew and his attendants were being ushered into their coach, she and Tessie bade farewell to Mistress Dalton, and set off the way they had come. Sybil said: 'Until that coach is out of sight, we go on walking as though we were going to our lodgings.'

'Aren't we, madam?' Tessie asked, puzzled.

'No. When it's safe, we shall change direction. We are going to see Lord Burghley, or at least send him a message. I am known there. If he's busy, they will let me write him a note. As we were following those men across the courtyard, I heard something interesting. Lord Burghley ought to know.'

It wasn't much. It hadn't even been said by or to the Duke of Norfolk. The junior chaplain and the clerk could have been talking of a matter that referred only to the bishop's business. But they had spoken of Baillie and on Norfolk's premises, and Norfolk had just had Father Andrew to dine. No, it wasn't much. But it was something.

TWENTY-ONE

Keeping Out of Sight

'What Sybil overheard in that courtyard,' I said, 'is a pointer. But no more than that.'

It was an hour later. The Brockleys, Ryder and I were sitting out on our vine-roofed veranda and now we had all read the letters. 'Yes, it's slender,' Ryder agreed. 'It doesn't prove anything. Mistress Jester clearly did her best, but nothing definite has come of it. A pity.'

'We've learned one thing,' Brockley said thoughtfully. 'We already knew that the Bishop of Ross has been in contact with Ridolfi but now we understand that he sent someone to meet Baillie – when and where?'

I hoped that because of the help his grace of Ross gave him, he would not be put in the Tower... I'm thankful I managed to meet Baillie in time. It was by a very narrow margin but still, I did it. Things might have been even worse for him if I hadn't!

I quoted the words from memory. 'My guess,' I said, 'is that when Baillie landed at Dover, the time he was arrested, an emissary from Ross got to him before he was seized, and if he was carrying any questionable letters, exchanged them for innocent ones. Cecil thought as much. Somehow, Ross must have learned that the arrest was planned. That's possible. He was free to attend court at the time.'

Ryder said: 'I doubt if we shall find out much more about Norfolk while we're here. Your principal business here is to find out what King Philip says to Signor Ridolfi. After that – if you succeed in it! – I insist that we leave and I suggest, Mistress Blanchard, that you start to plan that now. Think of some pretext.'

'I've already thought of that,' I said. 'My daughter is expecting her first child. I shall say that she sent word to me through you. She wants to see me. But how I'm to become privy to whatever is said between Ridolfi and King Philip, I just can't think.'

'I can,' said Brockley. 'I have been working on Giorgio Bruno. If Ridolfi succeeds in getting an audience at the palace, whether or not Bruno attends him, he will probably confide in him. Apparently, he often does. And Bruno,' said Brockley, 'is talkative by nature and a terror when he has a little good red wine inside him. I'm sure his master doesn't realize! If Bruno is ever arrested for anything, no one will need to put him on a rack to make him talk. All they'll have to do is to empty a wine bottle down his thirsty throat. He'll babble like a mountain brook, believe me.'

In the event, finding out how King Philip responded to Signor Ridolfi's appeal for support, was the easiest task I ever undertook for Cecil and the queen. There was no need for Brockley to get Giorgio Bruno drunk and I had no need to pick locks, wrestle with ciphers, hide behind tapestries or listen at doors. I had only to sit beside Donna while the two of us, embroidery frames in our hands but needles stilled, listened as Ridolfi stamped back and forth across the parlour and told the ceiling beams, the latticed windows, the massive settles and anyone who chanced to be within earshot, just what kind of reception the king of Spain had given him. Since he clearly wanted everyone who heard him to understand him, he talked in French. I followed him easily.

He had had no difficulty in arranging an appointment at the palace, far from it. The very morning after our arrival, before he had finished writing his request for an audience, a summons arrived from King Philip, bidding him to a private meeting at two of the clock that afternoon.

The Signor was pleased. Of course, he had already written to King Philip, and no doubt his majesty had thought matters over and had an answer for him. Dressed for court, he set off, escorted by three men, one of whom was Bruno. He was gone for four hours. When he came back, he was furious.

'He isn't interested! I present him with a scheme for returning the realm of England – of which he was once king! – to the true faith, for saving a myriad English souls from hell and *he isn't interested.* Oh yes, he had my letter but he has no help to offer – unless someone else does most of the work first! If someone else will prime the pump with the English and Scottish Catholics; if someone else will dispose of Elizabeth, assemble a basic invasion force complete with ships, decide on dates for all stages ... *then* he might be prepared to send a backup invasion fleet and some money, though as to the money...!'

Here Signor Ridolfi stopped short in the middle of the room, raised his eyes to the painted Judgement Day on the ceiling, and then groaned and dropped his head into his hands for a moment before declaring dismally: 'He called me to the palace because *he* wants to arrange a loan from *me.* Or through me, anyway. I have wide contacts. Keeping hold of the Netherlands is costing him a fortune, he says. I told him, *I told him*, that the Pope is behind us, backing us with his prayers. He said he valued the prayers but wished the Vatican had opened its coffers as well!'

It sounded as though both the Pope and King Philip had recognized Signor Ridolfi as the impractical dreamer he was. I was not surprised. I had heard many things about them but never that either was a fool.

Ridolfi grew calmer after a while and stamped off to his bedchamber, announcing that he meant to take some rest after such a trying afternoon. Later on, Brockley, to whom I had

263

described Ridolfi's diatribe, came to me to say that although we now knew all we needed to know, he and Ryder had an arrangement to go to a tavern with Bruno that evening and would keep the appointment.

They weren't likely to learn anything new, but it would be best, he said, not to make Bruno suspect that he was being used as a source of information. 'A sudden change of plan, just after such an interesting outburst as the one today, could look – pointed.'

I agreed. Bruno's chattiness was a two-edged sword. 'If he talks to you,' I said, 'he probably talks to his master just as much. And we certainly don't want Ridolfi getting suspicious.'

Once again, I thought of Robin Mayes and Timothy Kingham, and wondered what really went on behind Ridolfi's smiling face; and what really lived in his heart, beneath the surface of his generosity, his kindnesses.

Brockley and Ryder duly left in the early evening. My room had a window overlooking the street and I watched them stroll off with Bruno. The streets of Madrid, which tended to become quiet during the afternoons, which could be very sultry if there was no breeze, were filling up once more. Donna was closeted with her husband and Father Fernando, and Giulia was sewing in the parlour. Dale and I were by ourselves in my room, sitting by the window, which I had pushed open to let in some air. I intended to tell her that we would soon start for England but it was Dale who spoke

264

first.

'Ma'am, oh ma'am, are we going home soon? We've heard everything we needed to hear, haven't we? We might as well have been in the same room as the Signor and the king! And no one's ever mentioned the Duke of Norfolk that my lord Burghley is so worried about. Master Ryder is right. We're not likely to find out much about him now.'

'No,' I agreed. 'Sybil is better placed than I am for that. I am giving up on him.'

'So we really will go home soon?' Dale's eyes were big and anxious. 'I hate it here. There's something wrong.'

I was surprised. 'Something wrong? Well, what the Signor is up to is certainly wrong. But you mean something else, don't you? What is it?'

'It's this place, ma'am. This city. Something's not right with it.'

'I don't understand.'

Dale looked out of the window, and then turned to me, fumbled briefly for words and finally blurted out: 'I don't know how to explain ... it's ... this city ought to be a happy place and it isn't.'

'Go on.'

'It ought to be pleasant here. Beautiful buildings – lots of them. The park with its flowers and greenery, that we can see from the veranda. The grapevine over the veranda. Fountains. Sunshine. Happy things. But the people aren't happy.'

'How do you mean?'

'You can *see*!' Dale jerked her head towards the window. 'Look out there, ma'am! It isn't people just going about, visiting or marketing or making for the tavern or out walking. They're not meeting people they know and stopping for a gossip or a laugh. It's not like that at all. *Look* at them!'

Bewildered, I stared down at the street. At first I couldn't make head or tail of what Dale was trying to tell me. Groups of people, family parties with children were walking about, as far as I could tell, just as they usually did. Except...

Except that although I was too high up to see faces clearly, I should have been able to glimpse a smile here or there and I couldn't. Also, there seemed to be an unusual number of people gathered in small knots, talking quietly and earnestly.

'Everyone seems very solemn.' I drew back. 'Some seem to be having serious conversations. But what about?'

'I don't know, ma'am,' said Dale unhappily. 'I don't understand it either. But I started noticing it this morning and I don't like it. It's not natural. It's as if there's ... something hanging over the city. It's a brooding feel, as though a thunderstorm were going to break. I don't *like* it. We ought to get away from here as quick as we can, ma'am. That's what I think.'

Enlightenment came when Brockley and Ryder returned, which they did earlier than we

266

expected, in fact before supper. They had, after all, learned something from Bruno.

'The sooner we get away from Madrid, madam, the better,' Brockley said bluntly, echoing Dale. 'You know what was happening the day we arrived. You remember?'

I recalled that evil stench, the smoke in the distance, and nodded.

'It's going to happen again,' Ryder said. 'Bruno told us. He got it from Father Fernando. This is no safe place for any of us.'

'You mean another auto de fe?' I asked sharply.

'Yes,' said Ryder. 'Tomorrow, Bruno says. We'd better not leave then – we won't want to get entangled with any crowds or processions. We'll do better to stay inside. But after tomorrow, how soon can we reasonably set off?'

'Very soon,' I said with decision. 'After supper today, I shall tell Donna that my daughter wants me home.'

Someone tapped on the door and Donna's voice called my name. 'Madame Blanchard! Are you there?'

I nodded to Dale to let her in. She all but tumbled through the door, pale and distracted as I had never seen her before. I came hastily to my feet. 'Donna! Whatever is the matter?'

'Oh, *Ursula*!' Poor Donna was nearly in tears. 'Roberto has just told me – and Father Fernando says we must – that natural pity for human bodies mustn't overcome our care for human souls...'

'What are you talking about, my dear? Here – sit down.' I steadied Donna to a seat.

'There's to be a big auto de fe tomorrow. It's part of a purge that's going on, a purge of heresy. Roberto says we all have to attend. At least, I must, and Giulia and all our household. He can't command you but he advises it; people who don't attend may be looked at askance, especially if they're from heretic countries! Like England!' Donna hiccuped. 'I don't want to go! I know I'll be ill. I've seen one of these affairs before and I had such nightmares after-wards. But Roberto says I have to – and I thought I should forewarn you and...'

We did what we could to quieten her but when she finally left us, to get ready for supper, she was still white and frightened. We bolted the door after her and studied each other's faces.

'I'm not going,' I said flatly. Once more, sickeningly, I recalled the description of a burning that the uncle and aunt who brought me up had given me. 'I will *not* attend such a horror. I will *not*. I will hide in here. I'll pretend to be ill. I pity Donna with all my heart.'

'Where do the Inquisition find so many heretics?' Dale asked. 'When it's so dangerous to be one!'

'I fancy,' said Brockley heavily, 'that some of them are people of substance, and the Inquisition wants their property to swell the church coffers and maybe King Philip's as well. Bruno thinks so. I tell you, our Signor's butler and sec-retary is something of a cynic and freethinker

268

himself. He ought to be more careful what he says and who he says it to.'

'And I hope *you* are careful how you answer him,' I said. 'While you've been trying to get information out of him, I hope he hasn't been getting it out of you!'

Brockley looked injured. 'I said I was shocked to hear such a suggestion, madam. I shook my head at him most vehemently. But here in this room – I reckon he's right.'

'But does – can – King Philip really ... deliberately, gather wealth by ... by murdering his own subjects?' said Dale, horrified.

'It won't be as simple as that,' Ryder told her. 'I dare say he guesses, but he's never been officially told and when he's given reports on money seized from convicted heretics, and finds that a share is coming his way, on various pretexts, he just doesn't question any of it.'

'According to Bruno,' said Brockley in his most expressionless voice, 'he attends the religious services that begin these affairs, but doesn't stay to witness the executions. So he never actually sees – or hears – how that part of his income is earned. Or extracted might be a better way of putting it.'

'Ugh!' said Dale.

I shuddered, gripped not only by fear for us all, but also with loathing. Dale had been right. The beautiful city around us was tainted, by a miasma of evil that the mysterious sixth sense that most of us have, though we don't understand it, recoiled from by instinct.

'We'll leave as soon as we can,' I said. I added: 'I'll talk to Donna now – about my daughter! I shall say I'm tired and will take supper here in my room. The rest of you can please yourselves but I can't face Signor Ridolfi tonight.'

'I'll stay with you, ma'am,' Dale told me.

'We'll eat with the men in the kitchen,' Ryder said. 'We'll try to behave normally. I hope to heaven they don't talk about it too much down there.'

Afterwards, Brockley reported that the conversation in the kitchen had been muted, except for some traces of unhealthy excitement among a few of the younger servants. 'I think nearly everyone, secretly, is afraid,' he told me when he came to say goodnight. 'They never know where the Inquisition will strike next – or exactly what turns people into targets.'

Donna didn't protest when I told her about my imminent departure but I was sorry to see how miserable I had made her. In the morning, I would not have been surprised to wake up with a migraine. This didn't happen, but when I woke, at about five o'clock, I did feel nauseous. Dale went to the kitchen to make a soothing draught for me, and when she brought it Signor Ridolfi came with her.

'I hear you're sick, Madame? Do you have any fever?'

I said I thought not, but that I couldn't eat, and couldn't rise from my bed, either.

'A pity. It would have been best if we could

all attend today's big event – you know about it, of course. Donna said she had told you.'

'It's quite out of the question,' I said, wanly and truthfully, with one eye on the basin that Dale had placed within easy reach before withdrawing to the other side of the room. 'And,' I added, 'I wish Dale and my other companions to stay with me. If I need to call a physician, there will be someone to run with the message.'

'You'll find it hard to get hold of a physician today. Almost all of the city will be at the ceremony,' Ridolfi said. He looked worried. 'Mistress Blanchard, I am a man of note, known here as someone who has dealings with the king. People would notice if I did not attend. I only hope they won't notice if my guests don't! Everyone else connected with these lodgings will be present, but I will explain that you are ill, and order cold food to be left in the kitchen, for you and your servants. I hope you soon feel better.'

He seemed to be genuinely concerned, and as I had seen in a mirror that my complexion was tinged with green, this wasn't surprising. At least, I thought, he knew that my malady was real.

Donna looked in before they left. She was dreadfully pale. 'I wish we didn't have to go. I hate it so and it all goes on so long. It's going to be at the Plaza Mayor – that's a big square in that direction.' She pointed. 'The procession will come past here. You'll see it. We're going

271

straight to the Plaza. Yesterday I saw them getting it ready. There are platforms draped in black, with benches on top where the prisoners will sit so that all can see them, and another platform where there's an altar, and Mass will be said. And the pyres are ready, too...'

Her voice faded. Donna's soft brown eyes were distended, full of horror. 'I'm not surprised you want to go home to your daughter,' she said. I gave her a hug before she left. When she had gone, I was sick all over again.

I tried to go back to sleep after that. Dale sat beside my bed, while Brockley and Ryder sat talking quietly. We had an instinctive wish to keep together. I did doze, I think, for a little while but soon there were noises from outside which forced me awake. I sat up, relieved to find that I felt better. Dale said: 'They're coming.'

I didn't want to see the procession but at the same time, oddly, I couldn't refrain from looking. None of us could. Dale put a bed gown round me and inserted my feet into slippers and we joined the others. The window was closed but we could watch through the lattice.

It was a huge procession and spectacular, worth seeing, except for its ugly purpose. The street below was lined with people who had come to see it pass, 'Before following it to the Plaza,' Ryder whispered. To speak in a whisper seemed natural.

First came a priest bearing aloft a mighty cross, and followed by a number of men in

soldierly clothing, carrying swords. 'They're the Familiars,' Ryder said. 'You know about them?'

'Yes,' I said.

The servants of the Inquisition; its soldiers, hunters, jailers and worse. They were followed by another priest who walked under a red and gold canopy, held up by four more Familiars. As he went by, the crowd on either side of the street sank to its knees.

'Who's he?' Dale wanted to know.

'The one who will celebrate Mass,' Brockley said. 'Bruno told us a few things about this.'

There were more Familiars behind him. The Inquisition really did have a private army, I thought fearfully. Behind them marched a crowd of monks, all in black, hooded habits, with the hoods drawn over their heads. They made me shudder for every man of them looked like Death taking a walk. Then came the prisoners, shackled, some hobbling, some visibly scarred, some needing to be supported on either side, by each other, or by priests or Familiars, many weeping helplessly. The sound of frightened crying reached us even through the closed window. I saw two of them vomit as they stumbled along. Most, probably all, had been tortured. As they passed, a murmur began in the watching crowd, rising to shouts of abuse. Things were being thrown: stones, rotting fruit, eggs. There was a gap and then the next part of the parade began to come into view and Brockley suddenly pulled Dale back.

273

'Don't look! It's corpses, people who were declared guilty of heresy after they'd died. They've been dug up and tied to poles. The Inquisition hunts you down even after you're dead.'

'Corpses!' Dale uttered a sound of disgust, but resisted Brockley's attempt to keep her from looking. She jerked herself free to get to the window and bumped against it. Window and lattice were all one, with a single catch, which wasn't firmly shut and Dale knocked it half open. A fetid wave of corruption came up to us. I saw its source. Then I reeled away to grab my basin and throw up anew. Brockley and Ryder hauled Dale back and shut the window. Brockley was pale with anger.

'Fran! That was a stupid thing to do. I saw people looking up at us. Now some of them know there are folk in here who aren't attending the ceremony. Maybe they'll wonder why.'

'I don't suppose it matters,' I said wanly, looking up from the basin I was clutching. 'You're staying in to tend the sick. Me!'

'From all I've heard,' said Ryder, 'the Inquisition doesn't go in for listening to reasonable explanations. They'd be likely enough to ask why anyone should fall sick on a day when they ought to be rejoicing so much that illness goes into retreat.'

'We leave the day after tomorrow,' I said. 'I think I'll need a day to recover from this illness. It will look better, anyway. Less ... less panicky.'

'Less suspicious, I suppose you mean,' said Brockley. 'I wish to heaven we'd left yesterday!'

The day dragged. Ryder and Brockley fetched our cold food from the kitchen, and I managed to eat a little. Brockley, still angry with Dale, took her to their own room for a while and I don't know what passed between them. They came back with Dale subdued and red-cyed and both Ryder and I worked hard at conversation until the atmosphere returned to something like normal, and then we waited through the long, hot hours until, at the end of the afternoon, Dale took our used dishes down to the kitchen and came back with a wrinkled nose. 'It's that smell again. Smoke, and...'
'Don't!' I said.

We didn't see the Ridolfis again that day, but Donna came to find me in the morning. 'I haven't slept,' she said. 'It was so ... so horrible, and I had to pretend I didn't mind. Roberto said I must. I wish you weren't going away, Ursula. I feel better for having you here.'
'I'm glad of that,' I said. 'But, Donna...'
For the second time, I embarked on a description of Meg, unwell because of her first pregnancy, nervous, badly wanting her mother, appealing to me to come home. Donna's mouth drooped unhappily but once more, she didn't try to argue. I said I must explain to her husband as well. We found him on the veranda,

writing letters. I wondered who the recipients were likely to be and whether any of them were in England. I was relieved to find that Ridolfi seemed to understand my reason for leaving.

Donna, who had come with me, cried a little but Ridolfi told her, quite gently, that she must not be selfish. I took her to her room and handed her over to Giulia, saying I must help Dale pack our hampers. On returning to my room, I found Dale, very white in the face, tightening the straps on a bulging hamper while Brockley and Ryder stood watching by the window, their faces as grim as tombstones.

'What is it?' I said.

'I've been lending a hand in the stable yard, the way I often do,' Brockley said. 'There was a horse there that belongs to another hostelry, on the other side of the town. Some messenger or other left it here because it had gone lame. It had recovered, and I said I'd take it back to its rightful stable. So I did. There was a horse in need of exercise anyway. I could ride him and lead the other. I did that. I was just starting back when a party of horsemen arrived – at the other hostelry, you understand.'

'Yes. Yes, go on, Brockley.'

'A man with an escort came in. I got out of the way and I don't think he even saw me, let alone knew me. But I knew him. He was William Barker, madam. Secretary to the Duke of Norfolk.'

'William Barker? Here? In Madrid? But, Brockley...!'

276

'Quite. He would recognize us at once. He knows the part you played in damaging the plot in London two years back. If he's here in Madrid then it's probably to find Ridolfi. What else? Ridolfi and Norfolk were co-conspirators then and I reckon that here's the proof that they still are. We've been looking for that. Well, now we have it. But when he comes here...'

'We should leave,' said Ryder. *'Now.* Before Barker finds his way here and finds *us.* If we're gone when he comes – perhaps all he'll hear is that a Madame Blanchard was recently staying but has now left. He may not know that name. How are you feeling, Mistress Blanchard?'

'Well enough to travel if it saves my life!' I said.

The Ridolfis were surprised, and Donna very upset, to learn that I intended to leave so suddenly and that Brockley and Ryder had already arranged to hire horses for us. We would change mounts on the way and send these back. We would have to change mounts a number of times for we needed speed, to put Madrid behind us as quickly as possible.

To the Ridolfis I explained that I was so worried about Meg that it was gnawing at me; I knew I wouldn't sleep that night unless I was on my way to her; I was seriously concerned about her, I said, and that was why I had been ill yesterday...

At any rate, they could hardly prevent me from going, whatever they felt about it. I kissed

Donna, and then we were hurrying into the courtyard where the horses awaited us. In an undertone, Dale said: 'Ma'am, I'm thankful we're going and not just because I'm frightened. We ought to get on our way before riding's too dangerous for you. It's risky enough now!'

'What do you mean, Dale?' I asked, though I already knew the answer.

'You were seasick coming across from Italy, though the sea was flat as could be,' Dale said. 'And look at you yesterday. No migraine, but you were throwing up as if you wanted to empty yourself right out. And you might remember that I look after your linen. Who was it? Matthew de la Roche, I take it?'

'Yes,' I said. 'I hoped it wouldn't happen, but it has. He rescued me, Dale. I was so grateful. And in Catholic eyes, we are married.'

'As long as it was him and no one else,' said Dale.

I looked at her in alarm. 'Who else could it have been? *Dale!* What in the world have you been imagining?'

'Nothing, ma'am. I know it had to be de la Roche. You was always – bemused, like, by him. When will it be born?'

'Late January, if nothing goes amiss,' I said.

'Pray God it doesn't go amiss between here and Oporto!' said Dale.

TWENTY-TWO
The Shortest Route

Ryder had been to Spain twice before, as part of ambassadors' escorts, and had a fair idea of its geography. He told us about it as we rode. 'In a straight line, it's about a hundred and seventy five miles to the Portuguese border. We'd do best to avoid main routes but we can keep more or less to the shortest route out of Spain and find inns and hiring stables as we go. We'll still have to pass through a sizeable town called Plasencia. The Portuguese border is only six hours' ride beyond. Only...'

'Only?' I said.

'Plasencia is a big place and it's bound to have a branch of the Inquisition. A good many of the nobility have houses there and there are a couple of cathedrals. We should plan to reach it during the day and go through without stopping.'

'But will we really be pursued?' Dale asked in alarm. 'If this man Barker only hears that a Madame Blanchard was staying recently with the Ridolfis, why should that interest him?'

'Ridolfi only has to mention that he knew

Madame Blanchard in London two years ago, and then she was called Madame Stannard,' I said, 'and Barker's ears will prick up. If he asks who was with me, Ridolfi will mention the name Brockley. Barker will realize who we are at once.'

Brockley, with unusual ruthlessness as far as Dale was concerned, said: 'He'll then tell Ridolfi how madam worked against him, back then, in London, and Ridolfi will be outraged. He'll also see how unlikely it is that any of us have really converted to what they call the true faith. He'll almost certainly set the Inquisition on our tracks. The Inquisition has a particular dislike of lapsed or spurious converts. All Ridolfi and Barker will have to do, is tell them.'

'But...' Dale's eyes were huge with fear.

'Quite,' said Brockley. 'The faster we ride, and the less time we spend in big towns with cathedrals in them, the better.'

'We'd better not give our real names anywhere, either,' Ryder said. 'I suggest that Mistress Blanchard and I should become father and daughter – no, father and daughter-in-law; then we can have the same surname. It's simpler. We both speak French so we can pretend to be French. We'll call ourselves ... oh ... Pierre and ... and Eloise Devereux. You Brockleys will be our servants but as your French isn't good, you'd better be Netherlanders. You can be called van something – Van Hoorn will do. Johannes and Marie van Hoorn. Remember those names!'

Presently, Brockley rode up close beside me and said, very quietly: 'You have your knife?'

I pressed my hand to my side. 'It's here, quite safe. But if it comes to it, will Dale be able to use hers? Will she have the courage? She isn't very brave. Brockley, you frightened her just now.'

'I know. But she can be careless and I want her to understand she mustn't be,' Brockley said. He added: 'If necessary, I will look after her.'

Neither of us said anything more. Fear was heavy on me and no doubt on Brockley too. It was better not to speak of it.

We covered the best part of sixty miles that day, changing horses twice. Ryder's knowledge of Spanish was a blessing. We had water bottles with us, which we refilled at every stop, and it did help, during the hot noons, to be able to drink water at will. We were all very weary by nightfall. I gathered that Brockley and Ryder both knew of my condition. Dale had told Brockley the previous day, and he had told Ryder. They looked as though they were worried about me.

We found a reasonable inn and rose early next morning, to take a hurried breakfast and get into the saddles of fresh horses. We had been lucky and had got hold of a couple of amblers, complete with side saddles, which made things more comfortable for Dale and safer for me.

In fact, except for fatigue, I did not feel unwell. My nausea had vanished, as though the relief of being on my way home had cured me.

'Today and tomorrow will bring us to the border,' Ryder said encouragingly. 'Once we're into Portugal, we need not worry so much. Relations between Spain and Portugal aren't good just now. The king of Portugal is getting old and has no direct heir, and King Philip has been dropping hints that because of various marriages in the past – you know how all these royal houses intermarry – he ought to be the heir. The Portuguese don't agree. We'll be a lot safer in their country.'

Two days of hard riding, I thought. For a moment, I did quail, wondering if, after all, I could endure it. Then I straightened myself. I had only to hold together for two days. I would do it.

When and why did unease first begin to set in? I think it started shortly after noon on that second day, as we were passing through a hamlet that was mysteriously quiet.

In fact, it wasn't really mysterious. It was the time when, in summer, many people in Spain, having eaten their midday meal, take a siesta until the heat of the day grows less. Then they return to their fields and their crafts and work on, later than we would in England. Yet there was something eerie about that hushed village, with its closed doors and shuttered windows and complete absence of human life – visible human life, at any rate. The only living things we saw were a scrawny cat, asleep in a patch of shade, and a couple of goats grazing beside one of the unfriendly houses.

I didn't like it. We had passed through other villages on the way to Madrid but they had never been quite as lifeless as this even at noon, and Madrid, for all the horror of the ghastly procession we had witnessed, was in other respects a city like other cities. But this place made it clear to me, in a new way, that I was in a land not my own and not friendly to me, and that England was far distant, and I might never reach it.

We didn't achieve sixty miles that day. I began to flag that afternoon and at length, Brockley said: 'I think we'll have to stop, for madam's sake. I don't think it's safe for her to go on.'

'But you said we must ride fast,' Dale reminded him.

'We should, if we're being hunted,' I said. 'And we could be, by now. Dale's right. We should press on.'

'But if you fall ill, that will slow us down much more than a brief halt,' Brockley pointed out.

'There's an inn quite close; I remember it. I can see its chimneys from here,' Ryder put in, pointing to a clump of fir trees. A chimney, smoking thinly, could just be glimpsed beyond them.

I said: 'Perhaps we could just have a short rest there. It need not delay us too much, surely. I think...'

I stopped, because something seemed to have gone wrong with my eyes. Dark spots were dancing in the air in front of me, like a snowstorm, if snowflakes could ever be black. Then, without any sense of time having passed, I found myself lying on the ground, my shoulders held by Brockley's right arm, while Ryder was pressing the lip of a water bottle against my mouth. Dale, still mounted, was staring down at me. She looked, somehow, as though she were a long way off.

'It's all right,' Brockley said. 'You fainted but I caught you as you started to slip from your saddle. We got you safely down. You didn't bump yourself in any way. But you can travel no further today.'

'It's so hot this afternoon,' said Dale nervously. 'Perhaps we could go on when it's cooler.'

'Fran,' said Brockley, 'there are risks we daren't take. Don't keep arguing.'

'I'm sorry,' said Dale. She slipped from her saddle and came to loosen my clothing while Ryder coaxed me to drink from his water bottle. She was gentle and helpful. But her eyes were cold. I knew she was afraid and I could sympathize because I was frightened too. I hoped I was just fancying that she looked as though she hated me.

We spent the night at the inn. In the morning, Dale asked me anxiously how I felt. 'Do you have any pain, ma'am? Or ... or any bleeding?'

284

To her and my relief, I was able to say no, I had neither of these things. A good night's sleep had helped a great deal. I was ready to go on.

However, our original plan of arriving at Plasencia by day and going through it without stopping had been destroyed. Evening was near as we approached the place and we would have to spend the night there.

'There are no tavernas close outside the city,' Ryder said. 'I think the innkeepers of Plasencia don't want their custom stolen. All the same...'

We had turned aside from the road and pulled up in a fir wood, in order to talk. 'I've been thinking,' Ryder said. 'If Ridolfi did go to the Inquisition, it would take a day or two to set matters in hand – to get interviews with the right people, for instance. With luck, there's been enough delay to give us a head start. Only, something else has now occurred to me and I don't like it.'

'What?' asked Dale fearfully.

'Changing horses as we have, we've left a kind of trail. We've changed our names but our descriptions might be recognized. If the Familiars send horsemen after us, we won't be that hard to trace. And there's another possibility. They'd soon guess that we're likely to pass through Plasencia. There are ways round, but then it would take us longer to reach Portugal. They might send a hard-riding messenger, who could travel faster than we've been able to do, to Plasencia by one of the main roads. He could be there ahead of us, delivering a message to the authorities there. We could find our pursuers waiting for us, and innkeepers already informed of our description.'

'So what are we to do?' Brockley asked.

'I'd say that we should ride on, go straight through the city as we intended – buy some bread and fruit and fill our water bottles but quickly, without lingering – leave the city behind and then bivouac by the wayside. Sleep under the stars.'

'Under the stars?' said Brockley, and pointed, through a gap in the trees, towards the sky.

'Oh, dear God,' said Ryder. 'It's going to rain.'

Plasencia terrified both me and Dale. We had seen Madrid and been both impressed and oppressed by it, but this was worse. For one thing, it had obviously been built originally as a fortified town. It had walls, immense and strong, with mighty towers at intervals, and impressive gateways. It warned enemies off. It also warned them that if they once took the risk of entering, they might never leave again.

Dale looked at it in horror. 'Everything's so full of ... of *power*,' she whispered. 'Those walls! And those gates! Are they shut at night?'

'Not these days,' Ryder said. 'There is a garrison, but no one is threatening Plasencia now. Ever since the last century, Spanish grandees have been building houses here, both inside the city and outside, and they're a sociable set. There are comings and goings in and out of Plasencia half the night, as a rule. I've been here before and I was billeted quite near a gateway. I don't think the noise of horses and people laughing and talking ever let up all night. We won't look for lodgings near any gateway! But we'll have to lodge somewhere. Somewhere small, I think – with a landlord who puts business before piety.' He glanced up as he spoke, at a sky which was steadily growing darker and darker. 'And we'd better hurry.'

The town was busy. We found a market still in progress, drawing crowds. Brockley pointed out a possible hostelry and Ryder, telling him to hold the horses while the ladies looked at the market stalls – 'That will look natural enough; it won't attract attention' – went to inspect the inn.

He came back shaking his head. 'What's wrong with it?' Brockley asked.

'You see that archway at the side?' Ryder said. 'It leads into the stable yard. It's the only way out apart from the main front door. There's no back exit, not for horses and not for people, either. Won't do. We need a place with a back door for emergencies.'

Dale looked more terrified than ever and I saw her trembling. I was trembling, too.

Ryder found a more suitable hostelry only a few minutes later. 'Not that small, but it's like a rabbit warren inside,' he told us. 'Side doors, back doors ... just what we want.' We then presented ourselves: Pierre and Eloise Devereux, father and daughter-in-law, accompanied by

287

their Netherlander servants Johannes and Marie van Hoorn. We arranged for fresh horses in the morning, ordered a meal that we all took together in a private room, and retired. Ryder and I had adjoining rooms and, claiming that we liked our servants to be at hand, Ryder arranged a room for the Brockleys next to his.

As we said goodnight to the Brockleys, he said: 'Best not undress. Sleep in your clothes. Just in case we have to leave in a hurry.'

I slept badly. For one thing, sleeping in one's clothes isn't comfortable, and for another, just after we went to bed, the gathering clouds broke in a thunderstorm. The rumbles and flashes went on for hours, accompanied by the swish of heavy rain. Also, I could not forget those frowning city ramparts. I could feel them all around, like dungeon walls, hemming us in. Even though the gates might be open, and even though there were numerous ways out of this rambling building, I felt imprisoned, vulnerable and afraid.

Yet nothing happened. I slept eventually, when the storm had passed and woke to a clear, warm morning. We broke our fast, paid our bill, collected our new horses and once more set off.

'It's unreasonable, I know,' I said as we left the city and took the westward road, 'but I feel I can breathe better out here.'

'You probably can,' Ryder told me prosaically. 'I think there was a midden near our rooms. Now, today we hope to reach the Portuguese border. We should do it in six hours, as I told you. I suggest a brisk, steady pace and a rest halfway. Then we need not change horses.'

'But if the Inquisition do come after us,' Brockley said, 'would the border really stop them? They represent the church – not Spain.'

'Once we're in Portugal,' said Ryder, 'there are places of safety. Cecil and Walsingham between them are well aware that any English travellers who go to Spain, may run into danger. Arranging refuges in Spain itself wasn't easy, but they've set up some in Portugal. A mile and a half the other side of that border, there's a farm owned by a man with English relatives and no love for Spain. He has a vineyard and a fine set of cellars to mature his wine in, some with doors that you can't see unless you know they're there. He'll shelter us. Then we can go on to the next refuge – to the north west. There's a chain of them all the way to Oporto. Now, let's shake these horses up and see what good time we can make.'

My troubled night began to catch up with me as we rode. Before we reached our midway halt, I was feeling queasy again. The halt, though it was only for half an hour, did help, but the queasiness reappeared soon after we started out again. I wished I had once more had an ambler, but no amblers had been available and my mount was both straight-shouldered and bumpy.

Our horses this time were a motley collection altogether. Dale's was a skinny dapple grey, barely fifteen hands and none too long in the leg, while I was on a broad-backed, hard-mouthed skewbald, striking in appearance but not in performance. Brockley had a brown cob which was an obvious slug, who intended to do as little work as possible while Ryder's bay gelding was too long in the back. Once when we broke into a canter, Ryder found that though the front legs of his horse were cantering, the hind ones were merely doing a fast trot, which was absurd.

The day had turned hot, too, as sultry as though there had been no storm the night before. There had been traffic on the road at first, well-to-do people on horseback and in coaches, farmers and their wives, riding double on mules, or driving carts of produce to various markets. But the further we went from Plasencia, the fewer travellers we met.

After our halt, the heat became hard to bear. We rode through another silent village where not a soul was to be seen. A small church and what was presumably the priest's house were the last buildings we passed. The church door was uncompromisingly closed and the windows of the house were all shuttered. The only evidence that someone did actually live there, was the neatly kept garden, and hoof marks on the path that led past the side of the house to the quite extensive stabling we could glimpse at the back.

I had felt worse with every mile and at last was forced to call out that we must stop for a moment. 'Sorry,' I said, and then leant forward and was horribly sick down my horse's left shoulder.

Once more, it was Brockley who steadied me down from the saddle and sat me at the roadside. 'We'll never get to the border today. The mistress needs rest and coolness. You've used this road before. Ryder, do you know where the nearest inn is?'

'Half a mile behind us,' said Ryder. 'In that little village we passed through. There isn't another inn between here and the border.'

TWENTY-THREE

Thunder in the Night

'Oh, no!' Dale whimpered. 'You mean we've got to go back – to that *dead* place?'

'I'm afraid so,' Ryder told her. 'Mistress Blanchard, can you ride that short distance?'

I said I could. We took it slowly and reached the silent village without further mishap. We passed the church, where the door was still closed and the priest's house, which was still shuttered, passed the entrance to a narrow lane, followed the road round a bend and there was the inn. I hadn't noticed it when we rode by earlier but this was hardly a surprise, for it was a ramshackle place unlikely to attract a second glance.

The main door opened into a public room with bare wooden tables and benches, a spiral staircase in one corner, and a door leading through into a kitchen. Not a clean one, according to Dale, who peered in. The landlord, a dismal-looking individual with dark, drooping moustaches and badly shaven, drooping jowls, greeted us without much enthusiasm and then handed us over to his wife, who was tall and dressed in black and had a face as stern and immobile as if it were chiselled out of teak. She showed us the sleeping accommodation. There was an upper storey with two communal bedrooms, for men and women respectively, bedded down on straw. But there were also some private bedchambers, with actual beds, in a single storey wing that looked as though it had been built as an afterthought.

A door from the public room led into what at first looked like a lobby with a big latticed window. However, the stern landlady, leading the way while we followed with our saddlebags, turned to the right as she entered the lobby and led us into a narrow passageway with a couple of doors on either side. She showed us two small rooms overlooking the stable yard. The acrid smell of horses penetrated strongly. We were quoted an exorbitant price but Brockley muttered: 'Ground floor, good. We could get out of that window if necessary, and get straight to our horses,' and Ryder said we would take both rooms.

There didn't seem to be anyone else in that wing. Brockley and Ryder, when they went to stable the horses, said that ours were the only ones there and the only grooms were a couple of hard-faced fellows who made it clear that they'd clean the stalls, but travellers would have to groom and saddle their own mounts.

'Though we would anyway. I wouldn't trust either of those fellows an inch, either for good work or honesty,' Ryder said grimly.

Our rooms at least were clean and fairly cool. Just as I was, except for taking off my riding boots, I lay down on a bed that was reasonably comfortable, thankful to be out of the sun, and fell asleep. When I woke, a murmur of voices from somewhere nearby suggested that the inn now had more customers. Dale was sitting by my bed, and the men were in the room as well, by the window, which they had opened to let in some fresh air. 'What time is it?' I asked.

'Well on in the evening. Do you think you could eat something?' Dale asked anxiously.

I said yes, and Ryder, as the only one who could make himself properly understood in Spanish, fetched some food. I couldn't stomach the meat, which was drowned in a heavy, aromatic sauce, but I made do with bread and fruit, some milk, and half a glass of a light white wine, a little too sweet for my taste but at least it warmed and stimulated me. All the time, either Brockley or Ryder stayed at the window.

'No one was waiting for us in Plasencia,' Ryder said, 'and maybe we're not being hunted after all. But I think we should stay vigilant. If we keep a good watch, we'll see anyone who arrives on horseback.'

I felt safer for their precautions. It would be unbearable, I thought, if we were caught when we were so near to safety – well, to Portugal, anyway, where we would be safer than we were in Spain.

While tending the horses, Ryder and Brockley had done some reconnoitring. 'There's a gate out from the stable yard, to the left,' Ryder said. 'Goes into that lane we saw, that comes out by the priest's house and rejoins the main track just past that bend. Could be useful to know.'

I hoped we wouldn't need to know. Dale must have been thinking along the same lines for she looked dreadfully unhappy and I was unpleasantly aware that but for me, we would have been across the border by now. I wanted to apologize but what was the good of that when we all knew it could happen again? I fretted in silence.

Ryder took the dishes back to the kitchen. He was gone some time and when he came back, he looked concerned.

'There are a couple of men sipping wine down there that I don't like the look of,' he said. 'They're ... types. I noticed them at once. Soldierly. Plain, dark clothes; not any nobleman's livery. Tough. Cold eyes. I hope they didn't notice me, stepping in with the tray and then slipping out again, but I suggest we all now keep out of sight. When I went in, the landlord was asking them if they had horses, and they said they'd left them in the priest's stables because they're staying there. I had the feeling that he was nervous of them. Sounds as if they're in good standing with the church but they're not chaplains, not those two. As the landlord turned away from them, they spoke to each other and I did just pause a moment – as if to steady the things on my tray – and I tried to hear. I *thought* I heard one of them say something like *they mustn't reach the border* but I can't be sure. But if I'm right, well, I didn't like the sound of it.'

'You think they're Familiars?' Dale asked tremulously.

'Can't tell. But if we try to leave now we could attract more attention than if we stay quietly here,' Ryder told her. 'And besides ... Mistress Blanchard, how are you?'

I looked at him miserably. I wanted to go to sleep again. Silently, I cursed my weakness. I cursed Matthew, too, who had got me into this situation. 'I still need to rest, at least for a while. If it's safe,' I said wanly. 'But if it isn't, I'll have to manage somehow.'

I tried to sound brave, but the thought of attempting to get up, perhaps to climb out of the window, and then trying to ride, was appalling. I feared that if I tried to stand, I would collapse then and there. Brockley looked at me, and I saw that he understood.

'I don't think madam should try to move yet,' he said concernedly.

Ryder nodded. 'Very well. The landlord thinks we are Monsieur and Madame Devereux, with their servants the van Hoorns. We will leave things at that. But we must be careful. Familiars like to make their pounce at night, when people are at their lowest, most easily frightened or flung into despair. *If* they're Familiars and after us, and they've realized we're here, they'll probably go back to the priest's house for a while and come out again during the night. You women can rest but don't take off any clothes. We'll stand guard.'

'The window in that lobby place at the front gives a view across the bend, into the priest's garden.' Brockley said. 'We can take turns there and see if anyone at that house is active after dark.'

'Wake me at need,' I said.

I turned on my side and began to drift. The queasiness had mercifully gone. I slid into oblivion. I was far down in slumber's deepest ocean when a hand on my shoulder woke me and I opened my eyes to find that it was night. But there was moonlight and by it, I saw Dale standing by my bed and looking down at me with big, frightened eyes.

'Ma'am – wake up. Roger says, wake up.'

'We must leave. At once. However you feel!' That was Brockley, who was by the window. 'Ryder's been on guard in that lobby place. He thinks they're coming. There are lantern lights in the priest's stable yard and the moon's bright – he's glimpsed horses being led out. At midnight! They're hardly starting on a plain straightforward journey! We can't risk waiting. Madam, you must get up!'

I sat up, pushing back the sheet that was my only bed covering and swinging my legs off the bed. To my relief, I felt better; not vigorous but no longer ill. Dale crouched to thrust my feet into my boots.

Ryder came softly into the room. 'Hurry. There's more than two of them – I've seen

297

several horses. I'm leaving money here for our rooms and food. Bring the saddlebags. We'll have to get out of the window.'

Dale flung my cloak round me. Brockley got the window open. Ryder went through it first and sprinted across the stable yard to the tack room, to start the saddling. Brockley gave me a heave on to the sill. I slithered feet first to the ground, turned and received my saddlebags. Then came Dale, all in a scramble, dragging her bags with her. Brockley threw his own and Ryder's out of the window and followed. We were out in the warm, moonlit night. Pale moths fluttered here and there. Across the yard, we saw Ryder run from the tack room with two saddles over one arm and all four bridles over the other. He wrenched the stable door open.

One thing we could all, even Dale, do quickly and efficiently, was saddle up. Travelling with Ridolfi and fleeing across Spain, we had had plenty of practice. Brockley dashed for the other two saddles while the rest of us bridled the horses. Saddling and tightening girths took less than a minute.

'Lead them out quietly,' Ryder whispered. 'We don't want to wake the grooms. Lucky the yard is earth, not cobbles.'

I remembered another occasion when Brockley and I had fled from danger at dead of night on horseback. That had been winter in the north of England, with deep snow on the ground. This could hardly have been more different, but the fear was the same, the jolting

298

of one's breath, the hammering of one's heart, the desperate need for speed, speed.

But even as we led the horses into the open, the hush of the night was broken by a furious hammering at the inn's front door, and voices shouting.

'Open, in the name of King Philip and the Inquisition!'

Hubbub broke out inside the inn. Doors slammed. Windows flickered with light as candles were kindled. Voices were raised in alarm. 'Get mounted!' Ryder barked. 'We'll use the side gate and the lane. It brings us past the priest's house but the Familiars are *here,* not there, so it hardly matters. *Hurry!'*

He flung the side gate open and then sprang into his saddle. At that moment, out of a door beside the stable entrance, tumbling over themselves, came the two grooms, one brandishing a lantern, which made my skewbald snort and plunge. For a dreadful moment I thought I would fall. I clutched at the pommel and Dale, who had just scrambled on to her grey, lost her head and shrieked: 'Careful! Mistress Blanchard, don't fall! Hold on!'

At the inn, a back door was flung open and men ran out. Someone shouted: *'Blanchard! Yes,we have them!'* in English, and on a baying note of triumph, like a human mastiff. A woman's voice, probably that of the formidable landlady, shouted what sounded like encouragement. The groom with the lantern held it up and by its light I recognized Norfolk's secre-

299

tary, William Barker. An Englishman running with the hounds of the Inquisition. A man who knew me and the Brockleys by sight. With Barker there, there'd be no talking our way out of anything; no pretending that someone had misheard Dale when she cried out the name of Blanchard.

The groom who wasn't encumbered by the lantern, lunged towards my horse's head but I was in control again by then and kicked the skewbald hard. It leapt forward. I was through the gateway. Dale was through ahead of me. We were both galloping. I glanced back and saw that Brockley, who must have used his spurs on his slug of a cob, was hard behind me with Ryder on his heels. We tore along the lane, swerved left to pass the priest's house and reach the road and there, amazingly, Ryder pulled up with a yelp of excitement. 'Look!'

The moonlight was bright, except for the lack of colour. Plain to be seen, before us, was a line of horses tied by their reins to the fence of the priest's front garden. 'They're *their* horses!' Ryder drew his sword and leant out of his saddle to slash at the knotted reins. 'Got to be! Go on, go on! I'll catch you up! But *they* won't! *Go!*'

We had all slowed down when Ryder did and now I hesitated, instinctively reluctant to leave anyone behind but Brockley, shouting to Dale to ride on, *ride on*, grabbed my rein and hurled the three of us into a renewed gallop. I doubt if his cob had ever had such a demon on its back before. We didn't slow down for half a mile. Then we heard hoof beats coming after us but when we looked round, we recognized Ryder's broad-shouldered silhouette. He joined us, grinning. Ryder was one of those people who keep their teeth well into middle age, and they shone white in that moonlight.

'I've scared off those horses; set them galloping for dear life in the wrong direction. Those bastards won't chase us far tonight. Now we ride for the border and if you're sick again, Mistress Blanchard, you'll just have to be sick on the move. We're not stopping. Now, *ride*.'

And ride we did, hard and fast through that warm, moon-blanched world. We met no one, and no sound of pursuing hoof beats reached our ears. We had left the hunters behind. Where the road crossed into Portugal, there were guards, but they seemed only concerned to make sure we weren't Spanish. The fact that we all spoke English impressed them, and when I produced a letter, in English, signed William Cecil, Lord Burghley, it was enough. We were waved through.

The final mile and a half to what Ryder called our first refuge was accomplished at an easier pace. Of that part of the journey, I remember only a little: the silvered road stretching ahead; a ford where our horses' hooves sent up splashes like showers of diamonds; an owl flitting across our path with a doleful hoot. There was little conversation, certainly not between Dale and Brockley. Brockley was angry; I knew it by the set of his shoulders and his voice when he came alongside me to ask how I was faring. The anger was not for me, but the undertone of rage was there.

Then a long, low farmhouse was before us and Ryder was pulling at a bell. The door was being opened, by a shadowy figure holding up a candle. We could just make out that the figure was in a nightshirt. We were being ushered in. Ryder was talking, explaining who we were. He and Brockley brought the saddlebags in and went to tend the horses. Dale and I were being shown into a kitchen. A woman, plump, grey-haired, swathed in a wrapper, joined us, rubbing her eyes but saying words of welcome. She gave us something hot to drink, mulled spiced wine by the taste of it, and told me, in halting English, that there was ginger in it to settle my stomach.

'Tearing about on horseback in your state; small wonder you were sick. Yes, yes, they've told me. You're expecting. Now drink up and I'll show you your bed. Your woman is exhausted. I will look after you.'

The place was one-storey. There were no stairs. I was being led to a room at the back. The woman was carrying my saddlebags. I sat on a stool while my good-natured hostess delved into a chest, fetched out bedlinen, and made the tester bed ready for me. Then she was helping me to undress and get a nightgown out of my saddlebag, and she was putting me into the bed, drawing the sheet up, murmuring in her awkward English: 'Sleep easy. You are safe here.'

'The others,' I said drowsily. 'Where...'

'Your man Ryder will sleep in the stables with the horses. Your two servants are next door. Sleep now.'

She left me. The mattress beneath me was soft, feather-stuffed. I could hear Dale and Brockley moving about in the next room. My head sank into the pillow. The warm spiced wine, the sense, at last, of being safe, the relief of not having to sleep in my clothes, were pulling me down into darkness. And then, in the adjoining room, the storm broke.

I sat up, muzzily. I could not hear any words, but I could hear Brockley's voice, the anger in it, the outrage, and the sound of Dale crying. Brockley said something, fiercely, and the crying subsided. I thought he had told her not to make such a noise; she'd disturb the mistress.

I had no right to interfere, but I had never heard Brockley speak to Dale so harshly before. He loved her. He had broken his heart for her when she was in danger, years ago, in France. In the morning I would have to find a way to ask him ... or perhaps he would tell me, or Dale would ... but for the moment...

I was asleep.

Dale came to me in the morning, a pale and silent Dale whose tired, reddened eyes showed what kind of night she had had.

'Dale,' I said, as she finished my hair and put

a cap on my head, 'we're fairly safe now, so what's wrong? Please tell me.'

The result of this question, which I put to her in a gentle voice, was astounding. Dale gulped, gasped, sank to her knees beside my stool, buried her face in my lap and abandoned herself to a flood of grief.

'*Dale!*' I said, and pulled her up so that I could see her face. Swollen and tear-streaked, she was hardly recognizable. 'What is it? What *is* it?'

'Roger is so angry! He'll never forgive me! Last night, when we heard that banging on the inn door and your horse was frightened and you nearly fell, I called out your name, that the Signor knows you by! I shouted out *Mistress Blanchard, don't fall!* Then somebody rushed out of the back of the inn, shouting *Blanchard, we have them* ... and Roger says...'

I stood up and steered her to the bed, where I sat us both down and put the coverlet round her. 'Yes, Dale, Brockley says?'

'He says I as good as shouted to those Familiars who we were and where we were! I screamed out your name, ma'am, as if I wanted us all caught. I betrayed us all but you especially because it was you, two years ago, who got in Ridolfi's way and ... and...'

'It's all over, Dale. You just panicked. I was near enough to panicking myself, God knows. The Familiars had guessed we were there anyway and Barker would have identified us. Nothing you did made any difference. Please

304

don't...'

'That's not all, ma'am,' Dale whispered, head drooping. Her fingers plucked at the coverlet.

'Not *all*? What else can there be?'

'Roger doesn't know this and I can't tell him but I have to tell someone – even if you turn me off. I don't even know if Roger would come with me. He might stay with you. He mustn't know, ever, but...'

'But what, Dale? What *is* it?'

Dale, now set on a course of dreadful confession, shuddered but said what she had to say.

'It wasn't all just a mistake, ma'am. I ... Roger loves you, ma'am. Not the same way as he loves me, but he *does* love you. I see you sometimes, looking at each other. You make jokes I can't share; you talk about times when you were together and I wasn't there. You've gone off adventuring together, so often, without me. When you came back from Bruges, rescued from that Northumberland woman, Roger was that relieved to see you again; you can't imagine. And now...'

'What on earth are you saying, Dale?'

'You're with child by Matthew de la Roche, ma'am, and I believe it now because Roger made me believe it last night. He was so angry that I tried to defend myself by being angry too, and I told him what I'd been thinking, that I was half afraid it wasn't de la Roche but Roger instead. You could have found moments somehow; there's always moments.'

'Dale, since the death of my husband Hugh, I

305

don't think I've ever been alone with Brockley for more than a few minutes at a time!'

'Yes, he said that. He was so very angry; it was frightening. He said never, never, that of course it was de la Roche. We quarrelled about you, just after you got away from that Countess woman. We keep on quarrelling about you. It's as if you're in between us ... I know you don't mean to be ... I'm sorry...'

'I've heard you quarrelling more than once. But what has all this to do with last night?'

Dale's voice sank to a whisper. 'I half wanted you to be taken. Then I'd have Roger to myself. I got through that side gate into the lane ahead of you. I did it on purpose. I hoped he'd leave you behind and perhaps you'd be taken and us not. I wanted *us* to get away ... it all went through my brain like an arrow, in seconds. For those seconds, I was a madwoman, out of my mind. Now I can't believe I did it! But I know it's too late and I don't expect you to forgive me and I know Roger never would, if he ever found out ... I looked back, once. He'd let you go first, anyway. I'd put him in more danger than you!'

'Dale!'

'I've felt sometimes as if I were going crazed, wondering about you and him. I got angry too, when you were ill on the road and we were held up and it put us all in danger. If you hadn't been with child ... and I *couldn't* stop thinking, whose child? Oh, ma'am...'

'Dale! Oh, really! Listen, Dale. I have said this to you before. Now I say it again and I beg you to believe me. There is nothing in the friendship between me and Brockley that threatens what is between you and Brockley. The child I carry is that of Matthew de la Roche ... oh, Dale, don't cry so!'

It would have been natural to be angry but I wasn't. I could only put my arm round the shaking, sobbing woman beside me, Dale, who had served me so loyally for so many years and been repeatedly put into danger for my sake; Dale, to whom I was so accustomed that the idea of replacing her with anyone else was unthinkable.

I raised my voice, but not to shout at Dale. *'Brockley!'* I bellowed.

He came at once. I suspect he had had his ear to the wall between our rooms, if not against my door.

'Madam?'

'There's no point in wasting words, Brockley, or mincing them. We're on our way home with information that Lord Burghley needs. Our business is to get there safely, not quarrel amongst ourselves. Dale has told me how sorry she is for her mistake last night, and she has also told me how our friendship has worried her, worried her nearly out of her senses. I have reassured her and I have already forgotten what happened last night, when we were all too frightened to be quite in our right minds. Now, please fetch me some warm water. I want to wash. Then you two can go to your room and be alone together for a while.'

Dale crept out of the room. Brockley and I looked at each other.

'She meant harm, madam. Oh, some of it was carelessness, perhaps; she's been careless all along. But there was an intention of harm as well. I know Fran through and through.'

'Please don't let her realize that you've guessed. Please. It was only for a few seconds, in a moment of terror. Dale loves you. She needs you to comfort her. Let her know that what is between you really isn't in danger.' I looked gravely at Brockley. 'We didn't mean to,' I said, 'but we have hurt her. It mustn't happen again. This has festered in her for a long time.'

Brockley hesitated but then nodded. The relationship between us had shifted, the gap between us grown wider, as though we were on ships that had been sailing in company but were now diverging on to different headings. We would henceforth be lady and manservant and if there were memories we shared, we would not speak of them except in necessity. I carried within me a part of Matthew de la Roche; Brockley had a duty towards Dale, to rebuild what had been damaged. An episode in our long partnership was over.

TWENTY-FOUR

Harvest Home

Our host's name was Senhor Braganza, as we learned when we gathered for breakfast. He was half English and spoke the language well though with an accent, and after all our dangers and alarms, he was as reassuring as a rock in quicksand.

'There's much bad feeling in Portugal, as far as Spain's concerned,' he said. 'The border guards let regulars through – trade's got to go on, and there are Spanish people who have relatives in Portugal and visit them. They're known. But the guards won't let just anyone through and they don't care to help the Inquisition Familiars. The church in Portugal, just now, looks after its own affairs and doesn't want interference from Spain. It doesn't harry foreigners, either. That can cause diplomatic trouble and with our own king getting old and Philip already putting in a claim to succeed him, well, we might need friends!'

'Thank God for it,' said Ryder gratefully.

'Now, for your onward journey. I'll get your horses sent back to their Spanish stables but by

309

a roundabout route, just to be on the safe side, and I can provide you with transport. I gather, Mistress ... er...'

'Here, she can be known as Mistress Blanchard,' said Ryder.

'Thank you. My wife says that riding isn't good for you just now. I have a two-horse wagon and I'll drive you myself. I know the way to Oporto.'

He and Ryder began to discuss routes, speaking of places I had never heard of. I left them to it and thought about Dale and Brockley. They were picking at their food and not talking to each other and I was sorry. When we set out, I would make sure they were seated together and I could only hope that the ice between them would thaw soon.

In this, I was disappointed. They were as silent as ever with each other when we reached Oporto, which we did without incident, on the afternoon of the third day. Senhor Braganza installed us all in an inn and by evening, Ryder had arranged passages for us on a trading vessel leaving for England in the morning. Shortly after dawn, we said a grateful farewell to Braganza and soon after that, we were at sea.

It was another smooth voyage but I was seasick, of course. Dale tended me most lovingly. My sickness vanished the moment the white cliffs of Dover came in sight. I was so thankful to see them that I knelt down on the deck of the ship and whispered a prayer of thanks. I felt as though something inside me had taken wing at the first glimpse of those cliffs and flown to their protection like a homing dove. They were England. My own land. Safety.

We spent a night at a Dover inn, where Ryder and I put together a report for Cecil, describing King Philip's treatment of Ridolfi and the suspicious arrival of William Barker in Madrid.

'It's still a dangerous situation,' Ryder said. 'It's a thousand pities that Philip didn't reject Ridolfi outright. As it is, he seems willing to provide backing if Ridolfi does the fund-raising and assembles an army, and who's to say that Ridolfi won't manage it? There's a lot of Catholic Europe.'

I said: 'We must put in the reason why you are travelling ahead of me. Cecil had better know of my condition and how it happened. Then perhaps he won't ever inveigle me to the Netherlands again!'

In the morning, Ryder hired a horse and left for London ahead of the rest of us. 'The sooner we get this report to Lord Burghley, the better.' I had decided to go on travelling gently, by hiring a coach or at least another wagon. Ryder left some extra money with me. 'My lord sent me off well supplied,' he said.

Brockley had no difficulty in arranging a two-horse wagon and a driver for us. Travellers come and go all the time in Dover and plenty of enterprising people make a living from hiring horses and vehicles to arrivals from abroad. That afternoon, we set out.

'Do you really want to go to London, madam?' Brockley asked me. 'Ryder has taken the report to Lord Burghley. Wouldn't you rather go straight to Hawkswood?'

I shook my head. 'No, I want to see Cecil. I may be able to fill in some details for him and besides, Sybil may still be in London. If so, I must see her.'

'I hope we don't have to chase Cecil up and down the Thames or worse,' Brockley said glumly. 'He goes where the court goes and the queen's always on the move. She could be in any of the Thames-side palaces from Green- wich to Richmond, or away on Progress. We'll be lucky if we find Lord Burghley at his house in the Strand!'

We were lucky. We took only two days over the journey and reached London before the queen set off on her Summer Progress. She was for the moment based at Whitehall, near enough to Cecil's London house to let him live at home and still attend court. It was only the sixth of July.

I was glad to get there, as the wagon bounced and shook every time it encountered ruts in the road. The Portuguese wagon had been much the same and I had become privately convinced that a side-saddle on an ambler would be a smoother way to travel.

I was happy to see, as we rumbled through the open gateway of Cecil House, that the court- yard was encouragingly busy with people. Servants hurried to and fro, a hangdog individual in a workman's sleeveless leather jacket was being berated by a dignified steward over something done or not done, a couple of dark-clad clerks were walking side by side, heads bent over a sheaf of papers, two grooms were checking the legs of a restive bay horse. All the indications were that the master of the house was in residence.

'Though he may be attending the queen and won't be back until late,' I said to Dale. 'But Lady Mildred will look after us till then.'

But again we were in luck. Cecil was at home. Lady Mildred welcomed us, said we were expected, and immediately had us shown to her husband's study. He was seated at his desk and rose to his feet as we entered. He looked older than when I had seen him last, and his hair had receded. *He's going bald,* I thought, with a pang.

Serving my sister was probably an ageing experience. I could well believe that.

He was not alone. Ryder was there, and standing beside him was someone I didn't recognize, a stocky young man with short ginger hair glinting at the edges of his dark cap, and a snub-nosed, almost boyish face – until you looked at the pugnacious jaw and the tucked back corners of the mouth and the stone-coloured eyes, and saw that he wasn't boyish at all. He wore a secretary's dark gown and neat white ruff, and he didn't look at home in them. And seated close to Cecil's desk, was Sybil, with little Tessie standing behind her, looking shy. Sybil

313

sprang up and came joyfully to hug me. Cecil offered us all seats and introduced the stocky young man.

'Roland Wyse, seconded to me from Francis Walsingham's office, to be an observer when you all arrived. We call him Mr Wyse – he has a preference for modern forms of address. Mr Wyse, this is Mistress Stannard and her companion Fran Brockley, and this, of course, is Roger Brockley, whom I think you have met...'

So this was the young man Brockley had so much disliked, whose colleagues said he was ambitious. Brockley had said he looked like an assassin. As we greeted him (which Brockley did with what I recognized as imitation warmth), I studied his face and came to the same conclusion. However, I didn't suppose he would want to assassinate me, so I decided not to worry about him. As the introductions ended, a maidservant, no doubt sent by Lady Mildred, appeared with a flask of wine and some glasses.

Sybil poured for everyone. Cecil looked at me in a contrite manner and said: 'I am very thankful to see you, Ursula, and your companions, safely home again. I have read the report that Ryder brought. I am sorry, Ursula, to have let you go into such danger. I was very shocked when I heard of Timothy Kingham's death. He had no close family – his nearest relative is a second cousin – but I know the fellow and it was painful to tell him that Timothy was gone. I said he was killed by footpads. I suppose it *could* be true – but you think it was ordered by

Roberto Ridolfi?'

'It's highly likely,' I said. 'We will never be sure.' I added: 'I don't understand Ridolfi. I can make no sense of him. I think he lives partly in a strange world of his own. In this world he's pleasant, even kind. In the other world ... I think he's different.'

'If I could get my hands on him, he would soon leave for some other world. Permanently,' said Cecil. 'But I doubt if he'll come within my reach again. I didn't foresee how dangerous he could be. However, you *are* safe home and bringing a valuable harvest. I gather from the report that King Philip has said no to Ridolfi but might change his mind if Ridolfi does all the donkey work first. Well, something must be done to stifle Ridolfi's schemes and the easiest way is to make sure that he will find no co-operation in England. Which brings us, once again, to the Duke of Norfolk...'

He stopped, and his face hardened. A silence fell. The study was a pleasant place, warm with the sunshine that poured through the patterned leading of the window, and full of the agreeable smells of beeswax polish and paper and the leather bindings of copious files and books. But the emotional atmosphere now was not agreeable at all. It was menacing. The ruthless side of Cecil had come to the fore.

'From the moment that I became aware that Ridolfi was scheming again, I feared that Norfolk might be involved,' he said. 'He would be very valuable as a conspirator, especially if he

315

is still prepared to marry Mary Stuart. That's an alliance that would make her far more acceptable to the people of England. In fact, I would say that he would virtually be the cornerstone of any conspiracy – worth his weight in gold bullion to the plotters. But he was oh, so very humble when the last plot failed and the queen herself wants to trust him – to feel she has bound him to herself and to England. She is afraid to know the truth in case it's the wrong truth. That's why she has limited my powers to investigate him.'

I nodded. I probably understood this aspect of her better than Cecil did. Cecil had been at risk in the past, during the reign of the Catholic Queen Mary Tudor when Protestants were persecuted but he had so well mastered the skill of keeping out of harm's way that he had not been seriously threatened. He did not know from personal experience what that was like. But in those same terrifying days, when Mary feared her sister as a heretic and a rival, Elizabeth had come very close to the axe herself.

Also, Cecil was a family man, secure in the love of wife and children. He was not, as Elizabeth was, dependent on the loyalty of friends and courtiers. From the start of all this, Elizabeth had, I realized, been desperate to feel that Norfolk was loyal. He was among the principal men of her realm and a kinsman too. She had been not just furious with him for becoming entangled in the earlier plot, but bitterly hurt as well. She had turned her head away from the idea that he might betray her again. She had decided that as she didn't know how she would bear such disloyalty, or the peril of death, yet again, then the disloyalty, the peril, did not exist.

Only, they almost certainly did.

I said: 'It isn't proof, exactly, but William Barker *was* in Madrid when Ridolfi was there and he was with the Familiars who nearly caught us. He can only have found out that we were there if he had met Ridolfi. They have to be linked and that means – surely – that Norfolk and Ridolfi are linked as well.'

'Barker is back in England now,' Cecil said. 'He must have left his inquisitorial friends and ridden on through Portugal, overtaking you somewhere. From what you've told me, he would probably have been let through the border. He'd have produced credentials proving he was English. I agree with you. His presence in Madrid virtually amounts to proof that Norfolk is in this. And now, there is something else. Mistress Jester arrived here only half an hour before you did – that's why you found us all together when you arrived. She has news. Mistress Jester?'

'It isn't much in the way of evidence,' Sybil said. 'But the Duke of Norfolk has an estate in Shropshire, and the steward there – a Master Banister – often buys cloth from a Shrewsbury draper called Thomas Browne. Banister is a Catholic. Tessie learned that by chance, talking with some of the maids at Howard House.'

317

Tessie nodded speechlessly. Her eyes were wide with astonishment at the grave matters she had been hearing.

Sybil had paused, as if to collect her thoughts and Roland Wyse remarked: 'I am aware that Master Browne makes a journey to London every year, just before the queen leaves for her Summer Progress. It's a time when the men and women of the court often buy materials for new clothes.'

'Yes,' Sybil said. 'Browne calls at court and on the homes of courtiers and members of the royal council. If the Duke of Norfolk is in London, then Master Browne visits him to offer his wares.'

'He came this morning,' offered Tessie, half whispering.

Sybil nodded. 'We were calling on Mistress Dalton – I meant it to be my last visit before I go back to Hawkswood. We were in the great hall and Mistress Dalton was showing us some new tapestries that have just been hung there. Master Browne and the Duke came in together, at the other end of the hall. They took no notice of us but I thought I heard the Duke say something about delivering something valuable to Banister, and to remember that the matter was confidential. There was something in his tone ... I made believe to catch my foot in my skirt hem and sat down for a moment on a settle to put things right.'

'Quick-witted!' said Brockley appreciatively.

Sybil smiled. 'They paid no heed to us – I

think they saw us as just women discussing tapestries. But I listened with all my might. Master Browne is to take some packages to Banister, in Shropshire. The Duke was most anxious that Browne should take great care of them and deliver them as quickly as possible. He asked if Browne had any menservants with him and Browne said yes, three. The Duke said his secretaries Robert Higford and William Barker would give Browne the packages. Then they moved away and I shook my skirts out and said I must stitch the hem more securely. That's all. It may be nothing – perhaps the Duke is just sending a set of precious goblets or some gold plate to his Shrewsbury estate! But I heard that word *confidential*, and the secretary, Barker, has only just come back from a journey to Madrid. Mistress Dalton said so. She didn't approve – she said she couldn't think why the Duke should want to be in touch with anyone in such a Popish country as Spain.'

'It could be significant,' Cecil said. 'Or not. We can't tell. Those packages could be perfectly innocent but yes, I'd like to know what's in them. I gather that Browne is already on the road north, and hurrying, but no doubt he'll take the most obvious route and it shouldn't be too hard to overtake him. I was about to give instructions concerning that, when Ursula here was ushered in. Ryder, I want you in charge of this. You'd better take some dinner first, you'll need it, but be quick over it and then get yourself on the road and take a well-armed escort

319

with you.'

Brockley said: 'Can I go as well? If this does turn out to mean something, I'd like to be there.'

'So would I,' I said, without thinking.

'Ma'am!' said Dale, horrified, while Ryder, Brockley and Cecil all looked at me as though I had suddenly begun to speak in tongues.

'Ursula,' said Cecil, 'Ryder has told me of your expectations, and how they came about. They are why you have travelled from Dover by wagon. There is no question of you chasing Shrewsbury drapers to Shropshire! I would earnestly advise you to go home to Hawkswood, at once! I'll provide a coach.'

'I would rather stay in London until Brockley gets back,' I said. 'I will want to know the outcome of this – immediately!'

Cecil laughed. 'Then I suggest you stay here, you and Sybil and Dale. Mildred will enjoy your company. Wyse, if you like, you can join the hunting party. Walsingham told me that I might send you on any errand I wished and I believe you have a good horse. You and Brockley, go with Ryder, share his dinner and throw some essentials into saddlebags. Wyse, find a horse for Brockley.'

It must have been, I have since worked out, not that night but the one after, in a somewhat grimy Midlands inn, that Thomas Browne, draper of Shrewsbury, who had been growing increasingly uneasy about the weight of his saddlebags, sat in his candlelit bedroom, looking at them in doubt.

It was a very shocking thing for an honest man to contemplate. How could he rifle packages entrusted to him – and by a duke! – for delivery to somebody else? The somebody else, in this case, was Lawrence Banister, a steward on a ducal estate, and Master Browne knew him personally as a quiet-spoken, sober fellow, competent in his work, easy to deal with. Browne had no quarrel with Banister and the thought of questioning orders given by the Duke of Norfolk terrified him but...

The Duke had been in trouble in the past, plotting against the queen, even planning to offer his hand in marriage to that temptress Mary of Scotland, and ask for backing from Spain. The idea had been to restore her to the Scottish throne and then, somehow, to install her on the English one as well. And didn't the servants' gossip at Howard House in London say that the secretary Barker had just been to Madrid? Madrid! Where King Philip of Spain most likely was. Those packages were being sent northwards. To a Catholic steward. Were they ultimately bound for Scotland and Mary Stuart's supporters there? And why hadn't Norfolk said what was in them? Browne had carried things for him before and always known then what he was carrying.

He ought to have insisted on knowing this time, too. However afraid of the Duke he was, he ought to have done that.

Poor Master Browne was an efficient bargainer in business matters. Then he knew where he was and what he was about. He had no love for politics of any description. He was also a loyal subject of the queen.

Up in one corner of the unprepossessing room, was a spider's web with a nasty fat spider in the middle of it. His fevered imagination began to see the Duke as a spider, spinning plots like a web, ready to catch ... not just a queen, but possibly an innocent draper in his sticky trap.

He looked at the saddlebags, which he had dumped upon his bed. He bit his nails. He couldn't, no, he couldn't. It was wrong. It would be outrageous. But if he didn't, and something dangerous was going on, he might be arrested as a traitor. He might be executed. He might...

He rubbed a hand over his hair, which was growing scanty in his middle age, and shuddered at the thought of the things that happened to traitors.

He couldn't.

He must.

TWENTY-FIVE

The Lofty Cache

Brockley, Ryder and Wyse were gone. Cecil too had left to attend on the queen at Whitehall. Quietness descended on the house, and at the same time, a great weariness overtook me. Dale, who had taken to clucking round me like an officious hen, made me go to bed early, brought me supper on a tray, and once I had eaten it, virtually ordered me to sleep.

I rose late the next morning. Once more, Cecil had gone to Whitehall, leaving before I was awake. It was a sunny day and at my request, Dale put me into a loose gown with an open neck and I spent the morning with Lady Mildred, in the garden, reading. The Burghleys had an extensive library, with many books of travel and verse, as well as tomes on politics, science and history. But I grew sleepy again after dinner and Dale almost marched me to my bedchamber, saying I was to go back to bed and stay there.

The next day followed a similar pattern except that my exhaustion was wearing off and I declared that I would get up for the evening and take supper with the family. But I was awakened earlier than I expected, by someone calling my name. I opened my eyes to find Dale and Lady Mildred standing by my bed, beaming broadly.

'We are sorry to disturb you,' Lady Mildred said. 'Supper's still an hour away. But my husband has just returned home and is in his study and has something there he is anxious for you to see. Will you come?'

Those two happy faces were enough to convince me that the effort would be worth it. Lady Mildred smiled and left the room, while Dale helped me to dress, in a more formal style this time. Then she accompanied me down to the study.

It seemed crowded. As well as Cecil, Lady Mildred was there along with Sybil and Tessie, which was no surprise. But there were four others, travel-stained and tired, who were certainly unexpected.

One was a man I didn't know, a heavily built, middle-aged individual, holding his cap on his knee. He had scanty, dust-coloured hair, intelligent eyes and a worried expression. The other three...

'Brockley! I gasped. 'Ryder! Mr Wyse! I thought you must be nearly in Shropshire by now!'

'There was no need,' said Brockley. 'We weren't two hours on the road this morning before we met Master Thomas Browne and his servants, coming *back* towards London, and in a fearful hurry and mighty pleased at the sight of John Ryder's face, I may say.'

'According to him, I was just the man he most wanted to see,' Ryder said.

'You were,' said the thickset stranger feelingly.

'I am being remiss,' remarked Cecil. 'Ursula, this is Thomas Browne, draper of Shrewsbury. Mr Wyse decided that he should be brought here first, and by good fortune, I had just arrived home from court. Though we shall all have to go back there, after these gentlemen have taken a well-earned supper. I gather their horses are almost foundered and I suspect that they are, too. But we must confer with Francis Walsingham and I think it is time I handed Mr Wyse back to him. Sybil Jester was right to be suspicious of the packages Master Browne was asked to carry to Shropshire. Master Browne, perhaps you would like to explain? I have told you that Mistress Ursula Stannard is in my service.'

'I got suspicious of those packets,' said Browne. He had a country accent but not a heavy one; he was clearly both travelled and educated. 'Made my saddlebags weigh too much, they did, and they made clinking sounds and it was odd, too that Norfolk and his secretaries never said a single word about what might be in them. They just said it was a confidential errand, and said it in half whispers and it all seemed very peculiar.'

He hesitated, looking awkward, and Brockley

remarked: 'Master Browne says he knows about what happened two years ago and also knows Barker was just back from Spain, so what with one thing and another...'

He glanced at Browne, inviting him to take up the story again. Browne looked more uncomfortable than ever. 'I did what I did in case it was important, mattered – in case I were being mixed up in something that was wrong. But I didn't like it, because if there was nothing amiss, then what I was doing ... well, it was hardly excusable. I tell you, I sat for two hours or more in a scruffy inn bedchamber and didn't know right from wrong but in the end, I said a prayer to God to forgive me if I'd got it wrong, and then I opened one of the packets. There were three and I opened the heaviest. When I saw what was inside, I opened the rest.'

His face flushed and his voice faded. Cecil looked amused and Ryder laughed and took up the tale.

'There was coinage inside – two thousand crowns altogether. Worth five hundred pounds in all, and a letter that had Lawrence Banister's name on the outside but nothing else that made sense. The letter itself was a jumble of figures. I thought it must be in cipher. You didn't like it, did you, Browne?'

'No,' said Browne, recovering his powers of speech. 'No, I did *not*. It looked bad. If the Duke's just sending money to his steward to use on the estate, why not use his own men, not just my menservants? It looks as if he didn't want

326

attention drawn to my errand – and if letters can only make sense to folk who know how to read them, well, doesn't that mean whoever wrote them has something to hide? So I did it all up again, had a bad night worrying, and next morning, told my men we were making for London again and coming straight here.'

Ryder said soberly: 'We had a good escort with us, as you ordered, Lord Burghley. I sent six of them on to Shropshire to pick up this steward, Lawrence Banister.'

'I have already sent word to Walsingham,' said Cecil, 'to bring in those secretaries, Robert Higford and William Barker. Between them, I fancy they may have a good deal to tell us.'

'They'll try to lie their way out of trouble,' said Browne despondently.

Norfolk had played a dirty trick, I thought, in making a cat's paw of an innocent man. But Browne's innocence was tempered with a businessman's worldliness. He could recognize a dubious errand when he met one.

Cecil said: 'There are places in the Tower where the most taciturn people can be persuaded to become garrulous, sometimes within minutes. If the queen gives permission, that is.'

'Will she?' I said.

'I think so,' said Cecil. He added: 'I avoid being present at such – persuasions. I leave that to Walsingham, who doesn't seem to mind. Nor, I gather, does Mr Wyse here.'

Brockley had said that some of Walsingham's other staff didn't greatly care for Mr Wyse. It occurred to me that Cecil didn't, either.

'I shan't be present this time. I imagine that Sir Francis will wish me to tackle that cipher,' said Wyse. 'I have had no chance to start on it yet.'

I wondered if I should volunteer but decided not to. If Mr Wyse enjoyed watching interrogations by Elizabeth's rackmaster, then cheating him out of one felt like a virtuous act. Besides, Norfolk might not be using the same code as Ridolfi.

'I suppose one shouldn't criticize Walsingham,' said Lady Mildred mildly. 'He doesn't like traitors and therein lies his value. He is kind enough as a private man. He makes people nervous because he dresses like a black crow and looks as if he would peck out the eyes of a traitor without a second thought. The queen has a nickname for him – did you know? She calls him her Moor, because of his dark clothes and his complexion. He's nearly as brown as a Saracen. I do wonder if the queen will agree to drastic measures against those two secretaries, though.'

'If I think she will,' said Cecil, 'it's because of Norfolk. We now have strong evidence that he has betrayed her again and she will understand, however reluctantly, that the truth must be finally established. However hateful it may be.'

'So there we have it,' said Cecil. It was two days later and we were once more gathered in his study. It was evening and he had just returned from the court. He looked worn out, the line between his brows as deep as a newly ploughed furrow, but there was satisfaction in the set of his mouth and his intelligent eyes.

'On the queen's orders,' he said, 'the rack was employed. We racked that man Baillie – Ridolfi's messenger. We should have done it much sooner! I think we were too impressed by the fact that he's a Vatican courier, or the queen was. She doesn't like head-on confrontations with other heads of state, and that includes the Pope. Racking one of his couriers might count as such a confrontation.'

I laughed and he gave me a grim smile.

'She gave way,' he said. 'I think because this business has made her so angry, and bitter, that she lost her temper. Baillie gave us a good idea of just how much correspondence there's been between Ridolfi, Ross and Mary Stuart. Higford and Barker were also taken to the Tower and shown the rack. Higford took one look at it and couldn't talk fast enough, while Barker risked it, but started to babble within half a minute. None of the three of them could tell us everything we wanted to know, though, because obviously there were things they didn't know themselves. They all said they were given enciphered letters to dispatch but none of them did the enciphering. They think their masters, Ridolfi and Norfolk, did. They don't know what the letters said. Baillie and Barker both screamed out that they would tell us if they did know, and Walsingham, who was there, believed them. But Barker did tell us where to find a hidden cache of correspondence – Norfolk sometimes gave him or Higford letters to add to it. We can find that easily enough.'

'So Mary Stuart was a party to the plot?' I asked him.

'All three said that some of the enciphered letters were for her. We need those letters or at least her replies.' Cecil heaved a weary sigh. 'Do you know, I fear that her majesty may still baulk over arresting Norfolk unless we can present her with something she can't claim is a fairy story spun by terrified men on the rack. Elizabeth,' said Cecil exasperatedly, 'sometimes drives me frantic. As well she knows, which is why I can say it. I once threatened to resign my post and work instead in her garden or her kitchen, you know. I saw her today. My God! As I expected, she herself ordered the rack to be used but *now* she is saying that men in agony will invent things to please their interrogators! She says she won't take action against her cousin Mary, no matter what we discover, and she shudders and turns pale at the thought of condemning Norfolk. But if there are letters between him and Mary, incriminating him, she will have to, whatever she does about her confounded cousin of Scotland.'

'Did Barker admit that he met Ridolfi in Madrid?' I asked. 'Was it through him that Ridolfi realized who we were?'

'Yes, he did tell us that, and yes, it was your host Ridolfi who set the Inquisition on your

330

tracks. Apparently, the Inquisition dispatched Barker on a fast horse to warn their counterparts in Plasencia that you were likely to come through their city. You were lucky – he was meant to get there ahead of you but alerting the Inquisition took a couple of days and you'd already left the city before Barker reached it. He must have been hard behind you, though. You were *very* lucky. Tell me, does the name Giorgio Bruno sound familiar?'

'He's Ridolfi's butler and secretary,' I said.

'Was,' Cecil told me. 'While Barker was there, Bruno was arrested. Someone had overheard him in a tavern, saying that the Inquisition was corrupt – getting people executed so that their estates could be seized. Ridolfi apparently tried to get him released, though without success. A curious man, Ridolfi.'

I thought of him again; his impulses of kindness and his religious dream world; the death of Timothy Kingham and the death he nearly brought on me. He was an incomprehensible man, beyond my understanding.

'I would like to watch the search for the hidden cache of letters,' I said. 'There wouldn't be any danger to me in that, surely.'

Cecil smiled. 'I shouldn't think so. You can accompany me tomorrow if you wish.'

'You intend to be there yourself, Lord Burghley?' I said, surprised.

'You think it's beneath my dignity as an elder statesman? Perhaps it is, but once in a while, when events are weighty, I like to be a witness.

331

Walsingham says he is too much occupied but he has lent me Mr Wyse again, to be his representative. You will be quite as welcome. You've done more than anyone to put us on the right road.'

It was an impressive deputation that went to Howard House the next morning, led by Lord Burghley in his coach. Dale and I shared it with him and a couple of clerks, and behind us came a force of armed men led by John Ryder, while Brockley brought up the rear. Sybil had not wished to come. 'It would upset Mistress Dalton to see me. She might realize that I have been using her.'

As it happened, the Duke of Norfolk wasn't in his house. He was in residence, but had risen early and gone out. His gatekeeper looked at us in horror but dared not refuse entrance to Lord Burghley. The butler, more resolute, opened the main door, looked at us and then planted himself in the doorway as if to keep us out, until one of Cecil's clerks handed him the search warrant with the royal seal on it, whereupon his complexion turned grey and he stood aside. We trooped in.

Cecil led us straight to the great hall and then addressed us. 'Mistress Stannard, I shall wait here with you and Dale. I am not dressed for getting grimy. The rest of you' – he turned to Wyse and the other men including the clerks – 'will undertake the search. You know where to look. In the attic space, and pay special attention to the roof tiles. When Barker was on the rack, he shouted out something about roof tiles. I haven't seen them so I don't know what kind of hiding places they offer, but pay attention to them. Go now.'

I said: 'I shall come to no harm just climbing some stairs, quietly. I want to see the search with my own eyes.'

Cecil sighed. 'I might have known. Dale, go with your mistress and look after her.'

I had in fact not yet reached the clumsy stage or anything like it and mounted the stairs with ease, though the final stair was narrow and twisty, and I needed Brockley's hand to help me through the trapdoor in which the stairway ended. Once through, we found ourselves in a large, dusty space at the very top of the house. This space contained no furniture. Its purpose seemed to be that of holding a criss-cross tangle of beams and uprights to support the tiled roof above. Where there were gables, the tiling sloped. The roof looked as though it needed some repairs, for daylight showed in several places and there were damp patches on the floor, where the rain had come in.

Ryder said: 'We're to concentrate on the roof tiles. Spread out, lads and see if any of them seem to have been moved.'

The search began and went on for some time. Once, someone exclaimed that he had found something, but then poked with a sword hilt at the tiling above him and dislodged an untidy mess that looked like an abandoned bird's nest.

Unexpectedly, it was Dale, who was craning her neck to see overhead, who suddenly said: 'The tiles just above me must have shifted. There's a lot of light getting in and...' She took a pace backwards and then pointed excitedly. *'Look!* That wide beam! Surely...?'

I moved to her side and peered. She was right. The beam, wide enough to amount to a ledge, passed close below the roofing just here, and there was something on it. It looked as if the tiles above might have been disturbed when the something, whatever it was, was pushed on to the beam.

'Ryder!' I said.

He hurried over to me. Taller than either Dale or myself, he reached up. Only his fingertips could touch the beam, however. He pulled out his sword and used the tip to nudge the mysterious something. The rest of the party gathered eagerly round. The something suddenly shifted. Brockley started towards Dale but Wyse was faster, springing forward and pushing her aside just as a small leather sack fell with a thump, just missing her.

'Thank you!' Dale said to Wyse, and gave Brockley an unfriendly glance which I was sorry to see. Wyse stooped and picked up the sack. 'There's a box inside this. Could have hurt you, mistress! Lucky I was by.' He looked at Dale with concern and unexpectedly, I saw that the tough and ambitious young man with the pugnacious jaw and – if Brockley were right – a potential as an assassin, was at heart as

334

much of a chivalrous Sir Galahad as Brockley himself sometimes was. This time, more so. Brockley had been slow in going to her aid and she had noticed it. I wondered sadly if things would ever again be quite right between them.

The sack was closed by a drawstring. Wyse loosened it and pulled out a plain wooden box. 'Padlocked!' he said with annoyance. 'And no sign of a key. On my lord of Norfolk's key ring, no doubt, not that we can't break it open. Better do that in the presence of my lord of Burghley, though. But I rather think we've found what we want.'

Since I no longer feared the Inquisition, I no longer carried my tiny sharp knife. But my gown had my usual divided skirt and kirtle and inside the skirt was my usual pouch, containing, as ever, a purse of money, a little dagger, and my picklocks.

'We won't have to break it open,' I said.

TWENTY-SIX

Not All Bad

'So now we know,' said Queen Elizabeth bitterly.

She had sent a royal summons: to Cecil, Walsingham, Ryder, Wyse, myself, Sybil and the Brockleys. Her gentleman pensioners in their red and gold livery had admitted us to her private rooms in Whitehall, throwing open the double-leaved doors to let us pass in to a reception chamber, where we found Elizabeth awaiting us in state, seated in a high-backed chair on a dais.

The place was bare, though bright. Sunlight flashed on the gilded criss-cross pattern of ceiling beams and reflected the pattern on to the oak floor and Elizabeth's peach damask skirts. But apart from the fine tapestries on the walls and Elizabeth's own elaborately carved chair and one settle, pushed against a wall in a haphazard way as though it had got there by accident, there was no furniture.

I was relieved to find her seated. I had seen her the first time she learned that Norfolk had betrayed her and then, she had stormed about

336

like an infuriated lioness. But two years had passed since then and Elizabeth was changing. Her dress, her farthingale, her ruff, the ropes of her favourite pearls, were more sumptuous than ever before, and I suspected that the crimped red-gold hair had had its colour artificially deepened. Her pale, shield-shaped face was more of a shield than ever, hiding every trace of the thoughts behind those golden-brown eyes.

But they were still the eyes of a lioness; not, this time, a pacing, raging lioness, but a watchful one, who knew what it was to be hunted. She was my half-sister, but now, as I made my curtsy and rose to look her in the face, I had no sense of kinship with her, only a sense of awe, and something close to fear.

'So now we know,' she said again. 'We know it all. So very obliging – and stupid – of Norfolk to store the keys to his ciphers along with his correspondence. It took Wyse hardly one single day to decode the whole collection. We know now how much money has been raised for the cause of Mary Stuart; who has carried it into the country; who has contributed to it. These shores have been protected only because Philip of Spain – and therefore the Duke of Alva – cannot afford to launch an invasion. If they had, they would have found here, some who would welcome them – if sufficiently rewarded. And prominent among those, is Thomas Howard, Duke of Norfolk. Among the tiles of his London house, you, my friends, have found nineteen cipher letters to Norfolk from Mary Stuart and the Bishop of Ross, and Mr Wyse has decoded them. And any details not in the letters, have been obligingly revealed to us by the Bishop of Ross.'

She looked at Walsingham and smiled. It was a smile that made me tremble. 'I owe you much, old Moor. You sought the views of no fewer than eleven lawyers and they all declared that in a matter so serious, neither bishop nor ambassador can claim immunity from questioning. It was wondrous, what the sight of the rack did to loosen Ross's tongue. And what a loosening! He has been Mary Stuart's ambassador and supporter for years but to hear him now, you would think he had been her galley slave! He can't pour her sins out fast enough. Her beauty and charm have kept him chained, he says; he has been towards her like a rabbit fascinated by a snake, because yes, she did indeed have her husband Darnley murdered; she is no fit bride for Thomas Howard who will probably go the same way if he is so unwise as to marry her. He, Ross, has adored her and also hated and feared her...! What sort of woman is she? And what sort of man is John Leslie, Bishop of Ross?'

She sprang up and strode off the dais. She did it in a movement so swift and fierce that we were all taken by surprise. We scattered to let her pass through us. She strode towards the outer door, spun round, her long train swishing across the floor, and strode back. She had not changed as much as I had thought. The angry, pacing lioness was still there, had been there all the time. She had tried to present a facade of stillness; she had failed. Her anger was too great. It had flung her into infuriated motion.

She stopped pacing at last and faced us, standing at the foot of her dais. 'The first time Norfolk – my own cousin! – conspired against me, I was so furious and bitter; at first I wanted his head, then and there. But he confessed; he wept with his head in my lap; he soaked my skirt with his tears; he swore everlasting faithfulness to me and this realm. He spoke out of fear for his life and I pitied him. I have seen so many go to the block; I have known the terror of it myself. When he cried like a child pleading for forgiveness and mercy, yes, I truly pitied him. Besides, he *is* a kinsman. I gave him what he begged for. And now – this!'

'It was plain, your majesty, for some time before those letters were found,' Walsingham said. I didn't like Walsingham but I admired him for one thing. He was one of the few people who did not seem to fear Elizabeth.

'I didn't want to believe it,' said Elizabeth. 'Now I know I must. I called you all here to thank you for what you have done for me. But I promise you, I am near to being angry with you for discovering what you have. I have no doubt that Norfolk will come crying to me again but this time...'

'This time,' said Walsingham, 'there can be no mercy. I will go on my knees to plead against that. The man is dangerous.'

'I know. This time,' said Elizabeth, with terrible bitterness, 'he must be tried. And he will be found guilty. And he will lose his head.'

There was a silence. We all stood there, most of us staring at our feet. Elizabeth's white face and the rage in those lioness's eyes, were too difficult to look at.

'Leave us,' she said. 'Except for Ursula. We wish a few words alone with her.'

When the others had gone, the room seemed to increase in size. But Elizabeth appeared to diminish. The lioness was gone. Instead, I saw a woman past her youth, with lines of responsibility on her face. They showed at close quarters even though her skin was dusted with powder.

She beckoned me to sit beside her on the settle. Since I was also elaborately dressed, as one must be when attending court, there was only just room for the two of us, with our spreading skirts. We looked at each other.

'My sister,' said Elizabeth. 'And my aide. You have served me well and faced danger for me. And helped to bring me news that I needed to know but did not want. Norfolk will have a fair trial and a chance to defend himself but he will fail. And I shall have to force my hand to write my name on the warrant for his execution. Walsingham and Cecil will both insist. Walsingham most of all.'

I said nothing, because I couldn't think of anything that was safe. I didn't want to waken the lioness.

Elizabeth probably knew that perfectly well.

She considered me gravely. 'I like Thomas Howard,' she remarked. 'Not just as a cousin but as a man. And he was so like a child, when he pleaded with me for his life. It is hard to refuse a pleading child though now I must do so. Cecil tells me that you are with child, Ursula. Is he right? And was the child fathered by Matthew de la Roche, as Cecil says?'

'Yes. Did he tell you the whole story, ma'am?'

'Yes, he did. I know all about it, and I have no word of blame for you. I parted you from Matthew for England's sake and also, as well you know, for yours. I knew that it was a grief to you and I am sorry. I hope that this ... this new turn of events will bring you some comfort. When Cecil told me about it,' said Elizabeth, with a mercurial change of tone from regretful to brisk, 'I could see in his eyes that he was, as ever, sorry that I have never married and produced an heir of my own body to rule this realm after me; in fact, that he still hopes that I might – just – manage it. But I doubt that I shall. I envy you in a way, Ursula. You are not afraid?'

'Yes, I am.' Her enquiring expression encouraged me to enlarge. 'Bearing Meg was not easy and since then I have lost one pregnancy early while another led to a stillborn baby and nearly killed me. I can only hope and pray that this time will be different.'

Elizabeth nodded. 'I will hope and pray the same.' Her smile became wry. 'This country

341

needs a direct heir. Cecil is right, in a way. But it does not need a dead queen who leaves a child to replace her, and that is what I fear, should I make the attempt. I wish I were as young and healthy as you. Ursula, I will send your new son or daughter a rich christening gift, I promise. And there is one more thing. Cecil said that your child was probably due in late January.'

'Yes.'

'There will be talk. Clearly, it will be plain that it can't be Hugh Stannard's baby. When do you propose returning home? Are you going to Hawkswood or Withysham?'

'Hawkswood, ma'am. I am going first to visit my daughter in Buckinghamshire. She expects a child herself next month and I want to be with her. In September, I shall set off for Hawkswood.'

'Keep me informed, through Cecil, of your plans. I wish to send you with a fine, royal escort, to give you countenance. If the queen is seen to accept the situation and to honour you for your services to her, then it will be harder for the gossips to spread unpleasant rumours.'

'Thank you,' I said. 'I shall tell the whole story to my own households, both at Hawkswood and Withysham. But I know the power of gossip. I shall have to live with it until it becomes yesterday's tattle.'

I knew who would be the chief tattler, too. My tiresome neighbour Jane Cobbold would seize on my untimely pregnancy with spiteful delight; I could be sure of that.

'I shall be grateful,' I said, 'for your fine escort and your christening gift. Very grateful indeed.' Then, wanting to change the subject, I said: 'What will happen to Mary Stuart? She was as entangled as Norfolk in this latest conspiracy. After all, it was on her behalf!'

Elizabeth shook her head. 'I shall keep her fast and incommunicado. I shall see that no one rescues her from that. But I shall let her live. She is my cousin, as he is, but she is also an anointed queen, even though she is in exile. To behead Mary Stuart would be to set a very ugly precedent. God knows, I take no joy in killing members of my own family but Thomas Howard of Norfolk will have to stand – and die – for both himself and her.'

I was silent. It was the only time I ever heard her come near to criticizing her father King Henry, who had sent two wives to the block, one of them Elizabeth's own mother. She avoided speaking of her mother. But how often she thought of her – that, I believe, was another matter.

She rose and I rose with her. 'I hope next year, you will bring your new son or daughter to see me,' Elizabeth said.

I promised.

It was mid-September when at long last, I returned to Hawkswood. Sybil, with Tessie and Joseph, the young groom, had long since gone back there. Soon now, I would be there too, where Hugh's memory would keep me company, where, all around me, would be the things he had loved. A few roses might still be in bloom in his rose garden, and I would take some to adorn his grave.

I was happy. Dale and Brockley seemed to have become friends again, in a more muted way than before but still friends. And my fears for Meg had been unfounded. An easy confinement had brought forth a healthy and vociferous boy baby, who was to be named George after his father. A letter – sent via Hawkswood but dispatched to me by the steward, Adam Wilder – had also reached me from Margaret van Weede. She was looking forward to the arrival of her own first child, was happy and settled and reiterating that she was sorry that as a bride, she had been such a goose. She had found time to continue studying Latin and Greek, with the help of a retired pastor in the district and Antonio had encouraged her in this. Antonio was a kind husband, she said, and she hoped they would have a long life together and many children. Margaret, I thought, might never know the glittering emotional heights that I had known, but she might be all the more contented for it. She was safe, and off my conscience.

As for me, I now felt remarkably well. I was travelling by coach, of course. Following Elizabeth's orders, I had let her know when I proposed to leave Buckinghamshire, and she replied bidding me to Lord Burghley's house in

London first. I went there in Meg's modest coach, but was met in London by – as Elizabeth had promised – a most impressive escort, a fine horse for Brockley and a wonderful vehicle for me and Dale, its seating soft with thick cushions embroidered with Tudor roses.

Surprisingly, Mr Roland Wyse joined my party, though not as part of the escort. Walsingham had now returned to France, but he had passed Wyse on to Cecil's department and Cecil had given him a message to carry to Sir Edward Heron, the Sheriff of Surrey. Sir Edward was staying with the Cobbolds while repairs were being done to his own house. I agreed that the whole party should divert to the Cobbolds so that we could show Wyse the road. I also wanted to grasp the nettle that was Jane Cobbold. Since Sybil had gone to Hawkswood ahead of me, I had charged her with explaining my situation to the household and the neighbourhood, but I wanted to gauge how successful she had been with the Cobbolds, who were influential in the district. I also welcomed the chance to let them see my coach and escort and to see for themselves that the queen thought no worse of me.

Brockley, who decidedly did not like Wyse, grumbled at his presence. But a small incident just as we came on to Cobbold land somewhat altered his opinion. We were passing a solitary cottage. It had a newly thatched roof, but half of its garden was a wilderness, though the other half was a neat enough vegetable patch, and also contained a fowl run.

We paused to look because it was something of an oddity, as Brockley commented, and just then, a man came out of the cottage. He was probably middle-aged but it was hard to tell for he was as unkempt as the wild half of the garden, very skinny, dressed in patched old clothes, and with greasy greying hair trailing to his shoulders. Large red ears poked through it, one of them with a scar across it as if at some time, a dog had jumped up and bitten him. He had apparently stepped out to work in the garden, since he was carrying a trowel. He stared at the coach and the glossy well-bred horses and the livery of the escort in astonishment and called to us.

'You bound for the Cobbold place?'

Wyse, who was nearest to the garden gate, pushed his horse right up to it and called back: 'Yes. We're on the right road, aren't we?'

'Aye, you are, only there's a new track been driven, just a month ago, that's quicker. You'll see the fork just ahead. Take the right-hand way; cuts off a good quarter mile, so it do.'

'You're a Cobbold tenant?' Wyse enquired. Brockley, who had reined in beside my coach, leant down to whisper: 'Nosy, isn't he?' through the window.

'You could say that.' The fellow didn't seem to mind the nosiness. 'One of Mistress Jane's charities, that's me. Used to live near Guildford, raising sheep and grazing them on common land, and then the land was enclosed and

346

I'd nowhere for my sheep unless I paid for the grazing, and in the end I sold them to pay my rent and then got thrown out of my home anyway when that money ran out. Came begging on to Cobbold land. Well, Mistress Jane, when she heard my story and found out it was true, she said I could have this cottage, what was empty just then, if I'd tidy it up a bit. She got her husband to put new thatch on and fixed me up with half a dozen hens, and now I'm trying to get this bugger of a garden straight, though with the way weeds grow at this season, it's a struggle. But it's a home and I can earn a penny or two doing odd jobs up at the house. I'm a proper charity child, I am.'

He was as garrulous as Jane herself, I thought, but perhaps he was lonely. There were no other habitations nearby and he was hardly an attractive character to look at, anyway.

Wyse was holding his reins in his left hand and fishing under his doublet with his right. He pulled out a purse, balanced it on his horse's withers, extracted a handful of coins and reached over the gate, holding them out. 'Take these and welcome. They might buy you a couple more hens, or a rooster, maybe. Then you could raise chicks.'

'Well, if that's not the mark of a real gentleman!' The coins were fairly snatched. Wyse laughed. 'We'll be on our way. And I fancy we'll take the right-hand fork.'

Brockley leant down again. 'Seems Roland Wyse is not all bad. Maybe I'll have to change my mind about him.'

'Maybe you will,' I said, remembering that it was Wyse and not Brockley who had pulled Dale from under the falling box in Norfolk's attic. Our cavalcade started off again.

I was beginning to be tired and hoped that the Cobbolds would let us all take a break from our journey. The horses could do with some water and I would appreciate a cup of milk and a cinnamon cake. When we reached the Cobbolds' house, however, Mr Wyse was welcomed in, but Anthony Cobbold was not at home – which might have made a difference – and Jane came out of the house herself to tell me that she could not bring herself to invite me or any of my companions or escort indoors.

She had the decency to speak to me with her head inside my coach window so that the mounted escort couldn't hear but her words, nevertheless, were searing.

'I have heard the pretty tale that Mistress Jester has been putting about, but I'm not impressed. So, in France you met the man to whom you were once, allegedly, married though the marriage was long since declared unlawful, and within three months of being widowed, you were back with this old lover of yours. I do not offer hospitality to loose women. Be on your way, and don't come back. Or invite me to visit you. I shall have nothing to say to you, ever again.'

'As you wish,' I said, with dignity, and ordered that we should now proceed straight to

Hawkswood, with no further digressions. But as we did so, and the surrounding countryside grew more dear and more familiar with every creak of the coach, the pleasure of homecoming was dimmed. I had looked forward so much to seeing my household again; Sybil, my steward Adam Wilder, even gap-toothed old Gladys. Now I wondered how much rudeness Sybil had met when she tried to tell Jane my story.

Beside me, Dale must have been watching my face, for suddenly she said: 'Ma'am, don't look like that. Please don't. That Cobbold woman is a harpy. You mustn't let her upset you. She isn't worth it.'

I pulled myself together, straightening my back against the Tudor roses. Then, in the distance, I caught my first glimpse of Hawkswood's chimneys, and my spirits lifted. There, just ahead, was home and safety, and I didn't intend to be coaxed away from either again. Thinking of them created a warmth within me. 'You're right, Dale. And she isn't all bad, either. She's been charitable enough to that old man.'

The glow of homecoming made me feel charitable, too. Whatever Cecil and Brockley might think of him, Mr Wyse had indeed been fast on his feet in the attic of Howard House and he had given alms to the fellow in the cottage. Even Ridolfi wasn't a complete villain, I thought, recalling the amblers provided for Dale on the journey to Italy, and the fact that according to Cecil, he had tried to protect his outspoken butler. But my mind shied away

349

from wondering what had happened to Giorgio Bruno. It might well have happened to me, if Brockley and Ryder hadn't been such good bodyguards, if in the last resort I lacked the resolution to use my little knife, if Dale's insane moment of betrayal had succeeded...

But no, I must not think of that, and I hoped that by now, Brockley had thrust it out of his mind as well. He and Dale were still being just a little too formal with each other. I could only hope that the comfort and familiarity of home would smooth the bitter memories away, as a salve may soothe a wound.

'I hope Mistress Cobbold causes you no trouble, though, ma'am,' Dale broke into my thoughts. Her own were evidently still on Jane. 'You've had trouble enough and some of it through me. I'm sorry.'

'That's over and forgotten,' I said quickly. 'Let us forget Jane too, as far as we can. Listen, Dale, I intend to face her down.' I paused and then said it. 'I shall never see or be in touch with Matthew de la Roche again. That is final.' Ruthless words, but they came out more easily than I thought they would. I felt regret and sorrow, but it was like the lingering grief one feels for someone, once loved, who has been dead for many years, no more than that. I put a hand on my stomach and knew that I had all of Matthew that I now needed.

'He has a son at home in Blanchepierre,' I said calmly, 'and next year he will probably marry again and perhaps there will be more

children. He has no need of mine. But if my
child, God willing, is born safely, he or she will
bear the name of de la Roche and know who
their father is. I shall not hide the truth from the
child or anyone else. No pretences. No lies. I'll
make myself and my child accepted as we are.
I can do it, Dale.'

'I believe you will, ma'am!' said Dale.

Brockley appeared again beside the coach.
'Madam, do you see the chimneys? That's
Hawkswood!'

'I see them, Brockley.'

I was nearly there. I was going home. To
Hawkswood and – though his physical presence
was gone – to Hugh.